DOC FORD COUNTRY

Sulphur Wells

Gumbo-Limbo

Matlacha

Sandy Hook

CAPE CORAL

Bull Sharks

PINE ISLAND

St. James City

Sound

Woodring's Point

Sanibel Flats

Tarpon Bay

Causeway Blvd.

No Más

Doc Ford's Lab

Sanibel Marina

Dinkin's Bay Marina

Sanibel Lighthouse

anibel – Captiva Rd.

Periwinkle Way

Bait Box

Sanibel Lighthouse

Nave's

Casa Ybel Rd.

Tarpon Bay Rd.

Timbers

Bailey's General

W. Gulf Dr.

Gray Gables

FLORIDA

FORT MYERS RSW INTERNATIONAL AIRPORT (25 miles) →

D0122538

DECEIVED

WITHDRAWN

G. P. PUTNAM'S SONS
NEW YORK

DECEIVED

RANDY WAYNE WHITE

G. P. PUTNAM'S SONS
Publishers Since 1838
Published by the Penguin Group
Penguin Group (USA), 375 Hudson Street,
New York, New York 10014, USA

USA · Canada · UK · Ireland · Australia
New Zealand · India · South Africa · China

Penguin Books Ltd, Registered Offices: 80 Strand, London WC2R 0RL, England
For more information about the Penguin Group visit penguin.com

Library of Congress Cataloging-in-Publication Data

White, Randy Wayne.
Deceived / Randy Wayne White.
p.   cm.—(A Hannah Smith novel)
ISBN 978-0-399-16207-7
I. Title.
PS3573.H47473D455   2013   2013016785
813'.54—dc23

Printed in the United States of America
1   3   5   7   9   10   8   6   4   2

BOOK DESIGN BY EMILY S. HERRICK

This is a work of fiction. Names, characters, places, and incidents either
are the product of the author's imagination or are used fictitiously,
and any resemblance to actual persons, living or dead, businesses,
companies, events, or locales is entirely coincidental.

For Mrs. Iris Tanner,
a true Southern lady

See, when you are a kid, you do not listen to all this [stories from old fishing families]. It just goes whisp. Then, when it is too late, you wished you had listened to a whole lot of that stuff.

CAPT. ESPERANZA WOODRING
(1901–1992)

Quoted in
Fisherfolk of Charlotte Harbor, Florida
by Robert F. Edic
IAPS Books,
University of Florida

DECEIVED

ONE

Most fishing guides would consider it lucky to escape without injury or a lawsuit when, out of nowhere, a hundred-pound fish jumps into her boat and knocks two clients overboard.

When it happened on that clear, bright morning in April, the idea that a close call can also be a warning never entered my mind until later that afternoon. It was because of something a friend told me, a strange friend named Tomlinson whom some dismiss as a pot-smoking beach bum—which he is—but I like and trust the man anyway.

"I'd either move to Montana for a week or fire your clients," he counseled after giving my story some thought. "Could be a bad omen, Hannah—not the first time God sent a giant fish as His messenger."

Which was something I didn't take seriously because my boat was safely back at the dock and I had joined him in a hospital waiting room, hushed voices and the echoing footsteps of fear all around. Why worry about bad events in my future when there were people nearby with real problems? Some fighting for their lives, some recovering from near death—including a man I secretly hoped to date when he was well. Selfish thoughts didn't seem right in such a setting. Besides, the tarpon had appeared so unexpectedly, the blurry details weren't solid enough to carry the weight of a warning, let alone God's personal message to me.

"Some of the crazy notions you get," I replied, and expected a smile to signal he was joking. He wasn't. Tomlinson is tall and gaunt-faced, with long, scraggily hair that he fiddles with when fretful or preoccupied. He was chewing a strand now.

"This morning, a tarpon lands in your boat while you were under way—what are the odds?"

"I know, I know," I agreed. "My clients are lucky they weren't hurt. Me, too. Not more than a few bruises between us, which is a miracle."

"See?" Tomlinson said, then pressed, "A shark buzzed you, too. How big?"

The memory of that dorsal fin cleaving toward my client's legs caused a shudder—the fin had to be a yard tall. "Doesn't matter," I said. "They dropped the idea of a lawsuit."

Tomlinson shook his head in a way that suggested I had missed his point. "Go over it one more time. Close your eyes first. Picture what happened in your mind, and go slowly. It was only a few hours ago."

"You're serious?" I said.

"You see any magazines here you haven't read?" He looked around the room where, the previous month, we had spent six long nights waiting, and now we were back again. Tomlinson was jumpy, I realized, eager for a diversion. Truth was, I felt the same. Soon, we hoped, a physician would come down the hallway and tell us if a man we both cared about, a biologist named Marion Ford, could carry on with his life or would need a second heart surgery.

"Okay," I said. "I'll start from the beginning."

Something inside me feared the worst, but I closed my eyes, let my mind drift back, and did what I had been asked to do.

TWO

There are spring mornings so calm off Sanibel Island that in bays where islands block the breeze, saltwater bonds like blue gel, and, if you're in a good boat, the surface feels as solid as ice and as slick. I was in a good boat, a twenty-one-foot open boat, no top or canvas to get in the way, and powered by a fast Mercury outboard—a "flats skiff," as the design is known in Southwest Florida, where my family has lived for generations.

It had been one of those rare April mornings.

I'd picked up my clients at sunrise, and by eight a.m. we were nearing a shoal named Captiva Rocks when I saw water boil from the corner of my eye. An instant later, a huge fish jumped, floated high above us, then seemed to hurtle itself toward the boat. Because my clients were standing, we weren't going fast, but the fish came at us like a rocket. Dreamlike, that's the only way I can describe my surprise. What happened next took only seconds, but my eyes and brain processed the details in stop-action, as if viewing photos of a car wreck.

A tarpon, I realized. Six feet long, glittering like chrome, saltwater sparking from its tail. The fish froze for an instant, a silver pendant suspended from a cloudless sky, then the string broke and the huge fish fell. Instinct told me either to speed up or to yank the throttle into neutral and try to stop.

I did neither.

True, I was stunned, but a sudden change in boat speed is always risky. My clients, both men, had left their seats and gone forward. The youngest of them was wearing a photographer's vest but, fortunately, had left his cameras behind. The other, a big man in his sixties, had a belly pack strapped around his waist and had brought an old-fashioned wooden fishing rod, which he'd babied because of its age but was using like a walking stick for balance. Standing while under way is something I normally don't allow and I should have spoken up, but my livelihood depends on winning repeat charters, when I'm not tending to my late uncle's business—a private investigation agency that doesn't stay busy. The older man had made it clear that fishing was secondary, shooting photos is what he wanted, and he had hinted his project might require several trips. Besides, how could anything bad happen on a morning so calm and clear?

Seconds before the tarpon jumped, the older man—Delmont Chatham, as he'd told me on the phone—pointed and called over the sound of the engine, "Can you get us closer?" He was referring to a cluster of shacks built on pilings in shallow water, old fish houses, some almost a hundred years old. One was painted red, the others were gray weathered pine. It was a scene as pretty as any watercolor: tin roofs golden in the morning sunlight, pelicans and gulls hovering like kites. Seldom had I passed those stilt shacks that clients didn't want to stop for pictures, so I began a slow turn the moment Mr. Chatham pointed.

My eyes remained focused on the water, though. Most people believe May to be the start of tarpon season, but tarpon don't watch the calendar, and I'd been seeing pods of those big silver fish since March, so I scanned the surface for activity. Not just looking for tarpon either. April is a fertile time; a month that is as sweet and spirited as October. Bays come alive with oceangoing fish that move to the shallows to feed or spawn, often both. Turtles, too, hawksbills and loggerheads, appear, some the size of umbrellas. Manatees gather in families, the tip of a nose often the only warning a thousand-pound animal swims beneath. Cobia forage the flats, their periscope tails knifing the surface; schools of feeding redfish create oil slicks and can cause an acre of quaking water. The shacks would make for good photos, but a fishing guide's eyes are always on the hunt so my attention didn't swerve from the surface. Which is why I was the first to see the whirlpool swirl of a big fish flushing ahead of my skiff. Then another . . . and another.

My right hand, already on the throttle, tightened.

We were in an area of potholes and bars where depth changed abruptly from a foot or less to twenty feet in the channel. The water was shoaling fast, so what else but a bunch of tarpon could create such a disturbance? Bull sharks, great hammerheads, too, sometimes ride the flood into the shallows but seldom in schools.

Can't be sharks, I thought, and knew it was true when something moved to my left: a big silver tail stirred the surface, a tarpon swimming in the sickly way of a fish that has been played too long, then gaffed. The man wearing the photographer's vest—his name was Ransler—was kneeling on the front casting deck and saw it, too.

"What's that?" he yelled.

Which is when, before I could slow the boat or answer, the water exploded to our right and a hundred-pound tarpon arched high into the air in front of us. Both men threw their hands up to shield themselves while I tried to steer away, but there was no avoiding a collision. Like a silver wave, the fish slapped Ransler overboard, then slammed bone-hard onto the forward deck where Delmont Chatham stood frozen, his weight braced on the vintage fishing rod. Automatically, I reached and grabbed the man by the collar while I reduced throttle slowly, slowly, hoping the tarpon wouldn't slide off the casting platform into the boat, but it did. Even so, I thought I had things under control until the fish's wild flopping caused me to lose my grip, then knocked Chatham's legs from under him and he tumbled overboard, too.

Hannah Smith, you fool! You've just killed your clients!

That's what I was thinking. A nightmare so unexpected, it caused my brain to go numb. But I grew up on the water, fishing and running boats, so my hands and eyes knew better than to panic. With a glance over my shoulder, I located both men, shoved the throttle forward and circled back, the chines of my skiff skidding in a tight turn. Ransler, in his sodden photographer's vest, was already standing, water up only to his waist. Chatham, though, had dropped into a deep pothole and was struggling to keep his nose above water. The heavy belly pack, I realized, was pulling him down.

He's drowning, I thought. *I can't let that happen!*

The men were separated by a distance, so I pointed my skiff at Chatham, full speed, one hand trimming the engine while the other searched behind me for the anchor I keep in the transom well. The whole time, the tarpon was hammering the deck of my boat, slinging slime and saltwater in a frenzy, the engine noise was deafening, which was why I couldn't hear what Ransler was hollering at me—*Slow down!* most likely—but I didn't touch the throttle. Didn't do anything but keep a finger on the trim switch until I was two boat lengths away. By then, the propeller had cleared the surface, the angle seemed right, so I killed the engine while I dumped the anchor and then let the boat glide.

"You're gonna hit him!"

I could hear Ransler clearly enough now despite the thrashing tarpon, but I paid no attention. My skiff had lost so much speed, there was no need to wait for the anchor to pull taut and I didn't. I grabbed the bowline and jumped over the side, only a few yards from where Mr. Chatham was still struggling to keep his head up. I was wearing khaki shorts, a long-sleeved shirt, and leather boat shoes. The water was cool when it flooded my clothing and too murky to see much when I went under. I found the bottom with my feet and pushed off in what I guessed was the right direction. When I surfaced behind Chatham, it surprised us both, but him more than me because he yelped, "Jesus Christ!" as if he'd been bitten by a shark.

His reaction almost caused me to laugh, but I didn't, thank

god. There was no way of knowing there was a shark in the area, but there was—a big one, too. The wounded tarpon I'd seen moments earlier should have put me on my guard, but all I could think about was getting my clients out of the water and returning them safely to the dock.

"Stay calm!" I said into the older man's ear. "Take a big breath!" Then I got an arm wrapped around his huge chest and used the bow rope to pull us to the boat, which was settling itself in a shallower area. Chatham was scared and twitchy, I could feel it, coughing water, too, so he came along meekly enough until he found his footing and I tried to help boost him up onto the deck. He'd gotten enough air to reinflate his confidence, or his pride, though, and he pushed me away, saying, "I hope you've got a good attorney!" Then he floundered up onto the transom like a seal trying to exit a slippery pool but fell back. The man had to weigh close to three hundred pounds.

I was too stunned to reply, at first. Then felt such a flush of anger I decided it was best to ignore the comment, so I turned my attention to the younger man, who was wading toward us. "Are you hurt?"

Ransler was smiling, thank god, and sounded good-natured when he replied, "Ruined a camera lens probably, but I've got a great story to tell the grandkids—if I ever have any! You okay, Del?"

Delmont Chatham was still trying to pull himself out of the water but paused long enough to wheeze, "Hurry up, I want to get back to the car!" Which caused the younger man's smile to only broaden while he gave me a private look and made a calming motion with his hands that promised *He'll cool down, don't worry.*

I didn't believe it was true but appreciated the reassurance. It was in that instant the younger man became an actual person in my mind, not just a client, which is an example of how quickly and unfairly I sometimes judge people. That morning at the dock, Chatham had introduced the two of us, saying, "This is Rance—try not to act like he's so damn good-looking," then added the man's full name, which I heard as Joe or Joel Ransler but wasn't certain. We had shaken hands, but I'd made only brief eye contact because Chatham was right: the man was as tall and handsome as a pro athlete or a news anchor and I've never been comfortable around unusually handsome men, no idea why. So I had dismissed him as a "type"—one of those beautiful people who moved easily through life full of confidence and absent of worries. After a day on the boat, or even after several charters, we would still have nothing in common, I would never see him again—not that I was interested personally because I wasn't. Even so, it was a way of shielding myself, I suppose, but also the type of lazy thinking I dislike in others and try to avoid.

The man's small gesture of kindness, though, caused me to see his face clearly for the first time—a nice face with a boyish grin, brown hair done by a stylist, but not too prissy neat, especially now that it was wet, blue jeans, no belt, and a black T-shirt under the photographer's vest. I didn't know him well enough to use his nickname, Rance—that would have been unprofessional—but at least he wasn't threatening to sue me in court.

"Anybody hit their head?" I called while I moved to the side of the boat. "We need an ambulance if you're hurt." It was a question I should have asked Mr. Chatham since he'd booked the trip, but fishing guide etiquette had gone out the window as far as I was concerned. Fact was, Chatham's threat didn't have my full focus. The tarpon was knocking my gear to pieces, fishing rods and cushions flying, so I tried to get a hand on the fish's lower jaw while also steadying the boat—which was not easily done in water up to my chest. Mr. Chatham wasn't helping, either, with his attempts to belly flop aboard, which was frustrating for us both. Finally, after another failed effort, he yelled, "I can't do this with that goddamn fish banging around!"

I seldom use profanity, don't find it attractive, but rude talk was the least of my worries so I paid him no mind. But the younger man didn't like it. He snapped, "Watch your language, Delmont!" Which surprised me because of the sharp tone, plus he'd hardly opened his mouth all morning. Even more surprising was Mr. Chatham's reaction—silence. Just stood there, looking embarrassed, until Ransler got to the boat, leaned his weight on the gunnel, then said coolly, "After we get that fish in the water, you're going to apologize to Captain Smith. Okay, Del?"

"Just Hannah," I corrected him, aware there was something else I'd misjudged: Mr. Chatham was working for Ransler or was his subordinate in some way, not vice versa.

Joel was the younger man's name. I asked when he was close enough to shake hands a second time. Then the two of us, by using our weight to lower the gunnel, slid the tarpon gently into the water.

———

MR. CHATHAM actually did apologize, muttering, "Guess I overreacted." By then, he was sitting with his feet dangling off the side of the boat, both men watching me revive the fish. Joel was in the water, standing waist-deep to my right, while I walked the fish back and forth, hoping its gills would soon show some color.

"Don't blame you a bit, Mr. Chatham," I replied, which prompted the younger man to give me a nod of approval. Thank god I looked up when he did it because that's when I saw the dorsal fin—a metal-gray fin, tall as a scythe's blade, thick as a steel bar. The fin cleaved the water in a lazy serpentine pattern, then disappeared behind Joel only twenty paces away.

"What's wrong?" he asked when he saw my expression change.

"Get in the boat," I said.

"What?"

"In the boat—*now*." I had stopped what I was doing but didn't raise my voice; didn't want the man to stumble and fall if he panicked.

He was carrying a bucket he'd been using to slosh slime off the deck and gestured with it. "The boat's still a mess."

"Hurry up," I told him, which is when he realized I was staring at something behind him, so he turned and looked. The shark wasn't coming fast, but it was pushing a big wake, and the fin had reappeared.

"Jesus Christ," he whispered—profanity that seemed appropriate in this situation. Then began walking backward, slowly at first, then faster, which got the shark's attention. When the fin turned on a line to follow him, the man swore again. "Holy shit!"

Mr. Chatham was fretting over his antique fishing rod, which had been damaged by the collision, so he was oblivious, his legs dangling in the water, when he demanded, "What's the problem now?"

The problem was that the shark would have to cruise past both men before it got to me and might attack one or both of them instead of the tarpon I was reviving—an injured fish, I felt certain, that the shark had scented and was its actual target. There's no telling what a feeding shark will do in murky water, so I called to Joel, "Don't watch the thing, just get in the boat!" I was already moving toward the shark, pulling the tarpon along beside me, its streamlined body buoyant in my right hand.

Once again, the shark submerged, this time in the hole where Mr. Chatham had nearly drowned, water so deep its wake disappeared and I lost track of the thing.

"Where'd it go?" Joel sounded anxious when he shouted, and no wonder. He had reached the boat but was too much of a gentleman, apparently, to leave a woman behind.

"He wants this tarpon, not me," I called, raising my voice for the first time. "Do you know how to handle a boat?"

"Why?"

"Get in and start the damn engine!" I yelled, and began pulling the fish toward the boat, taking leaping strides in the slow-motion way that water requires. My language must have surprised the man because he vaulted immediately aboard and was already lowering the motor while he asked again, "Where the hell did he go?"

Rather than answering, I continued my slogging stride because I didn't know. The whole time I was debating whether to leave the tarpon behind or try to save it. The fish's tail was moving, its gills were working, but it was in no condition to sprint for its life. I'm not sentimental when it comes to fish, but the sight of a rolling tarpon never fails to produce a glow in me. They're such lean, powerful creatures. They're never uncertain in their movements, and their scales reflect the sky like mirrors, so a six-foot tarpon is as close to liquid sunlight as anything alive. I've got nothing against sharks—well . . . except their goatish eyes and brutal ways. Even so, it seemed wrong to allow such a pretty fish—and one that had injured itself on my boat—to become an easy meal.

As I grabbed for the transom, I yelled, "Pull the anchor!" then felt silly because Joel had already done it—all but the last few feet of line, which had just broken free. The man had the line coiled in one hand and was leaning with an outstretched arm to pull me aboard. I refused to let him do it, though, until I'd yelled to Mr. Chatham, who was standing at the controls, "Put the boat in gear—slow idle. You know how to do that?"

"Look at the *size* of that thing!" I heard Chatham whisper, looking down at the water, which made me jump, so I was safely over the transom but still hanging on to the tarpon when the shark appeared behind us, the boat idling forward now.

A great hammerhead shark, twelve feet long, a couple of hundred pounds, its space-alien eyes were separated on a stalk of gray as wide as a broomstick. The shark had its bearings. Knew exactly where the wounded fish was and accelerated toward us with the slow stroke of its tail.

"A little faster," I told Chatham, then said to the younger man, "Help me slide him onto the deck." Meaning the tarpon. "Put a few hundred yards behind us, we can finish reviving him. No guarantees, but at least he'll have a chance."

"Smart," Joel replied, and got on his belly. Then, when we had the fish braced between us, he looked at the slime on his clothes and said, "It's going to take you days to clean this boat."

No, it took only an hour because my clients insisted on helping. The three of us had survived an adventure and rescued a fish, which changed the mood from businesslike to friendly. It was Mr. Chatham who suggested they help, saying, "How about we take a break, then finish the trip when we're done? Where can we find some towels and a hose with freshwater?"

My childhood home, where my mother, Loretta, still lives, that's where—and only two miles from Captiva Rocks. It's an old house of yellow clapboard on a paw of land where three thousand years ago people built shell pyramids as temples. Tourists new to Florida are always surprised to hear this, but it's true. From the water, the remains of those shell mounds looked like rolling, wooded hills as we approached. There was also a row of tin-roofed cottages—cabins, really—built along the bay, and docks where mullet and stone-crab boats floated, which raised Mr. Chatham's spirits even more.

"That could be a scene from the nineteen hundreds," he said, reaching for a camera. "What's the name of the place?"

"Sulfur Wells," I told him. "It's an old fishing village, and not easy to get to by car. Because the lots are so small, folks call the cabins Munchkinville. Most only have one bedroom."

Mr. Chatham was nodding as if he were way ahead of me. "Sure, Sulfur Wells. My family used to own property here, but it's been years since I've come by water. That's why I didn't recognize it. Good call, Hannah!" The man smiled at Joel Ransler, and added, "I told you I chose the right fishing guide."

It seemed like a pleasant compliment until I learned that Delmont Chatham was from a well-known family in neighboring Sematee County—Chatham Chevrolet, Chatham Citrus & Cattle—and they owned a lot of property. His deference to Ransler suggested that he had inherited the name but not the money, which wasn't unusual. Mr. Chatham collected antique fishing equipment, it turned out, which is why he'd been so upset when the tarpon shattered his vintage rod. His hobby, and his family's history, gave us something to talk about, because my great-grandfather—who'd built the yellow house—had also been one of the area's first fishing guides.

It got better after I tied up at the dock because my mother was on her way out. She and her friends were taking a courtesy van to play bingo, as they always do on Fridays, so there was no time to explain why a strange man—Joel—was escorting me up to the house. I was relieved. Loretta has never been an easy woman to deal with, and the stroke she had three years ago has not made her any less of a trial to me, her only child.

I FELT LUCKY the rest of the day. And my good luck held into late afternoon, when, at the hospital, a woman physician interrupted my story about the hammerhead shark and dispelled Tomlinson's warnings about giant fish and messages from God. "Your biologist friend has to take it easy," she said. "No strenuous exercise. But he's done with hospitals for now. I'll see him in a few weeks."

Tomlinson had been so relieved, he'd hugged the physician, and told her, "Float on, honey!" which was the sort of thing Tomlinson says even to heart surgeons.

The previous few weeks had been difficult for all of us, particularly Marion Ford. In late February, the surgeon had spent two hours removing the tip of a stingray barb from Ford's chest, then repairing what she had described in the waiting room as "a tiny laceration of the right ventricle." To comfort the dozens who had gathered there that night, she had added, "All he needed was a simple stitch or two—we'll know more in a few hours."

What the doctor knew, what we all knew, was that Marion Ford had nearly died. The week that had followed had been a roller coaster of good news, then complications that included one awful night that Ford had spent on a ventilator in ICU. Looking through a window at a person you love being inflated and deflated like a child's toy is painful and proves the line between life and death is as thin as a newborn's skin.

Now, six weeks later, I felt lucky indeed—as did Ford's many friends at Dinkin's Bay, on Sanibel Island, where we returned at sunset to share the good news.

That night, though, the biologist chose not to stay late at his own party. Instead, he invited me, alone, to his house for a "quieter celebration." We shared a bottle of wine and attempted to make small talk until the tension I felt made it impossible to speak a coherent sentence. After that, there was no talking—no conversation, anyway—despite the doctor's orders about strenuous exercise.

I didn't slip into my own bed until first light.

THREE

My mother peppered me with barbs and questions, saying things like, "Is that a bounce in your step or are you walking funny?" And, "Because you didn't phone last night, I worried about a car wreck or worse. Are you in some kind of trouble with the law?"

I've lived on my own for years, I didn't have to explain, but it was the opening I'd been waiting for. "No, Loretta," I replied, "but I'm tempted to call the police right now. I was in the attic yesterday while you were at bingo. The big trunk was open and some of the family things are missing. Know anything about it?"

I'd discovered it while attempting to show Delmont Chatham the fishing tackle stored in the attic, particularly a reel that had been given to my great-grandfather by Teddy Roosevelt. Roosevelt had come to Captiva Island in 1917 to harpoon giant manta rays and he'd been impressed by the young boy who would become Captain Mason Smith. The former president had also written a small book about the trip called *Harpooning Devilfish*, in which he had mentioned my great-grandfather. The book was gone, too.

Yes, Loretta knew something about it. I could tell by the way she sniffed and instantly changed the subject.

"Have you noticed that idiot dog's not barking?"

She was referring to the neighbor's toy Pekingese. The question was irksome because, fact was, I *had* noticed the unusual silence. My mother continued, "It's because of what happened last night. An owl snatched that dog while he was outside weeing and carried him to the tree above my bedroom. The moon was so bright, I saw the whole thing."

I sighed. Another one of my mother's stories. And, really, I didn't care. Nor did I care about my neighbors. They had finished their warehouse-sized concrete-and-stucco a few months earlier, after flattening a centuries-old Indian mound in the process, but had only recently moved in. The destruction of what had once been a shell pyramid was repellent, but I wasn't going to be lured off on a tangent.

"We were talking about that missing fishing reel," I insisted.

"How's a woman who gets no sleep expected to remember anything?" she said in an accusing way. "Lord A'mighty, you've never heard such a terrible yowling in your life, and pray you never do. You've seen that monster owl—he roosts in the oaks behind the house."

No, I hadn't, but I'd heard him calling, a baritone *boom-boom-boom* that was sometimes answered by owls on neighboring islands miles away. "Maybe some sweet tea will improve your memory," I said, and went to make it.

"I'm not going to sit here and lie," she continued, pressing her advantage. "I didn't like that ugly ball of hair. He'd hike his leg on my collards and pooed in the garden—any wonder I haven't made greens lately? That new neighbor woman and I had words about that, believe me! But the dog hasn't been born deserves to be eaten by a giant bird."

My mother sat back in her recliner, reached for the TV remote and added, "Suppose I could use something cool to drink, darlin'. This time, don't be so stingy with the sugar."

I had no idea, of course, that the missing reel would turn out to be significant or that its disappearance would convince me that my mother and her friends were being victimized by thieves whose conscience had been replaced by sickness, and who were capable of theft, and even murder. So I allowed my attention to waver. Had Loretta actually seen an owl swoop down and grab the neighbor's pet Pekingese? The woman's damaged brain followed strange branches and was sometimes confused. However, she was also smart enough to use that impairment to disguise her true motives or to conceal her own bad behavior. Truth was, I suspected that she'd probably sold the reel or traded it for marijuana, which she had never admitted using but was quick to praise as a healing drug. Loretta had always been tricky when it suited her needs, a trait I'd found irksome even as a little girl.

"There's no reason to make up stories," I warned, ice crackling as I poured tea into a pitcher. "I just want to know where the family antiques have disappeared to."

The reel and the book weren't the only items missing from the attic.

"The dog's dead," Loretta repeated. "You've been here, what, an hour? How many times you heard that little rat yapping?" She motioned toward the pitcher. "And don't forget the sugar!"

It was true that the dog barked all day most days, including yesterday when my clients had followed me up the shell mound to the house. But on this warm April afternoon, I'd yet to hear a peep.

"That is kind of strange," I said.

"Biggest owl I've ever seen," my mother replied, as she'd just proven her point.

"Maybe I should go next door and ask about him."

Loretta sat up straight. "Don't you dare! Say anything, those people will suspect I had something to do with it. Besides, they probably started drinking already. Afternoons, they sit on the porch and play tropical music. I can practically smell the booze."

My mother's tone forced an awful possibility into my head. "Loretta, please tell you didn't hurt their dog."

My mother didn't make eye contact. "What in the world you talking about?"

"You heard me. Did you run over that poor little thing last night or take him somewhere? Someone used Jake's truck—don't think I didn't notice it's been moved." Yesterday, my late uncle's old Ford had been in the carport where it belonged. Now it was parked in the shade of an avocado tree.

"How could I?" she answered. "You took my keys and cut up my driver's license."

The part about cutting up her license was fantasy, but I was thinking, *Uh-oh.* "*Someone* used that truck," I said, "and it wouldn't be the first time you snuck out on your own."

My mother glared. "Now you're accusing me of being a dog killer *and* a liar!" She got to her feet and shuffled toward the counter, where I let her slip past, then watched as she poured her own tea and dumped in half the sugar bowl.

"A neighbor borrowed it, if you have to know," she replied after a sip. "Check the yard for owl pellets. Also pieces of curly red hair and a blue ribbon. Bound to be spread all over the property. Probably a collar, too, but I doubt owls eat rhinestones."

Incredible, I thought, *she means it,* and had to fight back a smile. The ugly fact was, I wanted to believe her story. The Pekingese had been as mean-natured and snappish as the new neighbors themselves. Twice the little dog had cornered me on our dock, yapping his shrill head off, then nipped at my ankles as I went by, once breaking the skin. Had I filed a lawsuit, as some suggested, my worries about paying my mother's medical bills might be over because the neighbors were rumored to be wealthy. I didn't sue, of course. Didn't even bother to do a background check on the people to confirm if the rumors were true. My late uncle's business is a licensed, bonded private investigation agency, so I know how to access such information, but snooping into people's private lives is not a privilege I abuse.

One last time I tried to steer the subject back to the missing reel but gave up after listening, instead, to how Loretta's vegetables would prosper now that the Pekingese was gone. She had never been a particularly affectionate mother, we'd never been close, but I couldn't deny she was a first-rate gardener and loved tending her plants. First thing she did each morning was carry her coffee out to visit her collards and squash, then confirm the tomatoes were properly staked. The garden was her last call every evening, too, even on Wednesday nights when she had church.

I didn't want to hear about the garden right now, though, and I was about to manufacture an excuse to go outside and check my boat when an excuse was provided for me. A knock came at the screen door: a little man in a suit, holding a folder under his arm. Behind him was a deputy sheriff—a woman deputy, red hair, petite, one nervous hand tapping at her holster, a name tag that read *L. Tupplemeyer* on her uniform.

Now what? I wondered.

"MRS. SMITH?" the man asked.

"That's right," I replied, not hesitating to lie. It was a way of shielding my mother from involvement. Loretta gets jumpy when policemen come around—a guilty conscience, I've always suspected—which has only gotten worse since her stroke. "Let's walk outside to talk," I suggested, and let the two follow me away from the porch.

When we were near the carport, the man put a paper into my hand and said, "You've been notified." Then handed me several more sheets stapled to a yellow tag. "If you have questions, I can explain the basics or you can have your attorney contact our office. We don't have a lot of time today, sorry—lots more stops to make."

Deputy Tupplemeyer had parked her squad car around the bend, I noticed, midway between the house and a row of bayside cabins—*Munchkinville*, as I had told Mr. Chatham. The cabins had been built during the same period as the fish shacks and some weren't in great shape—unpainted boats on blocks, cast nets hanging among stacks of wooden stone-crab traps. Apparently, Loretta wasn't the only resident the man had plans to visit.

"Why in the world would I need an attorney?" I asked, reading what appeared to be a cover letter.

"That's something you should ask an attorney," he replied, which irritated me.

The letterhead read *Florida Division of Historical Resources, Bureau of Archaeological Research.* The first paragraph, which struck me as threatening, began *You are hereby ordered to repair/replace/ remove the structures and/or vegetation as listed on the pages attached. This must be done within 5 business days . . .*

I flipped a page to skip ahead and looked up, my eyes moving from the little man wearing the suit to the county deputy. "This isn't from the local zoning department," I said. "Who are you?"

As the man told me his name, I flipped another page and soon felt my face coloring because of what came next: *You are in violation of ordinances that: 1. Prohibit planting exotic vegetation. 2. Disturbing/altering property designated as archaeologically or historically important . . .*

That was enough for me, no need to continue.

"I think you have the wrong address," I said. "My family has owned this property for longer than you've been alive and we don't plant anything more exotic than jasmine or bougainvillea—which are flowers, in case you don't know, not illegal plants. Unless this is about the vegetable garden, which would be silly."

The smug look on the man's face told me *It is about the garden.*

"You can't be serious?" I said.

The man confirmed that he was with a nod. "Unless you planted native species, a vegetable garden doesn't belong here. In your packet, there's a phone number for the extension agency. This island has been redesignated and the agents know it, so they're expecting a lot of calls."

Which made me mad enough to forget I was impersonating Loretta. "Redesignated *historical*—I know that. It happened more than a year ago."

"Then you should be in compliance by now, shouldn't you?" The man smiled.

I'm not a violent person, but I wanted to slap the smug look off his face. "This is ridiculous. My mother could have another stroke if she sees this letter. You should have better things to do than pick on invalid ladies who enjoy gardening."

The man proved he didn't by studying my late uncle's truck, which was parked in the shade, then spoke to the deputy. "That tree? It's an avocado. That wasn't mentioned in the report, but it has to go. Avocados, mangoes—it's the same as citrus. They're all exotics. We should check the backyard before my next stop."

"That tree's a hundred years old!" I argued, which might have been true but probably wasn't. Then asked, "Is that why *she's* here? You've got to bring an armed deputy to protect you?"

The petite woman gave me a tough cop look that she'd probably seen in movies and spoke for the first time, her accent unmistakably Boston. "The state of Florida doesn't want any trouble with locals. That's why I've been assigned—*ma'am*."

I shot her a hard look of my own and replied, "Then the state of Florida should relocate to a place that doesn't attract hurricanes—or tourists from Massachusetts."

It took Deputy Tupplemeyer a second to remember where she had been born. "Hey! Are you looking for trouble?"

"No," I told her, "I'm looking for a reason not to order you off my property and I can't think of a single one." I indicated the neighbor's new house, a mountain of concrete that dwarfed the poinciana and coconut palms separating our properties. "*Those* are the people you should be serving papers. They trucked off most of an Indian mound to build that house, then terraced the landscaping. Where was your agency then? They dumped a thousand years of pottery and artifacts somewhere—they won't even tell the archaeologists. But no one from the government said a word! Now you're bothering me about avocados and some pole beans? If I had either one of your jobs, I'd quit and do something I could be proud of."

To signal I was done reading, and done with the conversation, I folded the sheath of papers but also used those few seconds to tell myself, *Calm down*. Right or wrong, arguing with a police officer is always a bad choice, and I didn't want to push it too far. Plus, my mother's garden was at stake, and Loretta, who does have her sweet moments, didn't have much in life but tending her plants, putting up canned vegetables, and bingo.

The little man was getting nervous, a bit of sweat showing above his lip, and I expected Deputy Tupplemeyer to put me in my place with something stern. Instead, she said, "I've never heard of Indian mounds in Florida," sounding cop-like and cynical but also interested.

"You're standing on one," I replied. "Pyramids made of shell before the Spaniards arrived."

The deputy turned to the little man. "She's kidding, right? I thought they were hills."

He was remarking on the subject's unimportance when his phone buzzed, which allowed the deputy to ask me a couple more questions before explaining, "I spent two weeks in Guatemala. The ruins there. Mayan—it was for a course I was taking. Copán, too. Three weeks, that trip, then a month when I was in college." She had her hands on her hips, looking at the topography, maybe trying to imagine if what I'd told her was possible.

I asked, "East-west pyramids, is that the way the Maya built their cities?"

"You'd have to see for yourself to understand the attraction," she replied as if mishearing. But then added, "Yeah, the Maya were astronomers."

"Same with the people here," I said, then pointed to a distant island. "See the high trees? That's the western pyramid. The first day of spring, the sun sets right over it. We're standing on the eastern pyramid—what's left of it anyway. Farther east, there're three burial mounds."

The deputy looked at the man, who was putting his phone away, then at the house next door, her eyes taking in the terraced lawn, construction residue, insulation, broken stringers stacked by the road. The tracks of a bulldozer, too, used to flatten the mound and load dump trucks that had waited in a line. Then she asked him, "How could they get away with something like that?"

The man shook his head, getting more nervous by the second. "Permits and variances don't go through my department," he responded, which was an attempt to distance himself, but it also confirmed the truth as far as the deputy was concerned.

"A thousand years old," she said, thinking about it.

"Some artifacts, they've dated back four or five thousand years," I told her.

"Here?"

"Right where we're standing, pottery and shell tools—the artifacts the neighbors didn't have hauled off to the dump, or wherever they took it. About fifteen or twenty tons of shell mound, just disappeared."

"There's something *very* wrong about that," Deputy Tupplemeyer told the little man. Then had to show her authority over me by adding, "You shouldn't be digging a garden either. Like the law says. Not if this is an archaeological site."

I was explaining that my grandfather had raised pineapples on the plot where vegetables now grew, so it was too late to apologize, we couldn't go back in time, but we had drawn the line at bulldozing history. That's when I noticed that the neighbor woman had come outside and was watching. Alice Candor was her name, a medical doctor, local gossip claimed. She had a dog leash in one hand and was using the other to talk on a cell phone. A tall woman, bulky but not obese, with whom I'd never spoken but had seen a few times, distinctive in her appearance, always wearing dark baggy clothes. Often caftans, and she liked scarves. She was dressed that way now, whispering into the phone and watching, until she realized I'd spotted her, then spun her back to me.

That's when a little light went off in my head. "That's who

complained about the garden, isn't it? The new neighbors reported us, that's why you're here."

"Who?" the deputy asked, then became official. "Doesn't matter who did it, the names are confidential."

The man said, "Of course they are," but gave it all away when the neighbor woman suddenly knelt to retrieve something off the ground, froze for an instant, then bolted away, shrieking, her screams so piercing they spooked crows from the trees.

The man panicked and began to jog after her, calling, "Something must have bit her! Dr. Candor's hurt!"

No, the doctor had found her missing Pekingese.

FOUR

When I returned to the house to check on Loretta, she was pacing and looked upset, but it wasn't because of the neighbor's shrieking. It was because she couldn't locate a childhood friend and bingo partner of hers, Rosanna Helms, whom everyone called Pinky. Of special concern was that Mrs. Helms's answering machine didn't come on, and three of her other bingo partners hadn't answered the telephone either.

"Second day in a row Pinky didn't call," my mother said, "but yesterday, at least, her damn machine answered!"

At the time, of course, I had no reason to suspect that Mrs. Helms had been given our family antiques or to fear that the woman had been murdered. Like most adult daughters, I assumed my mother's anxiety was baseless, which is why I treated her with the same gentle impatience she had shown me as a little girl. "You're worried for no reason, please calm down," I told her.

"Something's wrong, I *know* it," Loretta insisted, while I steered her toward the recliner. Which caused me to remark that her day nurse, Mrs. Terwilliger, would soon return, so why not swallow her five p.m. meds a little early?

"It'll settle your nerves," I added.

My mother pursed her lips to refuse my advice. "Pinky and me talk every afternoon, you know that. Especially today—she was expecting a new wig in the mail."

"Maybe she forgot," I said.

"Nope! When the game shows are over, that phone rings. She never missed a day until yesterday. Then I always call Becky Darwin and Jody and Jody calls Epsey Hendry and what's-her-name, the woman I can't stand. Now they've all disappeared!"

"All five of your friends?"

"What's-her-name is a damn gossip, not a friend. It's the other four I'm worried about."

"Loretta, you're upsetting yourself for no reason."

Angry and near tears, my mother wailed, "Pinky's hurt, maybe dying—that's not cause to be upset? Hannah Smith, you listen to me! Just a few minutes ago, in my mind, I heard her crying for help! At least drive to the old Helms place and check."

The poor woman looked frantic, rusty hair hanging in strands over her face and housecoat, her hands balled into pale, knobby fists. The sight of her so frail and frightened squeezed at the heart. My mother had once been sharp and sure and bullheaded, but now the years and a brain embolism had sapped the best part of her away. It had made her so childlike, I wanted to hug her close to let her know she was safe and protected. So that's exactly what I did before returning with a pillow and a fresh glass of sweet tea, then apologized to her because it was the right thing to do. It was also a way of explaining the cries for help she'd heard.

"I was wrong to doubt you about that Pekingese, Mamma.

What you told me was true about the owl. Just now, the neighbor lady found what was left—not far from the oak grove, like you said. That's what you heard, not Pinky. The woman started screaming. There's a deputy sheriff trying to calm her right now."

Loretta's eyes flashed for an instant, a triumphant look, which I expected, but I didn't expect her to reply, "Think I don't know that? I was watching from the porch when that evil bitch found the collar, then picked up a piece of his tail or whatever it was she slung into the bushes. Her bawling has nothing to do with Pinky." Then again pleaded, "Hannah, please drive me so we can check. Pinky might be dying right now!"

I sighed, unsure if I should take Loretta seriously. There were times, as a girl, when I'd wondered if my mother was a mind reader. Even during my teenage years, Loretta's intuition had been maddeningly accurate—although often aided by her snoopy behavior.

The grandfather clock opposite the fireplace was tocking solemnly. It read 4:20 p.m., which meant it was nearly five. At sunset, which was around eight, I had a date with the biologist, whom I'd allowed myself to phone only twice since leaving his bedroom in the early hours of the morning. Sunset was less than three hours away, and I still had to finish some work in my late Uncle Jake's office before I showered, changed, and then boated across to Sanibel Island. Marion Ford lived there in an old stilthouse next to Dinkin's Bay Marina, where, every Friday night, there is a party. I didn't want to be late, nor did I want to give Ford the impression I was a slave to the whims of my addled mother. What kind of man would tolerate such a partner?

What to do?

"Lord A'mighty," Loretta gasped, breaking into my thoughts. "You're in love with that fish doctor! That's why you're refusing to help poor Pinky!"

"I am not!" I shot back and instantly regretted my denial. It invited bad luck, as lying often does, and somehow cheapened the good feeling inside me. But I wasn't going to allow my mother to poke around in my private thoughts without a battle, so I stuck by the lie, saying, "What's Pinky's number? If she doesn't answer, I'll take the truck and knock on her door. But you're staying right here. Mrs. Terwilliger just pulled into the drive."

The keys to the truck, though, were gone from the storage shed, which was my latest hiding spot.

"Where are they, Loretta?" I demanded, which should have put my mother in a difficult position. If I was to check on her friend, she would have to admit she had been sneaking out and driving illegally or, at the very least, letting someone chauffeur her into town.

"How would I know?" my mother replied with some heat. "That poor little Thurloe boy is the one I let use the truck when he needs it. Ask him."

"You're making up another story," I said, because it couldn't be true. There was nothing "little" about Levi Thurloe. The man was the size of a field hand and older than me, but his development had been stunted by a fever in infancy or some accident. Local gossip varied. Levi walked everywhere, didn't even own a bike. I'd seen him miles from the island, going to or coming from the mainland, head down, earbuds always plugged into his ears, using music to block the outside world. Walkin' Levi, locals called him—or worse. He was a solitary young man, commonly seen on the roads, but he seldom spoke so was the target of jokes and nasty rumors that I, at least, didn't find entertaining. More than once, as a girl, I had backed down some taunting bully, then been rewarded with Levi's shy, "Thank you, miz." The man was harmless in my opinion, but a poor choice when it came to loaning the family pickup truck.

"Levi doesn't know how to drive," I reminded my mother.

"People say the same thing about me!" Loretta countered. "He's working for the new neighbors as a handyman, and I can't say no to a half-wit who needs transportation. If you want the keys, find Levi—don't believe he's as dumb as some say. And for god's sake, hurry up!"

Luckily, I checked the truck's ignition before setting off on my search. The keys were there. So was Levi Thurloe. He was sitting on the passenger side, a big arm hooked out the open window as if already enjoying the ride. His sad, slow eyes stared straight ahead to avoid looking at me when I climbed in.

"You can't go," I said gently.

"Can," he replied without making eye contact—something he refused to do.

"Please get out."

"I *can*," he said again but not forcefully. It was more of a request.

I looked at my cell phone to check the time, aware the sun had already begun its slide west. "Levi, you don't even know where I'm headed."

"Don't matter," he responded, staring at nothing beyond the windshield.

It was five miles to the Helms place, a spooky-looking house in the mangroves at the end of a shell lane. Because the last stretch of road was bad, getting there would take awhile. Levi wasn't wearing his earbuds, I noticed, which was unusual, so I made him an offer. "Don't you miss your music? We'll go for a ride another day when you're better prepared."

The man shrugged but didn't budge.

I sighed, thought about it for a moment, then started the engine. "Put your seat belt on," I told him, "and keep your hand inside the window once we get moving."

Levi didn't speak again until we had crossed the line into Sematee County, driving north.

"*You're* nice" was all he said.

"THE NEIGHBOR LADY threatened to hire Mexicans to shoot the owl," I told Marion Ford, cell phone cradled to my ear as I drove. "Then she threatened me. Said she'll have me arrested if I pick up clients at Loretta's dock because it's not zoned commercial— doesn't matter Uncle Jake chartered out of there before he died. Fifteen years? Longer—he was only forty when they retired his badge. Scariest thing is, the neighbor lady didn't sound crazy, just mean. One of those women who's used to getting what she wants."

The biologist had called to ask if I would be at Dinkin's Bay before dark, but his voice had assumed the role of comforter and counselor now that I was sharing details about my afternoon.

"I wouldn't worry about the owl," he said. "Mexicans, especially the illegals, are too smart to risk jail or their jobs. And the neighbor, it'll dawn on her a sheriff's deputy was there listening. She's a physician? She'll think it through and that'll be the end of it."

"A doctor of *some* type," I responded. "I was tempted to do a background check through the office, but it seemed sneaky."

Ford found me amusing. "It's a poor private detective who lets ethics get in her way."

The agency had been part-time even for Jake, which is why I replied, "I'm already the poorest one around. It hasn't cost me my principles, though. And it gives me something to do when the wind's blowing too hard to fish."

"Good, keep your license current," he agreed. "Personally, I wouldn't hesitate to check out someone harassing your mother. First the vegetable garden, then the dock. You want me to have a talk with her? Tomlinson says Loretta's a lot of fun, and it's about time we met."

Tomlinson, of course, smoked weed and said, "Float on, honey!" to charm-addled women. He didn't mind escorting Loretta to the mounds at night to eavesdrop on her conversations with an Indian-king who had been dead a thousand years. Ford, thank god, was from solider stock, which meant my mother would hate him at first sight.

"As soon as Loretta's feeling better," I lied. "She's still all torn up about that little dog."

"Sounds as softhearted as you, Hannah."

There was no way for me to reply to that without another lie. Fortunately, the biologist in Ford saved me by inquiring, *What kind of owl?*

As we chatted, Levi watched the scenery of Sematee County flow by: raw land that had been clear-cut decades ago, then had gone wild with palmettos and melaleuca trees, awaiting the next small-time developer to go bankrupt. Lots of billboards—*Chatham Subaru & Honda*, I noticed—then walls of vegetation that were interrupted by ATV trails or small housing developments, a couple of nursery farms, and a trailer park or two. The turnoff to the Helms place wasn't marked, and I hadn't been there in a year, so, after another few minutes, I had to tell Ford, "Mind if I call later?" Because Levi was sitting right there beside me, however, my words came out sounding formal and abrupt. It created a silence between us.

"You doing okay?" Ford asked. "After last night, I mean."

"Never better," I assured him, giving it all the warmth I could. Then abandoned my concern about Levi and said, "I bought something today I want to model for you. But maybe I should wait. The doctor was serious about no strenuous exercise."

The man laughed as if we were conspirators, then replied with a suggestion so bawdy I was taken aback—but only for a moment because secretly, in my mind, I had already pictured that very thing happening. Ford, whom I had never heard speak crudely to a woman, or even to a man, had just opened a private door to me, it felt like. Better yet, his intimate thoughts mirrored my own, which encouraged me to speak freely about my own secret wants when and if the chance came. I'm picky about men, I seldom date, so what I felt was new in my experience.

"Did you just say what I thought you said?" I smiled.

"You're offended."

"I'm not!" I said. "The doctor ordered you to stay in bed, so someone needs to be handy. And I've got some ideas about tonight myself."

Because my ears were warm when I put the phone away, I sat stiffly, both hands on the steering wheel. Didn't risk a glance at Levi, who rode in silence, while I downshifted into second and watched for landmarks. Ahead, opposite a hand-painted *Acreage for Sale* sign, a mailbox gathered weeds at the intersection of a shell road. The box, which looked too small to hold mail-order wigs, had been shotgunned, the pellet holes rimmed with rust. Same with a yellow *Deer Crossing* sign and another that read *Dead End*.

"Redneck graffiti," I muttered, turning onto the shell road, then downshifting again. The road was a mess of potholes and ruts. It hadn't been graded for years—not since I'd brought Loretta to console Mrs. Helms after her son, Mica, had been sentenced to prison for operating a meth lab. Her daughter, Crystal—the sweetest, quietest girl in my fourth-grade class—was already in jail for other drug-related crimes, so Loretta had treated the occasion like a funeral, bringing along a basket of baked goods and a pan of lasagna. My mother's actual intentions were to convince her childhood friend to move into the village, which Mrs. Helms had done, but she had recently returned to live alone in the family home. No idea why—the bay-front cabin she'd inherited was the nicest in Munchkinville.

After several hundred yards of zigzagging, I told Levi, "Hold tight!" because we were approaching a hole deep enough to hold water. It hadn't rained for two weeks, so I expected the truck to bang hard and it did. Levi, still in a trance, seemed not to hear but awoke when his head banged the roof.

"Ooh-ee!" he said, which is the equivalent of *Ouch!* to a Southern child who had not progressed beyond the age of ten. Then his eyes widened and his head began to swivel, taking in details as if trying to figure out where we were.

"Tighten that seat belt," I advised. "We've still got a quarter mile to go and there's another big hole ahead."

"No," he said. "Stop!"

I couldn't stop. Water might have killed the engine, so I spun the wheels and worked the clutch until we had cleared the second hole, Levi repeating, "No! . . . No! . . . No!" the whole time.

"What's wrong?" I asked, when we'd reached a smooth stretch.

The poor man was terrified. "Can't," he said. "I want to go back."

It had taken us twenty minutes to travel a few miles; the sun was now above the trees, which didn't give me time to waste. "We will," I said patiently. "Soon as I'm done with my business. We'll stop at the marina, too, and I'll buy you a bottle of pop. How's that sound?"

"No!" Levi yelled, fighting with his seat belt.

I reached to comfort him by patting his arm, but that only scared the poor creature more. There was nothing I could do but sit and watch as he kicked open the door and took off, running. Not toward the main road either. He bolted into a thicket of buttonwood trees that signaled the beginning of mangroves where, a hundred years ago, the Helms family had homestead a piece of high ground on what had once been a cattle trail that led to the bay.

"Pay Day Road," locals still called the shell lane. The name dated back to the 1990s when off-loading marijuana bales required a remote place that was hard to find by land or water. *Pot hauling,* as it was known, had saved some fishermen from going broke, had made a few others wealthy, but had spelled trouble for the Helms family, particularly their young children, who had learned the trade too early to save themselves.

I thought about getting out and calling to Levi but decided against it. The decision wasn't purely selfishness, but my eagerness to get to Sanibel Island played a role. By truck, it was several miles to Sulfur Wells, but there was also an old horse trail through the backcountry that cut the distance in half. Walkin' Levi would know the trail, so he'd probably be home long before me.

But what was it about Pay Day Road that had scared the poor man? The Helms family had once kept pit bulls, I remembered. Not fighting dogs—not since old Mr. Helms had died, anyway—but for protection.

Levi's afraid of dogs, I thought. Shy people who traveled on foot had every reason to fear pit bulls. It made sense.

Even so, I felt a creeping uneasiness that caused me to take a precaution. My cell phone showed only one bar, but it was enough to include a locator map when I messaged Marion Ford and another friend, Nathan Pace, who is a bodybuilder but a sweet man nonetheless.

Here checking on Loretta's friend. Will text again in 30.

I signed the note *H4*, a signature I reserve for friends, and also to remind myself I'm the fourth Hannah Smith in my family, so have more reasons than most to be cautious. My great-great-grandmother—known as Big Six because of her height and strength—and my wild aunt, Hannah Three, had both come to violent ends due to their own recklessness and their poor judgment in men. The history inherited with my name, although I've never admitted it, is a secret reason I'm careful about dating. The fear that history repeats itself is silly and superstitious, I suppose, but I'm also aware that my own judgment is often less than perfect.

I sent the text, waited for the message to clear, then put the truck in gear.

Ahead, mangrove trees leaned in to form a tunnel that sprinkled sunlight on the windshield. The shell road became sand and showed tire tracks coming or going. Both maybe. Definitely fresh.

A UPS truck, I hoped, delivering the wig Loretta had mentioned.

FIVE

The house where Rosanna Helms's husband, Dwight, had been born, and where *his* mother had been born, resembled a tobacco barn on pilings that, for a hundred years, had been jettisoning the junk that now surrounded the place. Oil drums, trailers, crab traps, pieces of Mica's Harley-Davidson scattered around a hot-water heater, rusting near a satellite dish, and a bicycle frame perched trophylike atop a sheen of glass fishing net—Crystal's bike, I remembered the pink streamers.

Crystal and I had played in this yard as children. She had been a shy, big-boned girl who enjoyed Barbie dolls, which I'd tolerated out of boredom more than politeness. But she was also game enough to paddle a canoe I'd found in the mangroves, then patched with roofing tar. We had never been close, but childhood is a powerful link, so it felt strange to be here alone, an adult woman sent to check on a playmate's mother, a mother who had chosen to live amid the wreckage of her own shattered family. I had never liked the feel of this place. I didn't like being here now.

Like a few other outposts on the coast, the Helms property had prospered when commerce was conducted by water, but the first roads had bypassed it, and better roads had left it as isolated as an island, the acreage not worth much because it was the only high ground in a tract of mangroves now protected by law. Yet the house remained as I remembered, a resolute structure two floors high, wood black as creosote, with four small holes cut for windows and a fifth added for a door.

From the truck, I could see that the front door was open now, hanging lopsided on its hinges—unusual in a place where mosquitoes swarmed.

I considered getting out to check but was reluctant. Instead, I honked the horn to get attention, then honked again, expecting Mrs. Helms to appear in the doorway. She didn't.

After another minute, I hollered out the window, "Miz Helms? It's Hannah Smith!"

Overhead, an osprey whistled. A mosquito found my ear, whining the good news, while trees filtered a gust of wind, then clung to the silence that was my answer.

It made no sense. Rosanna Helms's car was parked beneath the plywood shed—an old Cadillac as swaybacked as a horse but still hinting at the wealth her family had enjoyed during the pot-hauling years. She was a competent driver—better than Loretta, anyway—and had no trouble getting around. Unless the car wouldn't start, which was possible considering its age and the years of abuse dealt to it by Pay Day Road.

I recalled the fresh tire tracks I'd seen on the way in. Maybe that explained the woman's absence. Even so, the possibility didn't excuse me from checking inside the house—but what about the pit bulls I remembered? They hadn't come running at the sound of my truck, which suggested I had nothing to fear. On the other hand, the dogs could be a hundred yards away, where the shell road dead-ended, enjoying sunlight and water on the commercial-sized dock that had been rotting there since Dwight Helms had died—shot by drug dealers, most believed, even though the murder had never been solved.

No . . . it was safer, I decided, to try dialing again from my cell and hope the woman answered. At the very least, I would hear her phone ringing through the open door, which would have been a comfort because my mother had used the absence of an answering machine as evidence her friend was in trouble.

Twice I hit *Redial* before realizing the problem: *No service.* I moved the phone around, touched it to the windshield, even held it out the window, before finally giving up. No way around it, I had to go inside that house.

Please, God, don't let Loretta be right about this. That's what I was thinking when I slid out of the truck and hurried across the yard to the porch. Every step, my eyes were moving, worried about those dogs. When I got to the door, I had something new to worry about. The door was leaning on its hinges because someone had used a crowbar to shear the doorknob off, then rip the dead bolt free of the framing.

No . . . not a crowbar, I saw when I looked closer. The door, which was plain but solid, had been split down the middle by a single blow, only weather stripping joining the two pieces.

An axe, I thought. *A strong man with an axe did this.*

I took a step back. Where was the man now? Where was the axe?

"Miz Helms! *Pinky!* Are you there?" I had never used the woman's nickname before and embraced the absurd hope it would shock her into responding. It did not.

The house was as dark inside as it was outside, just as I remembered. Through the open doorway, in the shadows of the living room, I could see a mix of antique furniture and modern appliances, a wide-screen TV that was on but muted. A game show, one of my mother's favorites, same with her bingo partners. A topic they squabbled about on the phone.

Eyes scanning the trees to my left, to my right, I backed to the porch railing and checked my cell. Still no service—but why was the Helmses' satellite dish working?

Does it matter?

No, it did not. My brain was avoiding the real question, which was: *Should I bolt for the truck and get help or go inside the house to see if Mrs. Helms was hurt?*

What if it was Loretta in there? my conscience argued. *Your own mother injured, maybe dying?* Then it asked a more painful question: *What if it was you thirty years from now? A helpless widow unable to cry out!*

My pounding heart urged *Run! Get out of here now!* but I couldn't do that. Why is the most difficult choice almost always the right choice in a tough situation? The good and decent person in me ignored a final reproach—*You have only yourself to blame!*—then took charge of the situation. I had to find a weapon. Something I could swing or throw to fend off a strong man carrying an axe.

Propped against the porch steps was a shovel I hadn't noticed until now. It seemed a handy discovery until I hefted it and saw that the blade was soiled with dog feces. Which caused me to notice other unseen details in the yard: a bucket nearly empty of water; a galvanized chain clipped to a tree where the earth had been trotted into a circle; a second tree and another chain where there were mounds of dog spore fresh enough to draw bluebottle flies. Midway between the two dog runs was a cushion that had been shredded and a bone the size of a steer's leg that had been gnawed in two.

My hands began to shake. I held the shovel tighter to steady them, then cleaned the blade by jamming it in the sand. *Pit bulls.* Mrs. Helms still owned pit bulls. She had lost her husband, Dwight, to drug dealers, and her children to drug dealing, but the progeny of the family's dogs had survived it all.

Where were they?

Not in the house. I was certain of that—they would have charged me by now. Suddenly, the house seemed a safer choice than standing alone on the porch.

I slipped past the door and went inside.

MRS. HELMS used snuff, Peach Blend, which wasn't uncommon for women her age. "Rubbing snuff," Loretta calls the practice, and believes it relieves menstrual cramps and gives energy, which is why the odor was familiar when I entered the living room. But why so strong?

The muted television darkened the room, so I flicked the wall switch and my question was answered. A can of Peach Blend lay open on the floor, the sweet tobacco spread on a shattered coffee table. Within easy reach was the woman's vinyl recliner. The recliner had tumbled over backward hard enough to crack the wood floor, landing amid a litter of what looked like pamphlets. Glass from a china closet crunched beneath my feet—its walnut facing showed the divot from a single blow of an axe. Mrs. Helms had used a frozen orange juice can as a spittoon. It was there, too. Or was that sticky black mess beneath the can blood? I couldn't be sure, and the possibility caused me to freeze for a moment.

A crime scene, I thought. *Don't touch anything.*

I had finished three semesters toward my A.S. degree in law enforcement before Loretta's stroke and had at least learned the basics. But then I ignored my own counsel by hurrying across the room to retrieve the telephone, which was also on the floor.

Nine-one-one. I hammered the buttons with an index finger. The signal tones suggested the phone was working, but it was dead when I put it to my ear. My god, Loretta had been right about the significance of no answering machine! I was already frightened, but this realization pushed me close to panic.

Pinky's hurt, maybe dying! my mother had said, or something similar. I couldn't escape to the truck; not now, I couldn't, because what my mother had feared might be true. I had to continue searching the house.

"Miz Helms! You here?" How unnerving it was to hear my own voice tainted by the coward that is in me. It caused me to take stock. I am an oversized woman, fitter and stronger than most. Poor, tiny Mrs. Helms was in her seventies, had survived family tragedies and cancer yet continued to live her life with a woman's energy, still fussing over clothes and her looks. If an intruder was in this house, Mrs. Helms was the one who had a right to be frightened, not me!

I picked up the shovel, noticing the pamphlets when I knelt. Dozens of the things on glossy paper, all the same:

PRESERVE OUR HERITAGE
JOIN FISHERFOLK of SOUTH FLORIDA, Inc.

The words were printed in white over an old-timey photo of a pioneer woman stirring a cauldron. Below it was an architect's drawing of a modern building—it appeared to be a museum.

A charity project, I thought. Had I seen the same pamphlet among my mother's magazines? If not, there was something similar, which was no surprise. Elderly women were easy targets for solicitors seeking donations. Loretta, because she was lonely, took every automated phone call just to hear a human voice. Same when a solicitor came to the door. Pinky Helms would have been no different. I dropped the pamphlet and continued on through the house, flicking on lights as I went.

In the hallway was a heavy metal floor lamp with twin globes, milky white, that came on when I hit the wall switch. The staircase to the second floor was there: wood beneath carpet worn bare by the passage of children and time. Crystal's room was up there.

Mica's, too. Mica was three years younger but already taller than me when he entered middle school, and already smoking cigarettes and weed. By then, Crystal and I were strangers, separated by interests and school districts, since the village of Sulfur Wells was on the line that separated Sematee County from Lee County. I hadn't been up those stairs in twenty years. I didn't want to go up them now. Wasn't it smarter to search Mrs. Helms's bedroom first? A woman in her seventies, even if fleeing for her life, wasn't likely to charge up the stairs.

There was a door, though, that separated the stairs from the rest of the house—typical of old houses that had been pieced together before air-conditioning. I knew the woman's bedroom was somewhere off the kitchen, which meant I would have to open the door before continuing: a cheap door, painted green, with a white ceramic knob. I stood staring at it for several seconds, aware that the dread I felt was irrational. A man with an axe would have bashed the thing to pieces; at the very least, would not have closed a door behind him. But an elderly woman on the run *might* have.

A competent investigator searches buildings systematically, always clearing one room before proceeding to the next.

Textbook training from the degree I had failed to complete. Competence, I realized, could also be a handy excuse for cowardice.

I turned away from the door and went up the stairs, wood creaking beneath my weight with every slow step, my eyes focused on lace curtains white with sunlight at the top of the landing. They streamed with dust beams that pulled me forward as if on a tightrope while I used the shovel for balance. Even so, it was a clumsy weapon to carry. Halfway up, when I turned to glance behind me, the blade clunked against the banister so loudly, it startled me and I almost fell. Then I dropped the shovel, which made even more noise when it sledded down the stairs, banging each step like a cymbal.

To steady myself, I leaned against the wall, my heart pounding again. Should I retrieve the shovel? Or continue without it?

To postpone the decision, I used my voice again. "Anyone up there?" Then added a lie in case I had cornered an intruder. "The police are here! We're worried about you, Miz Helms."

The silence I expected was jolted by a new sound coming from outside the house; a distant noise that touched my ears as the random snaring of a drum. Then the sound deepened and took form, and I thought, *Barking dogs!* Dogs coming toward the house at a run; a slathering chorus I recognized from hunting with my Uncle Jake in the Everglades as a girl. It was the bellow of catch dogs that had picked up the scent and were on the heels of game.

Pit bulls. The Helms dogs had returned.

Dear god, I thought, remembering: *You left the front door open!*

The oversight had left me unprotected. Nothing at all to slow those animals if they struck my scent and came after me—me, a stranger, not only on their property but inside their owner's home.

Run!

Because I panicked, that's what I did. Hand on the banister, I vaulted down the steps, but then hesitated, the green door to my right, the living room to the left. The door offered protection, but only temporary. The living room exited to the porch, then my truck, which was the only sure means of escape. Drive half a mile on Pay Day Road, I would have a cell signal again and could call

the police. But the wild barking of the dogs was so close now—
would they catch me as I crossed the yard?

Not if I hurried! So I turned left. Stumbled over the shovel,
hesitated again before picking it up, then sprinted down the hall
toward the living room. The pine floor was slick. A shovel is also
an awkward tool to run with. I had to slap a hand on the wall to
make my final turn, skidded on the broken glass, and then continued more cautiously. I kept my eyes on the open doorway. It was a
beacon, an airy rectangle bright with daylight and freedom, that,
oddly, had muted my own hearing as abruptly as the wide-screen
TV, where, on the game show, a young woman was weeping,
whether for joy or in despair I neither knew nor cared. Three
strides from the door, though, I stopped, my head tilted, straining
to hear.

The dogs—they had stopped barking. *Why?*

I wasn't deaf. I banged the shovel on the floor to prove it to
myself. The thunk of metal on wood registered in my ears, but my
attention was already riveted to a more chilling sound: claws clattering on gravel; a heavy, wolfish breathing so close that the slap of
a panting tongue was unmistakable. I took a step back when the
panting stopped. It was replaced by the rumble of a dog growling.

No . . . two dogs. Their silhouettes trotted across the lighted
doorway. Both pit bulls, their heads the size of concrete blocks,
stubby horns for ears, on dwarfed bodies of brindle-yellow fur and
muscle, drifted past unaware of my presence. I pressed my back
against a wall and didn't move, didn't breathe. It didn't save me.
The odor of my skin, my clothing, the odor of my fear, was in the

air, and one dog stopped, lifted his nose to taste my scent, then returned to the doorway and looked inside. Soon, he was joined by the other dog, both animals alert, intense, their tiny eyes now so focused on me that the flooring vibrated when they began to growl in unison.

SÍX

I have been charged by dogs while jogging and know it's best to take the offensive. I've backed down collies and retrievers and even a pit bull, who was so instantly sweet that he had begged me to scratch his ears, then followed me home.

It was a strategy worth trying. "Get out of here!" I yelled, and banged the shovel hard on the floor. I took a step toward the door and did it again. "Get!"

These dogs, however, were not sweet-natured. They looked half starved, all jaws and instinct, and they came at me when I moved. The lead dog—there's always an alpha dog—came first, trotting toward me, then lunged, stiff-legged, and roared when I jabbed the shovel at it. She was female, judging from the absence of the testicles that hung so prominently from the second dog, who was larger and also slyer. He slunk into the room without barking, teeth bared, and disappeared behind the overturned recliner. When he reappeared, he was to my left, and moving toward the hall, an attempt to corner me, I realized—two dogs who hunted as a pack. I began to sidestep toward the bigger male because the hallway was my only escape.

When the female charged again, I swung the shovel too hard and the thing almost flew out of my hands. The near loss frightened me so badly, I felt an electric sensation between the ears. With it bloomed a horrible certainty that these animals, if they got me on the ground, would not just maul me, they would feed on me. I could not lose the shovel. I could not lose my footing. Turn my back on either pit bull, even for an instant, and that would be the beginning of an assault so horrible I couldn't allow myself to contemplate it—nor would I tolerate the indignity these animals were forcing on me!

I was terrified, but I was also getting mad.

"Get the hell away!" I hollered, jabbing. The alpha dog grabbed at the shovel when I thrust it, teeth striking the blade with the metallic sound of flint striking sparks. At the same instant, the larger dog snaked his head at me, teeth clacking near my calf, then retreated to a safe distance. Twice that happened, which gave me an idea. I feinted at the female again to lure the male closer, then swung the shovel blindly to my left, hoping the larger dog would attack. He did. The shovel blade glanced off the animal's head and spun him sideways, yelping. The alpha dog was in such a frenzy that a yelp of weakness invited attack and she did attack him, slashing her teeth at the larger dog's flank before returning her attention to me.

Too late. I had jumped into the hallway and was already backing away, holding the shovel in both hands like a spear. The female stalked me but kept her distance. Behind me, the garish green door I had dreaded was now my rescuer—if I could get the thing open and closed before I was bitten. That was key. Once a pit bull locks its jaws into flesh, there is no breaking free. It could still happen. No matter how I used the shovel for protection, there would be a moment when I had to turn and leave my legs unprotected. If the dog buried her teeth in me, no matter how hard I fought, I would be dragged to the floor, and they would both have me.

The alpha dog seemed to sense her chance would soon come and was biding her time as the male rejoined her. She paused to award him with a quick sniff, then continued to follow, her throat rumbling, as I backed past the stairway where the floor lamp cast its milky light. I was within reach of the doorknob now. But I had to invent something to distract the dogs to allow me the free second needed to slip into the next room and slam the door.

What?

I risked a glance over my shoulder at the porcelain knob. It was threaded through a metal plate that had a keyhole. A terrifying thought flashed into my mind: *What if the door was locked?* If it was locked, the diversion I was considering would hinder me more than help. It fact, the decision would leave me disfigured for life, or worse.

Can't be locked, I told myself. *No one in their right mind would lock a door in a stairwell.*

Well, I would soon find out.

I had been edging toward the staircase, an angle that gave me more protection but also put me in a corner next to the lamp. These pit bulls were hunters and instinctively saw their advantage, which they secured by separating a few feet to trap me. They were barking again, trying to back me against the wall with mock charges, working themselves into the frenzy that I knew prefaced a full-on attack. I had to do something—and did. The floor lamp was made of pot metal and heavier than expected when I grabbed it and slammed it toward the dogs. The twin glass globes shattered, but the pop of incandescent bulbs wasn't as loud as I'd hoped.

Even so, both dogs yelped and jumped away. It gave me time to yank the door open and back into the next room, but I did it in such a rush I dropped the shovel after banging my wrist on something.

BOOM! . . . BOOM! The pit bulls had recovered quickly and were already throwing themselves at the door, their barking a slathered garble that made it impossible to think. I put my shoulder against the wood, breathing hard, my heart pounding. To add to the chaos, the room I'd entered was a mystery of shadows and dark shapes, only two westward windows allowing light. I felt around until I found the dead bolt and latched the door tight but still kept my weight against it.

BOOM! . . . BOOM! . . . BOOM! With each assault, the wood vibrated like a drum. The dogs weren't giving up.

I was in the kitchen, I realized. I could tell from the odor of linoleum and Lysol and garbage that had begun to rot. Also, I could see the glint of pans hanging, the shape of a refrigerator. A sink, too, with twin faucets set beneath a window too small for the room. A lancet of light came through the glass, though not much. It was hot in here; a space built to fend off tropical summers but, instead, only denied sunlight.

Get to the truck, I told myself. *Do it now before the dogs circle around back! Mrs. Helms, if she's here, if she's alive, will have to wait for the police.*

I hadn't given the woman a thought, of course, since the pit bulls had attacked. She came into my mind now, however, because my eyes were adjusting to the shadows and I recognized the shape and gleam of something near the sink, although it took me a second.

A wig?

Yes, a woman's wig; silver hair cropped short and combed to a sheen, a style for business luncheons. Loretta had mentioned that a wig would be delivered today, which proved Mrs. Helms had been here, and probably still was.

No . . . I might be mistaken about that. Since her chemotherapy, the woman had bought several wigs, usually inexpensive brands made of nylon. This one, even from a distance, looked expensive, like natural human hair, and why would a woman as fussy as Pinky Helms leave a new wig by the sink? Someone else could have put it there. So it proved nothing, and I wasn't sticking around even if it did.

Scratching and panting, the pit bulls were digging beneath the door now. Determined to get their teeth in me, but I felt secure enough to step away, then sag against the wall for a moment. After several deep breaths, I pushed off and hurried across the room in search of a light switch and an exit. On the way, I allowed myself to detour near the sink because the window provided a lighted footpath. Passed close enough to realize the wig wasn't near the sink, it was *in* the sink.

I stopped; felt a chill that made me reluctant to step closer. Yes . . . the wig was sitting or floating in water on what might have been a Styrofoam base. Rust-stained water, copper red, beneath a window that boiled with late-afternoon sunlight. Bad pipes would explain the reddish color; a country well that blackened water with minerals, sulfur and iron, explained it, too. The village of Sulfur Wells had been named for that very reason and supported what I desperately wanted to believe. My nerves couldn't handle another explanation. I had to get out of this place!

Dazed, I hurried toward the darkest corner of the kitchen, where reason told me there would be a door. There was. No doubt about it because the door cracked a few inches as I approached, filtering an expanding band of light. I felt the heat of the sun thatch my body, but what appeared within that band of daylight paralyzed me. A man was there—a wedge of face wrapped in a scarf, one dark eye staring. One black glove, too. His big hand braced something against his shoulder, a tool of some type on a hickory-thick handle.

An axe.

I AM NOT a woman who screams when surprised. Even as a girl, Loretta, her friends, too, had commented on my stoic, tomboy ways. The accusations that were always hidden in their comments had been troubling to me until I was older. By then, I knew I was attracted to men, so I have accepted those early criticisms—along with many others voiced by Loretta—as proof I've inherited solid qualities that, despite my secret weaknesses, make a stronger woman and give me confidence.

When the man appeared, I did not scream. Even when he shifted the axe to his other shoulder to slide into the kitchen, I didn't scream, although I did back away. But when he slammed the door behind him, cloaking him in darkness, I couldn't help myself. A whimpering sound escaped my lips, which I instantly retracted by calling, "If you hurt Mrs. Helms, mister, you'd better run while you have the chance!"

No reply. Instead, I heard the rattle of metal, then the thunk of a dead bolt burying itself in the doorframe. He had locked us in.

I stayed on the offensive. "Police are on their way! In fact, in fact"—I fumbled to retrieve the cell phone from my pocket, then held it up—"they're listening to every word I say!"

The man turned to face me, his body as wide and shapeless as a raincoat. I couldn't see details, just the bulk of his shoulders, the contour of his head, a momentary glint of something that mirrored a shard of light—the axe blade? Then he walked toward me, but so slowly that shadows swirled around him like displaced fog. Was it confidence or caution? The kitchen was dark, but, if he kept coming, I would soon get a better look at him. Or had my threats made him uncertain? The dogs were still at the kitchen door, their barking frenzied—another possibility.

I couldn't just stand there, so I ran to put a table between us, then waited. Either direction, I was trapped. I looked at the window above the sink. It wasn't much wider than my shoulders. I could wiggle through if I shattered the glass, but not fast enough to save my legs and lower torso from at least one blow from the axe. Just imagining the impact caused a numbness in me. It dulled my movements and my thinking. The coward in me was urging *Be submissive, beg for your life. Earn his kindness!*

Beneath the window, a floating ball of woman's hair ridiculed that coward. The anger I'd felt toward the dogs returned, and it, too, ridiculed any display of weakness. Guarantee my humiliation by welcoming an assault? No—I wouldn't do that.

"I warned you!" I yelled. Then put the phone to my ear and spoke too loudly, "That's right, Officer! Send a couple of guys to the back door." When my attacker appeared to stiffen, I added, "Yes, he's armed! Shoot him, if you can—I don't think you have a choice!"

In some quiet corner of my mind, questions formed: *Is it smart to convince a crazy man he's cornered? Or that you've just ordered him killed?*

My doubts vanished when the man ducked backward for a moment and blended into the shadows, where he did . . . *something*. I couldn't see. A moment later, though, I knew my bluff had failed. I heard a grunt of rage, and the axe reappeared near the ceiling. There was the sound of heavy footsteps, then the man was beneath the axe, holding it over his head and striding toward me.

I had opened several drawers while standing at the table— nothing but dish towels and plastic plates. Frantically, I turned toward the window—an impossible choice. Use a towel to shatter the glass? Even if I'd found a hammer, there wasn't time.

The pit bulls had quieted but were scratching at the door— chewing at the wood, too, biting off chunks and growling—their eagerness probably fired by every word they'd heard me speak. Open the door, they'd be at my throat before I took a step. Unless I was willing to risk the worst on the chance of saving myself.

I pulled out a drawer and flung it into the man's path. He stumbled but caught himself while I sprinted to the kitchen door, put my hand on the dead bolt, and turned to face him. There was enough light now to see that he *was* wearing a baggy raincoat. It hung to his ankles . . . rubber gloves, too, and what looked like a sun mask, the stretchy, tubular type that fishermen pull over their heads to prevent skin cancer. Two black eyes peered out; just a hint of design on the material, but the design was common enough for me to recognize.

I hammered my heel against the door and yelled, "Get out or I'll loose these dogs on you!" which caused a renewed frenzy of barking. At the same instant, a terrible thought came into my mind: *What if he owns the dogs?*

It didn't matter. My threat stopped the man, but he also drew the axe back as if to throw it, which left me no choice. I yanked the door open and jumped behind it, my back pressed flat against the wall, and I held the doorknob tight with both hands. For the next several seconds, only sounds and fear dominated my senses: a din of clattering claws, a slobbering growl, the thunder of a man running . . . furniture crashed—or was it the sound of an axe shattering a door? Then, from what might have been outside, floated a wild howl of pain. Animal or man, I couldn't tell. I didn't care.

I peeked around the door, then sprinted to my truck. Not until I was almost to Burnt Store Road did I use my cell to call 911—the whole time checking the mirror, afraid I was still being chased.

SEVEN

Standing amid a fireworks of flashing blue lights, I said to a detective, "I've already sat in the back of two squad cars and answered that very same question. I don't feel like sitting. And don't see the point of repeating myself."

The most troubling question, out of the dozens I'd been asked, was, "Are you sure you saw something in the sink?" Two detectives and a sheriff's deputy had varied the wording, of course. "Tell me again about that wig." And, "In a dark room, what caused you to think the hair was human?" And, "How did you know the water was bloody if you couldn't find a light switch?"

I hadn't said *bloody*, I had said *reddish-colored*, so it had been an attempt to trick me. Not the first or last either.

The questions by themselves weren't upsetting, but the fact I was being asked so delicately, and repeatedly, told me what the police would not: the sink had been empty when they arrived. Nor had the pit bulls returned, and maybe the wreckage in the living room had been removed, too. No way to guess specifics, but I was convinced that someone had returned to the house and neatened up the crime scene. They'd had time to do a good job, too, which was my fault. I had refused to park at the intersection of Pay Day Road and await help as the operator had insisted—sit there alone and risk the axe man having a fast truck or ATV? Nope. Instead, I'd driven straight to a Publix parking lot, six miles away, where there were bright lights and witnesses. Even police GPSes didn't list the pot hauler's nickname for what amounted to a long driveway, so thirty minutes or more had lapsed by the time I'd led police back to the old Helms place.

"It's not that we don't believe you, Mrs. Smith," the detective was saying now. "It's procedure. People under stress sometimes forget details. Sometimes even imagine details that—"

"It's *Ms.* Smith," I interrupted. "And I didn't imagine a door beaten down with an axe. And I didn't imagine the man who tried to kill me with that same axe."

"The *same* axe?" the detective said, trying to draw me out by sounding intrigued.

I ignored him by offering advice. "As to the pit bulls, take a walk around the yard, then be sure to check your shoes before you step in a car. Detective? I don't care if you believe me or not. Find Rosanna Helms, that's all I care about. Someone broke into that poor woman's house and there's no telling what they did to her."

The man frowned and started to say, "Ms. Smith, it's not my job to believe—" but then stopped to concentrate on a radio message by touching a finger to his ear. I listened to him say, "Yeah . . . Yeah—if you say so." Then, "Yeah, well, I'm not crazy about the idea, but—" Then, "Sheriff, if that's what you want, no problem. She's right here." Then the detective stood taller, looking for landmarks, saying, "We're by the house, the whole perimeter's taped off, so we're standing in the drive by the . . . Well, hell, if he knows the woman, he'll recognize her, right?"

I wondered who it was who knew me, while the detective, looking peeved, adjusted a knob on the transceiver in his breast pocket. "There's someone wants to speak with you," he said finally. "He's on his way."

"A relative of Mrs. Helms?" I asked.

The man shook his head. "You're welcome to sit in my car. The mosquitoes, I spent a couple of nights camping on Cayo Costa, but they weren't this damn bad. How about a bottle of water?"

To the west, an orange sky topped the tree line but could not penetrate the haunted-house shadows of the Helms place. I sighed in the heavy way people do when they're tired of cooperating and replied, "I'm late already. If you're not holding me as a suspect, I have the right to leave. Anything else, sorry. It'll have to wait 'till tomorrow."

The detective's pleasant attitude vanished as if a switch had been thrown. "You an attorney?"

"No, but—"

"How do you know you're not a suspect? I'm going to be real honest, Ms. Smith, parts of your story don't match up with what we found in there." He motioned toward the house. "So far, all we have is a probable vandalism and a reported assault. The victim— if that's what you are—is usually eager to cooperate."

Because I was getting mad, the temptation was to inform this plainclothes deputy that I was a licensed private investigator bonded by the state and there was nothing I had signed or sworn to that obligated me to tolerate his bullying. The risk, though, was his questions would become even more aggressive and reveal I was a novice, not an actual professional in that field. A private investigator is something very different from a woman who has an investigator's license because she inherited a business from her uncle and who has only one successful case under her belt.

The little experience I've had, however, told me that threatening a cop wouldn't hasten my release. Especially here, across the line in Sematee County, where my family owned no property. So I backed off, explaining, "Thing is, I've got to get home and tell my mother. I dread it. She and Mrs. Helms went to school together. Best friends for something like sixty years, and she's going to take the news hard."

"As far as we know," the deputy reminded me, "the woman who owns this place is just fine. The lab guys are in there right now." His head swiveled, then he ordered me to stay right where I was by adding, "Don't wander off, I'll be back in a second."

Within reach was a key lime tree. I yanked off a leaf, tore it, then used its sweet odor to clean my hands and also calm myself. It was almost seven o'clock! Earlier, from the Publix parking lot, I had texted Ford rather than call because I feared he would hear the distress in my voice and offer to cancel. But there was no hiding my upset when he telephoned seconds later. Now, instead of postponing our date, he was on his way to Sulfur Wells because, as he said, "I don't need the whole story to know you shouldn't be alone, especially alone driving a boat."

His thoughtfulness had almost unleashed the tears I'd been holding back since arriving at the parking lot. Maybe he had sensed that, too, because his voice had softened when he said,

"Pack a bag, you're staying with me at the lab. I'll make dinner—fresh pompano and potatoes on the grill. How's that sound?"

Ford, as I had learned, referred to his stilthouse as "the lab" because it was equipped for marine research projects, so his offer sounded like sweet relief to me.

That was half an hour ago, though, and now I was having second thoughts. Ford's boat is even faster than mine, and he knows the backcountry almost as well, so he was probably waiting at our dock right now, which was a new source of anxiety. I could picture Loretta interrogating the man, terrifying him with examples of my family's genetics—he was a biologist, after all. He would be alert to emotional oddities that might be hidden in my personality. Why hadn't I thought to warn him!

An unmarked car, I noticed, was idling toward me, the detective walking alongside and speaking to the driver through an open window. Someone new coming to ask questions. I still had time to text Ford and I did:

Almost done. Oh—Mother hasn't been the same since her stroke, so be patient and pretend to believe her 'till I get there.

After a moment of indecision, I added, *Miss you, H4.*

I hit the *Send* key twice before remembering there was no signal. By then, I could see that the unmarked car was, in fact, a sporty-looking Audi that had somehow survived the bad road. I recognized the driver, too, when he stepped out, although it took a moment. The face was familiar, but didn't belong at a crime scene where pit bulls and hooded men attacked women.

It was my charter client from yesterday, the good-looking younger man. Joel Ransler.

IF MY CLIENTS offer a business card, fine, but I never ask their occupation, nor do I contact them unless invited. As my late Uncle Jake had counseled me, *What is said on a boat, especially a small boat, is private and has to stay that way. I've fished movie stars, a bunch of pro ballplayers, even an astronaut, but I never brag about them by name, let alone ask for an autograph. For all you know, your clients told their wives they're attending a funeral in Cleveland. Be respectful, do your job—leave gossiping to Yankees and amateurs.*

Which is why I didn't need to pretend to be surprised when the detective introduced my client, saying, "Mr. Ransler is the county special prosecutor, so you can tell him anything you'd tell me." He turned to Ransler. "We haven't filed any charges yet, Joel. You sure you've got the time for this?"

Ransler had a face and smile that reminded me of an actor I had yet to recall; an actor who was old now, maybe dead—I don't see many movies—but had been equally good-looking, with a white smile and charm that filled a room even from a TV screen. He was showing that smile now, his eyes seeing only me, when he gave the deputy's shoulder a pat and said, "Ms. Smith and I are old friends, Billy. I would've been here sooner, but I was in Arcadia when I heard the dispatcher mention her name."

Arcadia is inland Florida, a beautiful little town, but a two-hour drive, and it wasn't in Sematee County. Instantly, I felt safer, even special. Just as fast, the detective's attitude toward me changed. "Sorry, Mrs.—*Miz* Smith—if some of my questions seemed rough, but—"

Ransler let the man off the hook by interrupting, "Billy's one of the best we've got and that's what he's paid to do. She understands that—don't you, Hannah?"

Time to make peace, and I did. "He couldn't have been more polite—same with the other deputies. What happened here was so crazy, it's a wonder they could make sense out of a word I said."

Fifteen minutes later, Joel Ransler had his hand on my back and was steering me away from the house, where I'd just taken the special prosecutor step-by-step, describing what had happened. I had been right about someone returning to remove evidence. The recliner sat squarely in front of the television, which was still on. The kitchen sink was empty; maybe they'd wiped the place clean of fingerprints, too. The back door wasn't broken as I expected, but there was no denying someone had used an axe on the front door and smashed the china cabinet, too, although the floor had been swept clean—even the Fisherfolk Inc. pamphlets I'd seen were gone. When I told Ransler my suspicions, he didn't pamper me by remaining neutral.

"It's what stupid criminals do if they don't panic," he said. "Or a sociopath whose mood swings back to normal. They realize what they've done, so try to erase it by neatening up afterward."

I said, "Even charity pamphlets?"

"Chaos becomes the enemy," he replied, then got down to business. "Your attacker wore a raincoat, you said. What color?"

Ransler had been so nice I didn't want to be rude, but it was now twenty after seven and I'd mentioned a couple of times I was in a hurry. Sensing my impatience, he added, "I believe your story, every word. Question is, who did this? And where's Rosanna

Helms?" Then gave me a squeeze before removing his arm from my shoulder. "The reason the raincoat is important is—well, there are a couple of reasons. A killer with an axe knows there will be a lot of blood, so it shows premeditation. You described him as big and sort of shapeless."

"It was one of those cheap, poncho-type rain slickers," I said, "but looked bigger, I guess. Sorry, you're right. I left that part out."

Ransler thought about it. "Sort of like a tent, and he was wearing a hood."

"No," I said. "A few years back, fishermen started using sun masks. Skin cancer is a real problem. They're tubular, sort of a stretchy material you pull down over your head."

"You sound sure."

"Patagonia sells some with shark jaws below the eyeholes. You know, a great white shark's teeth where a fisherman's mouth would be? It's popular. Right away, even with the lights off, I recognized what he was wearing."

"Shark jaws," Ransler said with a wince that told me he was thinking about the hammerhead we'd seen. "A big man wearing gloves and a sun mask."

"As tall as me," I said. "Taller, maybe."

"But shapeless because of a rain poncho, or whatever it was draped over him."

"You saw for yourself how dark it is in that kitchen."

Ransler paused to consider the careful wording of what came next. "Then how do you know it was a man, Hannah?"

The question surprised me. "Well . . . his voice, I guess. The way he handled the axe. You know, *strong*." But then had to admit,

"I guess it is possible. He didn't actually say anything, just sort of bellowed when he came at me. I suppose it could have been a woman, but I'd bet against it, I really would."

"Did you know Crystal Helms was released from Raiford three weeks ago?"

Another surprise, but I shook my head to refuse the idea he was suggesting. "I haven't seen her in years."

"Was she a big girl?"

"Well, yes, but Crystal could never—"

"Hurt you or her own mother?" Ransler cut in. "I'm not saying she did, but I want you to be aware of the situation. And the son—I forget what Billy said his name is—he was paroled in early March."

"Mica's out, too?" I said softly. "We had no reason to stay in touch, even with Crystal—not since grade school. Our mothers stayed friends, that's all, but my mother never said a word."

"In the morning, I'll check the records, but I know the Helms family has a long history of felonies related to drug dealing. The daughter especially—again, I have to pull the file—but one of my guys said Crystal spent some of her time in the psych ward." The man squared himself and placed his hands on my shoulders in a comforting way. "That's just between you and me. I wouldn't share this with most people—I'm not allowed to, in fact."

He waited until I looked at him before adding, "I like you, Hannah. An attractive woman who can handle a boat—can handle just about *any* situation, from what I gather. I trust you, and I'm worried because you're an unusual woman—and the person who did this is insane. My opinion, of course."

I moved slightly, thinking Ransler would remove his hands. He didn't, but that was okay. "I appreciate it, Joel," I said.

"I take care of my friends, Hannah Smith—even the few who've proven they can take care of themselves."

My eyes had tried to drift away, but now I had no choice but to reply, "You did a background check after our charter, didn't you? Or was it before?" There was a long list of information he could have discovered—I'm single and live alone, for one thing. From the way he said *proven* I could take care of myself, though, I could tell he was referencing an incident that had put my name in the news some months back: I'd shot and wounded a man who'd threatened to rape me.

Ransler's hands tightened on my shoulders while his expression asked *Does it matter?* "I'm going to have the sheriff's department keep an eye on your mother's place, okay? Just until we know more about Mrs. Helms. And tonight I'm following you home to make sure you get there in one piece." Now his smile told me *Don't argue!*

The feeling of his hands on my shoulders wasn't uncomfortable, and he kept them there even when I replied, "Thanks, but I'm meeting a friend. In fact, I'm so late now I wouldn't blame him if he's mad."

"Him," Ransler replied. "You know the guy well?" Normally, the question would have struck me as intrusive, but his tone conveyed worry. Women are usually assaulted by men they know.

"We're dating," I said. "And he's not the violent type—just the opposite. So don't worry."

"The guy's a lucky man," Ransler replied in a sweet way that made his own disappointment a gift to me.

"You'd like him," I said, smiling back. "Next fishing trip is my treat. The three of us, or bring Mr. Chatham, too, if you want. He's a marine biologist on Sanibel and pretty good with a fly rod."

Ransler started to comment but turned when a deputy called, "Hey, Joel, take a look at this!" He was jogging toward us, carrying a camera.

The deputy had photos to show the special prosecutor. I wasn't invited to view them and was glad, because I knew from their conversation they had found the body of one of the pit bulls.

"Put his head in the freezer!" was the last thing I heard the deputy say before I excused myself with a wave and hurried away.

EIGHT

The previous night, when I had slipped into Marion Ford's arms, then into his bed for the first time, I had pretended to be reticent—despite the smoky shakiness of my voice—because I don't share my body out of fondness, nor for sport, and I wanted Ford to know it.

Tonight, though, my nervous system was so overloaded, the words *No* and *Slow down* weren't within a thousand miles of the next morning. I wanted to lose myself in private sensations, disappear into the secret oneness we were beginning to create, and I did—*we* did—Ford looking at his watch, finally, and saying, "Gezzus, no wonder I'm hungry, it's two a.m. You still want that pompano? Or try to hold out until breakfast?"

His bawdy openness on the phone, and in bed, had cut me free, and I said, "There *is* something I've imagined trying . . . if you wouldn't mind . . ."

But before I could say more, he was already doing it, and when we were done, the tears I had been holding back were unleashed, which soon became embarrassing.

"I can't seem to stop," I sobbed. "I don't know why."

"One of us has to stop," Ford responded dryly, "or we'll both die of dehydration. I've got beer, but Gatorade's probably a better call."

The pretense that he had misunderstood struck me as the funniest thing I'd ever heard. It replaced my bawling with laughter, and my laughter became something fun we shared, letting it flow back and forth between us, two naughty adults joined by a tide that neaped when a strange sound seeped beneath the door. A gonging sound; repetitive, like a doorbell that is stuck.

"Damn it," Ford said, throwing the covers back, "that's not supposed to happen."

"Something wrong in the lab?" I asked. I figured it was an alarm of some sort; a warning that one of the dozens of fish tanks there was leaking water or an aerator had gone bad.

"Phone call," Ford explained. "This won't take long," then hurried out of the bedroom, his weight causing the stilthouse to vibrate.

A telephone? Ford's cell phone buzzed as an alert and his landline had an old-fashioned ringer. It was not a story a man would invent, especially a man as honest and plainspoken as Marion Ford. So maybe he had changed his ringtone or he owned a third phone—none of my business, but I was aware that only an emergency or a drunken friend would cause a phone to ring at two in the morning.

I listened to a screen door slap shut, and soon the gonging stopped. I stretched, yawned, and lay there, luxuriating in the contentment I had just shared with a man I might be falling in love with. Maybe was already too far gone in love for my own good—it was way too early to have discussed commitment—but I didn't care. It felt natural to lie there in my own skin, unashamed, letting moonlight show my body to the window and anyone who might be outside peeking—which was not a possibility, of course— Ford's house, actually two small houses built on stilts in shallow water fifty yards from shore. That fact made my boldness a silly fiction, but I maintained it by walking naked to the bathroom. I felt a great closeness to my new lover, true, but I was nonetheless shy about using the toilet—the result of spending most of my life sleeping alone. So I made use of the opportunity but didn't use the light switch. Vanity was the reason. I'll never be considered beautiful by fashion model standards, but I do have a long, full body that moonlight treats kindly, and reality was something I'd seen enough of for one day.

After a few minutes, I surmised the phone call wasn't an emergency or I would have heard Ford's voice spike through the wall. It allowed me to relax while I stood at the window. Dinkin's Bay Marina, down the shoreline, was speckled with dock lights where houseboats and cruisers shimmered beneath the moon. Still a few wandering souls awake: two women huddled together on the aft deck of a Chris-Craft; the boney silhouette of Tomlinson sharing a joint with a friend. I had met the two women when Ford was in the hospital, so I recognized them from the name of their boat, *Tiger Lilly.* The women had been chilly toward me at first but that had changed. Tomlinson, of course, still flirted openly, he still probed my availability with words and his eyes while urging me to *Float on!* But that was changing, too.

I like it here, I thought. *Good people in a place that feels safe.*

I slid beneath the covers; arranged my hair, then folded the sheet across my breasts for maximum effect. After several more minutes, I decided to read while I waited. Books were something Ford and I had in common and they can bring two strangers together faster than anything I know. We both liked nonfiction, especially natural history, which is always a safe topic of conversation. Gradually, though, books had allowed us to reveal our more personal tastes. Reading Marjorie Kinnan Rawlings had somehow led me into British classics. Now I'm fascinated by the complicated lives of George Eliot and Charlotte Brontë, among others, and we had been trading favorites, him reading *Jane Eyre*—or pretending to at least. I had been switching between Carl Hiaasen and Peter Matthiessen. *Killing Mister Watson* was on the bedstand, but I soon put it away because the subject matter— violence set among mangroves—was unsettling after my visit to the Helms place.

I lay back, rearranged the sheet, then my hair. Next thing I knew, I had been transported by a nightmare from Dinkin's Bay to a doorless mansion where pit bulls eyed me from a hallway, then gave chase. The worst part was the terrible guilt I felt—the guilt of sneaking into the concrete privacy of a neighbor's house without a permit or an excuse to shield me from a faceless woman's axe.

Marion!

Maybe I screamed his name. More likely, I dreamt that part, too, because I was sitting up alone in bed when I awoke. There was no clock in the room, but I felt that a long space of time had passed.

I put my feet on the floor and found the baggy shirt I had been using as a robe. Dew dripped off the tin roof; the boom of a distant owl interrupted the rustle of mangroves and the chiming of chuck-will's-widow birds. Yes, it was *very* late.

Where was Ford?

FORD'S LAB was walled with bubbling aquariums, its pinewood interior old, like most fish houses, but furnished with stainless tables, a marble countertop with chemical racks, and a metal desk, where I found the biologist sitting. He was so deep in thought, he was startled when I came into the room.

"Marion?" I said gently. "Is everything okay?"

Lighting from a gooseneck lamp was harsh, but only over the desk. It showed an open book—a world atlas—and what looked like a complicated cell phone near a legal pad where Ford had made notes, his block printing tiny but as concise as the orderliness of the room.

"Oh . . . *Hannah!*" he said, as if he'd forgotten I was visiting. "Sorry, I got preoccupied." Then swiveled his back to me, closed the atlas, and slid the legal pad beneath it. The cell phone wasn't as easily hidden, but the thought was in his mind, I sensed it, even though he pushed his chair away, straightening his glasses, and invited me closer with a wave.

"I'm interrupting," I said. "I should have knocked."

"No. You never have to do that. Not with me, you don't."

I wasn't convinced. We all have secrets, as I am aware. We all deserve the privacy of our own minds, but Ford's attempt to hide what I'd already seen was disturbing. "This is your work space," I responded. "You're busy—no need to apologize."

I hadn't intended to sound chilly but did. That changed when Ford stood, moved into the harsh light, and I got my first real look at him, shirtless and unprotected by bedroom shadows. The man was too muscled to appear frail, but he had lost weight after a week in the hospital, then three weeks convalescing. Fishing shorts hung on the bones of his hips, he looked gaunt and vulnerable because of the fresh scar beneath his heart—a scar new enough to be startling.

I couldn't take my eyes off the thing. Only two days ago, after pretending reticence, I had been celebrating Ford's good news in bed. Now I was being cold to the man I'd nearly lost—a man I might be falling in love with and didn't want to lose again.

"I should have put on a shirt," Ford said when he saw my expression. "Hang on, I'll grab a lab coat."

I caught the man's arm as he passed, then framed his face between my hands and kissed him. "I've got vanity enough for both of us," I said, "so don't bother. I thought you left the lights off to make *me* look prettier."

When he grinned, I kissed him again, then leaned for a closer look at his chest. "Stand still, for heaven sakes! Get your hand out of the way."

The scar was a pink weld of flesh that angled four inches across his ribs. I had touched the scar with my fingers, my lips, too, but always in bedroom darkness. So I kissed it again as if saying, *Hello,* then stood, taking care not to look at the desk. "I'm going back to bed. Get your work done, then come along. A man who shirks his work isn't going to get far with me."

"Hey," he said when I turned to go, then pulled my body close, his eyes staring into mine. "When you came in, I did something else stupid. I tried to hide something from you. It has to do with the phone call. Want to talk about it now? Or wait 'till morning?"

Ford's willingness was enough for me. "Or not at all," I replied, then steered his hand to a place that promised *That's okay, too.*

SITTING ON THE DECK, sipping coffee, wearing jeans and a purple tank top that had to belong to Tomlinson, I told myself, *Instead of prying, set an example. Ford will get around to discussing the phone call when he's ready.*

Or maybe not. Hadn't I told him there was no need? It was a matter of respect and like-minded behavior. Last night, Ford had treated me with care by not pressing for details about what had happened at the Helms place. So it seemed right to satisfy his curiosity before dropping a hint or two in hopes of satisfying my own.

"That's exactly how I remember it," I said, concluding my story. "It all happened so fast, but, at the time, it just kept getting worse and worse. Like it would never end—you know how that is?"

Ford wanted to hear more about Levi Thurloe and Loretta's new neighbors—tangent issues, it seemed to me—before asking, "You're sure you're not hurt? If the guy did something, you can tell me, I'll understand." Then explained he'd read about victims blaming themselves, not their attackers, which is why some women kept the facts secret to hide guilt they didn't deserve.

"I've got a little bruise," I said, touching my wrist, "but it's because I almost slammed the door on my own hand. Maybe you haven't noticed, but I have my clumsy moments."

Ford is mild-tempered, but I could see that he was too concerned to smile. Part of me was glad. It meant he cared. But I also didn't want a man who studied fish for a living to get involved in a matter that was dangerous and best left to experts.

"I was at the wrong place at the wrong time," I explained. "That's what it comes down to. The lunatic with the axe— whoever it was—he never touched me, I *would* tell you. So he has no reason to come after me—or Loretta. But the special prosecutor has deputies checking on her just to be safe."

Ford had yet to ask about Joel Ransler, although the coincidence of Ransler being my new fishing client had caused his attention to zoom. He alluded to the coincidence now, but obliquely, saying, "You two had a wild couple of days. A tarpon jumps in your boat, then you're assaulted in his jurisdiction."

"That's why he's giving Loretta extra attention," I reminded him.

"It's a powerful bond," he agreed, "and the timing couldn't be better. I remember when the governor appointed a special prosecutor in Sematee, but I'm surprised the position still exists. The small county with a big drug problem. Whatever the reason, I'm glad he's there."

"Their commissioners made it a full-time job," I replied. "Sort of like a state attorney, but a smaller area. That's what Joel told me anyway."

"Joel," Ford said, but not in an accusing way—more like he wanted to remember the name.

"He's about my age, that's what he said to call him, so, yeah."

"An attorney who likes to fish in his spare time, that's not unusual. He and his friend were taking a lot of photos, too, you said."

"I didn't know why until Joel mentioned it last night. The man who actually booked the charter is about thirty years older, Delmont Chatham."

"As in citrus groves and car dealerships?" Ford asked.

"Minus the money, I'm guessing. Mr. Chatham works for Sematee County, too. He's been cataloging examples of old Florida architecture because it's disappearing so fast. Something to do with restoring historic buildings. He loved Loretta's house—it's the oldest house in Lee County, did you know that? When I was showing him the attic, that's when I found the trunk open—an old Army trunk—and noticed things missing. Quite a bit of old fishing gear was gone, and some family books I'd put in a Ziplocs to protect them."

It was another tangent Ford found interesting, so I explained about the Vom Hofe reel and Teddy Roosevelt's little book, *Harpooning Devilfish*, which I had enjoyed as a teen.

"Vom Hofe," Ford said, familiar with the name, "and Chatham is a—did you say he's an *expert* or a *collector*?"

I had said neither, only that Delmont Chatham's antique fishing rod had shattered when the tarpon jumped in my boat. "Probably a little of both," I replied. "That's why he wanted to see the reel. He was disappointed, and asked me to call if the reel showed up."

"Your clients chose the right fishing guide, didn't they?" Ford said, then referred to last night when he'd spent twenty minutes alone waiting for me to return and listening to Loretta. "Your mother said those two were very sweet to her."

"She didn't even meet Mr. Chatham," I laughed, "and she only said a quick hello to Joel." As I said it, I was remembering that Loretta, by phone, had raved to me about how good-looking Joel Ransler was, and probably rich, too. Had she told Ford the same thing? More than likely, knowing her, which is why I added, "Loretta enjoys meeting people, but she tends to confuse them with actors she sees on TV. She was on her way to play bingo, so I'd be surprised if she remembers Joel at all."

Ford chuckled. "I *like* your mother, no need to worry about that."

I rolled my eyes. "I just hope Mrs. Helms is safe somewhere, off on a trip with a friend. She and Loretta are close. The Helms family has had enough trouble as is."

"That's the problem with gerrymandering," Ford responded, which made no sense until he explained. "What I mean is, where they live. Sematee County has got that one little section of panhandle that juts west to the bay. It's only a few miles of waterfront, and all mangroves, so it's an invitation to drug trafficking because the county seat is so faraway." Then he asked a few questions about the Helms family, before adding, "I'm not surprised they still have problems up there."

"Where aren't they having drug problems?" I said. "Half the people I went to school with screwed up their lives that way. The Helms kids, they're not even the worst examples."

"Crystal and Mica," Ford remembered, filing the information away. "And Mrs. Rosanna Helms—your mother's closest friend."

Ford meant something by that, I could tell, but I was eager to get off the subject and put him at ease. "It's out of our hands, that's what I'm telling you. *We* don't need to worry. If something comes up, Joel gave me his cell number, plus cell numbers for the head detectives, too. The sheriff's department gets paid to find criminals, Marion. And Joel's already sent two texts, which proves he's keeping me in the loop."

I had offered to show Ford the messages, but he'd been satisfied with my paraphrased versions. The first message read *No news. Call if U need me day or nite*, and the second had asked if I was available for a charter on Monday. I hadn't responded but intended to reply *Yes*, which Ford also knew and had accepted without comment. Now he voiced concern, saying, "Does it seem odd the guy wants to fish when there might be a psycho loose in his county?"

"No," I laughed, but soon sobered and amended, "Wait . . . you're right. A seventy-year-old woman missing—even if it's Joel's day off, he and everyone else should keep at it until they find her."

Ford, though, was also thinking about it and decided he was wrong. "The man's a prosecutor, not a violent-crimes investigator.

Until the police have a suspect, there's nothing he can do. You two are friends, he hears a dispatcher say your name, so it's natural that he shows up as a favor to you." Ford nodded, his expression saying *Good for him*, then seemed to swing the other direction, asking, "You think he has a romantic interest?"

Was this jealousy? If so, it wasn't in his tone, which was reflective, even clinical. There was no reason to duck the question, but my own inclination toward privacy can behave without reason.

"Interested in *me*?" I asked. "How would I know?"

Ford cleans his glasses whenever he needs a few moments to think or to regroup. Wire-rimmed glasses. He cleaned them now. When he was done, his clinical tone was newly visible in his eyes.

Right away, I knew I'd made a mistake. *I just lied to you,* that's what I should have said. But I didn't. Instead, I told myself, *It's such a minor thing,* then sat there and watched my new lover smile his understanding. "The guy's a fool if he's not interested in you," Ford said. "Either way, I'm glad you're in touch—like a safety net, just in case. The thing is, Hannah"—Ford stood—"that phone call I got at two a.m. I'm debating on whether to leave for Venezuela tonight or try to postpone."

It caused me to almost spill my coffee. *"Where?"* He hadn't mentioned a trip, let alone a trip to another country.

Ford held out his hand, meaning he wanted to talk inside. "The call was about a consulting job—out of the blue. They need me right away. I'd like you to stay here, but not just to look after the place—because it's safer."

I realized he was waiting to help me to my feet. It was a gentlemanly gesture that didn't fit a lover who, without warning, packs up and flies off to South America. I took his hand anyway, unsure whether to fall into his arms or wait for an explanation. "Sorry, I'm flustered," I said. "Worst-case scenario, I figured it was one of your old girlfriends, or that your dog was delayed, or . . . I don't know what I thought. But a *new job?*"

Ford's smile was sympathetic, but the careful, clinical look had not left his eyes. "I almost forgot about the dog," he said, meaning the retriever he had bought and who was scheduled to arrive on Thursday. Then he reassured me by wrapping an arm over my shoulder. "I'll only be gone a week, ten days at the most. Before I leave, though, I want to make sure you're not in danger. Mind if I have someone I know call Joel Ransler? Or one of the detectives? Depending on where they find Mrs. Helms, and from what you told me, I'm not convinced it was a random attacker." When I didn't reply immediately, he added, "Is that a problem?"

I loved the warmth of his closeness and was relieved to hear he wouldn't be gone long, but I also didn't want Ford, a biologist, to invite danger—or even ridicule—by poking his nose into business that belonged to law enforcement professionals.

I pulled away. "Marion, I've never had any trouble taking care of myself. I'm more worried about your health. The doctor said to avoid anything stressful. And didn't I read about some kind of war going on in Venezuela?" Which was another lie, but a white lie. The fighting I'd read about was somewhere in the mountains of South America, and my geography was rusty.

"A war, huh?" Ford replied, which told me it was the first he had heard of it. His eyes hadn't left mine, but he looked away, as if deciding something. "I want to trust you, Hannah."

"You can!" I said.

The man nodded, his glasses glinting momentarily before his sharp eyes returned. "Let's go into the lab. We need to go over a few things."

"You can tell me anything," I said, and came very close to adding, *I might be in love with you.* Rather than risk it, I hugged him, hoping he would feel what I was feeling. Maybe he did, from the way he kissed me, yet I had a sudden, nagging fear there was now something wrong between us.

The next morning, a Sunday, I awoke in my lover's bed and was soon aware of a pleasant but peculiar odor on his hands when he returned from the lab. Just a hint of a chemical, or some solvent, that soap could not wash away. A familiar odor to me, but it didn't belong in the laboratory of a marine biologist—Ford and I had been workout companions before we became lovers, so I would have known.

Hoppe's Gun Oil, I finally realized, an almost fruity scent. My nose would soon track the memory to my late Uncle Jake's office, and then his holster, which he had carried as a Tampa detective. A bullet had retired Jake to fishing and running a small private investigation agency, but he loved to shoot and often took me along as his student.

Why had a biologist, who'd never mentioned owning a weapon, used gun solvent?

By then, it was Sunday night and too late to ask. Marion Ford was on a plane to Caracas.

NINE

When Joel Ransler parked his Audi near the dock on Monday morning and walked toward my boat, he was alone, which was unexpected, but then I saw his grave expression and knew the reason. They had found Rosanna Helms.

"Bad news?" I asked, wiping my hands on a towel.

My instincts were correct. Yesterday at sunset, deputies had noticed vultures circling a few hundred yards from the house. They were unaware that a footpath led to the area, so they had cut through the mangroves, using lights when it got too dark to work. There was a circular clearing there, a small pond in the middle— the beginning of a sinkhole. The woman was found facedown in water that was just deep enough to float her body.

"No sign of a struggle," Ransler said, "and no obvious injuries. The medical examiner thinks she's been dead since Thursday, but that's preliminary."

"That's awful," I said, getting to my feet. Loretta, of course, had heard Ransler's car and was trying to eavesdrop from the porch. She would soon have to be told about her friend, but the job required gentleness and planning. Mrs. Terwilliger was in the kitchen, making their breakfast, so now was not the time.

I got Joel's attention and nodded toward the house. He confirmed his understanding by taking a seat close to my skiff before explaining, "The only reason I mention the condition of the body is because the media might go into detail. You should be prepared. It's not . . . *nice*, the way she died, so the less your mother knows, the better."

"Are you sure Mrs. Helms wasn't running from someone?" I asked, meaning a crazy person with an axe.

"She'd already been dead for at least a day when you were attacked," the prosecutor reminded me. "I suppose the perp could've come back to rob the place. But why?" He thought about it, then shook his head. "No . . . what happened is, I think you surprised someone in the middle of a burglary. He—or *she*—wouldn't have used an axe on the door if they knew someone was inside. That bothered me from the start."

An insane killer might, I thought but stuck to reason, asking, "Then why was he wearing a mask?"

"Whoever it was probably came by boat—the dock's only fifty, a hundred yards from the house. And you said yourself sun masks are popular with fishermen. The perp probably had it stuck in his pocket and put it on when he heard you drive up. Maybe the sound of your truck brought the woman's dogs on the run, too. Those animals were half starved, apparently."

Ransler paused and tapped a knuckle at his teeth, thinking about it before adding, "What he did to that dog, though, that *does* bother me. And what he might have done to you. Whoever the person is, I think he's got a screw loose."

"Anyone could have wandered into that house and surprised him," I said, wanting to believe it.

Ransler nodded. "Unless the medical examiner says different, we think Mrs. Helms wandered off and got lost. That's usually the case when an elderly person goes missing. It gets dark, they panic, then just sort of give up and die. Or maybe she got so thirsty, she tried to drink from the pond."

"That's . . . terrible," I murmured.

The man shrugged and allowed me some privacy by looking at his hands. "The important thing is she didn't suffer for long—the medical examiner has dealt with a lot of these cases and the old ones go quick. But please don't tell your mother right away. Not anyone until the lab sends back DNA confirmation. We should get it late today."

"That's just a formality, right?" I said. "You're *sure* it's Mrs. Helms."

"We're sure, but it's more than a formality. The sheriff's department located the daughter, Crystal—she's living in a trailer park not far from here—but there was no point in asking her to identify the body. So we've got to wait to make it public."

The significance of that came so slowly I sought another explanation. "You mean Crystal was too upset . . . or she's using drugs again?"

The prosecutor's pained expression read *I didn't want to tell you* but he did, saying, "Vultures weren't the only thing that got to the body, Hannah. You grew up in this country, you know better than me what lives in those mangroves."

Crabs, snakes, feral hogs, rodents—I didn't think about it for long.

"Enough," I said. "Poor Mrs. Helms." Then we both sat in the silence of an April morning while, nearby, baitfish panicked beneath a sortie of pelicans and warring seagulls.

"There is one thing that might make you feel better," Ransler said finally. "The pamphlets you saw but were missing? Deputies found a stack wadded in a trash bag behind the house. Under a pile of junk."

"Trying to hide them," I said. "Why do that?"

"Irrational people do irrational things. What interests me . . . Well, if we'd found one pamphlet, no big deal. But Mrs. Helms had a whole stack. It has nothing to do with her death but might lead to something you could maybe help me with. I have a couple in my briefcase, if you're interested . . . and have the time."

I said, "Time to do what?"

"Consumer fraud is a big issue for my office. Especially schemes that target the elderly. It's a billion-dollar business in Florida, but I'm so short-staffed I need to hire outside help to—" Ransler was interrupted by the ping of his cell phone, which he looked at before saying, "Sorry, I've got to take this."

I busied myself rigging new fishing leaders while the special prosecutor stepped away to talk but was wondering if the man had come because he had a romantic interest in me. Or had he come to give me the news about Mrs. Helms, then offer me a job?

I spun a Bimini twist around my knees and waited to find out.

JOEL RANSLER had called the previous afternoon, saying he and Mr. Chatham wanted to do some fly-fishing and also take more photos—concentrating on the area between Sulfur Wells and where the Sematee and Charlotte county borders met. Did I know the water and was I available?

I HAD ANSWERED yes to both. He was referring to a short stretch of coastline, less than five miles, all shoal water and mangroves, as Ford had described it. Access to the area was through a tricky slalom of cuts and creeks, and I had been looking forward to the challenge because it would give me a break from worrying about Ford. Instead of thinking of him, I would have to concentrate on running my boat and then finding fish in a series of bays where limestone reefs were a threat—an oddity in Southwest Florida. Ransler had arrived dressed for work, though, not fishing, in his blue pin-striped shirt and tie, and he was alone, so I figured the trip was off.

Which is why, when he finished his phone call and had returned to the dock, I offered him a bottle of water, saying, "I feel sick about Mrs. Helms, but I appreciate you driving down to tell me. I know you're busy, Joel, so let's make it another day."

"Rance," he corrected me, "and what gives you the idea I'm canceling? That was Del on the phone. He's dealing with some family issues, so it looks like it'll be just you and me." He knelt to take the bottle of water and opened it. After a sip, he asked, "Is that okay?"

Do a fishing trip so soon after Mrs. Helms's body had been found—just the two of us? My uneasiness must have shown because the man gave me a look that mixed patience and understanding. "I'm just the prosecutor. There's nothing I can do about the person who assaulted you until the cops have their ducks in a row. And there's nothing either one of us can do for Mrs. Helms. In my job, I see some of the most horrific stuff you can imagine, but life goes on, Hannah." He smiled. "Right?"

I tried the only excuse I could come up with. "I'm worried about my mother—you know, leaving her alone so soon."

Ransler looked toward the house. "She doesn't have a nurse?"

"A sitter, yes, but—"

"Then your mother will be just fine—unless she wanders off in the mangroves. But, tell you what, I'll have the deputies keep an eye on the place for another few days if you're concerned."

Sulfur Wells wasn't in Sematee County, which I pointed out, but Ransler replied it wasn't a problem. Then looked around, saying, "I've got clothes and my fishing gear in the car. Can I change in your mom's house? Or what about there?"

He pointed at what I still believe is the most beautiful little motor yacht I've ever seen: a twenty-seven-foot "picnic" boat, a Marlow Prowler, moored at the end of the dock. A client had rewarded me with a year rent-free if I made it livable, then maintained it. Problem was, as I should have known, the vessel was twenty years old, had seldom been used, so there was mold in the bathroom, and the air-conditioning needed to be redone. Yesterday, after kissing Ford good-bye, I had busied myself by moving the boat here so I could work on it and also keep an eye on Loretta.

"You're welcome to go aboard," I told Ransler, "but the head doesn't work."

"You own it?" He was walking toward the boat, his eyes taking in the midnight blue hull, the white upper deck, the teak and stainless fittings that I had stripped, then polished.

"I wish," I replied, then explained why the Marlow had become my project.

"She's a beauty," he said, "but a little small to live on, don't you think?"

"I'll let you know in a week. The new head and shower fittings arrive tomorrow. I've been working on it for months, but I hope to have everything finished and my things aboard by Sunday."

Joel Ransler had the ability to flex his jaw and smile at the same time. When he did it now, the actor he resembled came into my mind—the handsome one in *Butch Cassidy and the Sundance Kid*, although both actors had been handsome in their way.

"A fishing guide, a private investigator, and you're a ship's carpenter, too," he smiled. "Is there anything you can't do, Captain Smith?"

I don't blush but felt as if I came close, even though Ransler had just confirmed he knew I had worked part-time in my uncle's agency, which meant he'd done a background check on me. I told him, "Plumbing and wiring aren't hard if you just follow the directions. If there's something too heavy to manage alone, I've got a friend who's a bodybuilder. And another friend, Cordial Pallet— you ever hear of him? There's nothing that man doesn't know about boats, and he helps when I get stuck."

"He's the marine biologist you're dating?"

I shook my head. Cordial was in his eighties and runs the boat-yard at Fisherman's Wharf, which I was explaining when I noticed an odd glint of light from the balcony of the new neighbors' house. I shielded my eyes and climbed up on the dock to have a look.

Ransler asked, "What's wrong?"

"Hang on," I said, because I realized that someone was spying on us.

OUR FAMILY'S DOCK is two hundred feet long, and I was halfway to shore before I was sure of what I was seeing. Alice Candor was on the balcony, standing with a man who was four inches shorter and holding something to his face—a camera, I realized. Candor was directing while the man snapped pictures of me, using a tele-photo lens, which is why he soon knew he'd been spotted and ducked behind the railing. But I'd had time to recognize him. It was the officious little man who'd ordered the removal of Loret-ta's garden and fruit trees.

Another zoning violation, I thought. It explained why the man wanted photos of me with a fishing client. Or . . . had Alice Can-dor complained about the Marlow cruiser, a vessel big enough to live aboard at a private dock?

I looked over my shoulder at the boat, then walked until I had a view of the road and stopped again. The redheaded deputy, whom I'd actually sort of liked, was nowhere to be seen. Levi Thurloe was in the Candors' yard, a bag of cement under each arm, walking toward the side of the house. Fifty-pound bags, but no problem at all for Walkin' Levi. If police hadn't questioned him yet, they soon would, which I'd been fretting about because Levi frightened so easily.

"That's the man who rode with me in the truck," I said when I heard Ransler come up behind me. "I told you about him."

"The mentally retarded guy, yeah. Billy picked him up yesterday afternoon, but he took it easy on him." In response to my questioning look, he added, "I *promised* he would, didn't I?" Then explained, "Look, Hannah, it doesn't matter how long you've known . . . what's his name again?"

I told him.

"Well, it doesn't matter if you think the poor guy likes you. The detectives still had to check him out. Thurloe knew where you were headed Friday afternoon. He knew you were alone. Billy doesn't think the guy's smart enough to fence stolen property, and he has no priors. But that's the way law enforcement works. Keep eliminating suspects until you have your man." Ransler watched Levi disappear around the corner of the house before saying, "Holy cripes, he's a big one, isn't he? My advice is, avoid all contact because you never know what's going on in the mind of someone like that."

"Kids used to pick on Levi," I said. "Never once did I see him stand up for himself."

Ransler was nodding his empathy when I added, "You're welcome to change clothes in the boat. I'll be back in a minute after I check on something."

"We'll need bug spray," he said as I started away. "I'd like to see the Helms property from the water, then maybe get out and have a look around."

It stopped me. Before I could ask, though, the special prosecutor tried to put me at ease, saying, "I don't want to see the pond where the woman died, don't worry. This has to do with an old murder case. I brought along the file so I can orient myself."

"You mean her husband?" I said. "Dwight Helms's murder, is that the one?" As I asked, Alice Candor vanished into the house, too, so I'd missed my opportunity to flash her a nasty look or maybe even say something when I got close enough.

"Yeah, killed by person or persons unknown," Ransler said. "Do you remember the details? It was a long time ago—almost twenty years."

"I don't remember much about Mr. Helms, just that he looked like a giant to me. Wore a big cowboy hat. And that they never found the man who shot him."

The prosecutor had stepped off the dock and was opening his car but looked up when I asked, "Joel? Is it a coincidence you're reopening the case?"

"Unsolved murders are never closed," he began, then stopped and puzzled over something. After a moment, he asked, "Did you say *shot*? Is that what people around here believe?"

Now I was confused. "Yes, by drug dealers, outsiders supposedly. Shot once or twice in the back of the head. If the killer was caught, I never heard about it—"

"That's not what I'm saying, Hannah. Parents . . . Yeah, I can see why they wouldn't want their kids to know the details. This many years later, when locals talk about the murder, I'm surprised they don't . . ." The man paused to reconsidered. "*There's* the explanation. It happened so long ago, old-timers don't discuss it."

"That's true," I said, still confused. "No one's proud of something like that. But are you telling me Dwight Helms *wasn't* shot by drug dealers?"

Ransler's tone became dismissive as he opened the trunk of his Audi and reached in. "Forensic science wasn't very good in those days, that's why I'm bringing the file along. Until I see for myself, though"—he stepped away from the car, holding an open briefcase—"let's talk about that job I offered you."

Job? I had guessed right, but now he got down to details, explaining, "My office has a budget to hire outside help—Tallahassee money earmarked to track consumer fraud. That's how big the problem is. Here, does this look familiar?"

He handed me a manila envelope that contained the pamphlet I'd seen on the floor in the Helmses' living room. Same old-timey photo of a woman stirring a cauldron, an architect's drawing of a modern building beneath—the mock-up of a museum, I read for the first time—and in bold white typeface:

PRESERVE OUR HERITAGE
JOIN FISHERFOLK of SOUTH FLORIDA Inc.

"These things were scattered all over the floor," I said, then looked at the back where there was a simple pledge form that solicited donations of $10, $20, $50—just check the box—and a fill-in-the-blank space for *Other*. If it was a swindle, at least the con men weren't being overly greedy, which I told Joel.

"Maybe it's legitimate, maybe it's a soft pitch that leads to bigger money," he replied. "That's not unusual. I have only two people on my staff and we've got seventy, eighty of these so-called charities to check out. Those are just the ones we've flagged. There are fifty *thousand* charities registered in this state, did you know that?"

I looked at the pamphlet again. The fine print said that Fisher-folk of South Florida Inc. was a 501(c)(3) nonprofit, donations tax-deductible. The address was a P.O. box in Carnicero, a little crossroads town, inland Florida.

"Carnicero's in Sematee County?" I asked.

"Yep—I always picture carnival people because of the name. In the envelope there's preliminary information that'll explain why I flagged the organization."

"Your friend Mr. Chatham probably knows something about this," I said. "I don't know if his family fished, but the Chathams have been in Florida a long time."

"Del's never heard of it, and that's another red flag. So's the fact that Rosanna Helms had a whole stack of these forms. Chances are, she gave them out to her friends. Maybe *they* have a stack, too, which could mean it's some kind of pyramid scheme. I need someone local, an insider, to follow up in person and do the research. By law, I can only hire an investigator licensed and bonded by the state, so you're a perfect fit."

"Actually, it was my Uncle Jake's business," I replied. "And I've got a lot of charters already booked, so I—"

"This isn't high priority, so you can work around your charters. We'll pay whatever the rate schedule allows by the state. If this Fisherfolk thing is legitimate, you'll know soon enough—then I'll throw more cases your way." The man offered me a confidential smile. "For me, it's a win-win because hiring you gives me a built-in excuse to—"

Do what? Stay in touch? Meet for dinner? Try to lure me into bed—that *wasn't* going to happen. Ransler didn't offer a hint because his cell rang again, this time with important business.

"Gotta run," he told me, pocketing his phone. "An actual murder—they just found the body."

"What happened?" I asked.

"Can't say. Oh"—the special prosecutor looked over his shoulder as he walked toward his car—"can we postpone our trip until this afternoon? I could be back by one, maybe two."

I shook my head. I had a charter scheduled for the afternoon, a woman who wanted to learn fly-casting, and her son who was home from college.

"Wednesday morning, then," Ransler pressed. "I've got meetings tomorrow."

I don't like being rushed, and was also troubled by the man's subtle flirting, so I shook my head and lied, "The biologist I'm dating? He's already booked me for Wednesday. All day."

Ransler thought that was humorous. It caused him to smile as he opened the door of his Audi. "Your boyfriend has to book a date? Or do you mean you charge him to fish?"

"We're collecting *specimens*," I responded as if that explained everything.

"Then make it tomorrow, I'll change my calendar. Afternoon or morning?" Ransler, who should have been on his way to a murder scene, stood, loose-jointed and amused, awaiting my answer.

"Tomorrow same time," I told him, which was safer than risking another ridiculous lie.

TEN

Loretta was napping when I got to the house, Alice Candor and the nosy little man with the camera were nowhere to be seen, so I opened my laptop, still fuming, and searched for details on a murder that had gone unsolved for twenty years. I had a dozen more important things to do but couldn't stop myself. Joel Ransler had been evasive about how Dwight Helms had died. *Why?* My secret fear was that Helms, instead of being shot, had been killed with an axe, which was a wild suspicion but so unsettling I was determined to prove myself wrong.

The old newspaper stories I found, though, weren't helpful, because accessing the archives required a paid subscription. Should I find my wallet and use a credit card? Or wait until I was at my Uncle Jake's office where our computer was authorized to search restricted state and federal files? I decided to wait because the crime databases would offer more information than newspaper stories that were twenty years old.

No . . . twenty-one years old, according to the abstracts I read. Dwight Helms's body had been found in May after a tip to police from "an unnamed informant." Helms had also been arrested the previous month for leaving the scene of an accident and charged with DUI. A year earlier, he had been arrested but not charged after police found a bale of marijuana in his abandoned pickup truck.

Ransler had said Crystal Helms was living in a trailer park not far from Sulfur Wells, so I did a quick search on her, then on her brother, Mica. Like their father, the lives of both were summarized by a series of police reports that recorded the saddest of family traditions, but nothing so new as a phone number or address.

The Internet wastes a lot more of my time than it saves, which I remind myself about daily, yet it's hard to tear myself away from the keyboard once I get started. I had a ton of things to do—background searches on Alice Candor and Joel, among them, which required the office computer—but I found myself checking my e-mail in hopes of a note from Ford. No luck, which wasn't surprising because he had warned me that communication was difficult from Venezuela.

Steered by Ransler's claim there were thousands of charitable organizations in Florida—a few of them fraudulent—I moved on to the subject of scam artists.

He had been right about elderly Americans being a favorite target. Most of them owned property, they had retirement funds and money socked away. Scammers working from the safety of foreign countries—Jamaica, most commonly—preyed on their fragility and loneliness like carrion birds.

There was a long list of gambits: Make contact by phone, Internet, or, better yet, by registered mail—pose as an IRS agent and demand back taxes. Or claim to be a mortgage company that is foreclosing unless a forgotten lien is paid. Threaten to disclose an unnamed crime—by age eighty, we're all guilty of something, right? Deliver the good news that a million-dollar lottery prize will be shared once the "fees" are paid. If U.S. authorities expose or confront the scammers, so what? They change their cell numbers, invent a new scenario, and return to picking the bones of the innocent living. The scammers' greatest assets, I read, were America's inattentive adult children who confused the term *professional care* with *family care*.

These stories were so upsetting that when I heard my mother's bedroom door open and the sound of her shuffling feet, I found myself rushing to help her into the recliner and then fetched her tea after spending several minutes searching for the TV remote, which she had stored with the dish towels, God knows why.

"Are you drunk or did you bump your head?" Loretta demanded when I offered her a pillow. Then called to Mrs. Terwilliger, who was outside picking tomatoes, "Donna, get in here! Something's wrong with Hannah and she's scaring me!"

It was then my mother noticed the Fisherfolk of South Florida pamphlet I'd left on the desk. Instantly, her demeanor changed. "My dear lord," she moaned, "Pinky's dead, that's why you're being so nice. I told you when it was happening. Was she murdered?"

I hadn't received confirmation from Joel Ransler, but I also couldn't lie—not after the stories I'd just read about ignoring the elderly. "It's not official, Mamma, but, yes, Mrs. Helms was found last night. She wasn't murdered, though, she died naturally—out for a nice walk. She didn't suffer at all."

For several minutes, my mother cried, halting her tears long enough to tell me what a good woman Rosanna Helms had been, then mixing in stories about the fun they'd had as girls. "We were always there for each other," she sniffled. "Except for the years we weren't speaking, I've never had a closer friend!"

I said the things people always do under those circumstances while I knelt by the recliner and waited for Loretta to get hold of herself. She finally did, and was still in control after I'd returned with a fresh box of tissues, her eyes rheumy as grapes when she looked up at me. "You searched Pinky's house yesterday. Didn't you tell me that?" She had the date wrong, but I was struck by how unusually lucid my mother sounded.

"Yes, late Friday afternoon, but Mrs. Helms wasn't there," I said, once again omitting details about my attacker.

Her attention shifted to the pamphlet and she sighed. "So now you know the truth, I suppose."

"Truth about what?" I asked.

"You know what I'm talking about. Why torture me by not saying it?"

"You're upset," I replied. "You've got nothing to feel guilty about."

"I don't?" she asked as if surprised. Then she began her nervous habit of tapping thumbs against middle fingers, a sure sign her mind was working hard at something. It made me suspicious.

"Know the truth about *what*?" I asked again, voice firmer.

Loretta's thumb tapping stopped. It meant she had come to a realization or had settled on a strategy—seldom did it mean she was about to speak the truth. This time was different, apparently, because she replied, "Teddy Roosevelt's fishing reel. And the book you mentioned . . . And a bunch of other junk nobody cared about until you went snooping. I had Levi drive it all to Pinky's place."

I had been comforting the woman by patting her shoulder but decided she had received enough comforting for one day. I pulled my hand away and stood straight. *"Snooping?"* I said. "Granddaddy left those things to the family in his will. That Vom Hofe reel alone was worth a thousand dollars—I looked it up on the Internet. Why in the world did you give it to Pinky?"

Loretta exchanged her tissue for the TV remote and swung her face toward the television. "Don't begrudge a dead woman a bunch of old fishing tackle you never used in the first place."

"That's not an answer," I countered. "Besides, more than just a reel is missing. Where are the framed photos of Great-grandma and Aunt Sarah? There was a mesh gauge for weaving nets that was over a hundred years old. And a bill of sale for cattle from the Confederate Army signed by—"

"Which is why it belongs in a museum, not your Uncle Jake's Army trunk!" Loretta interrupted. Then snapped, "Pinky's dead—go to her house and steal the junk back, if you want it so bad. She's not around anymore to stop you!"

I had suspected a connection between our missing antiques and the drawing of a museum on the pamphlet, so what I'd just heard wasn't shocking news. What bothered me was the look of secret triumph fixed on Loretta's face. There had to be a reason. Had she intentionally steered me to the subject of Teddy Roosevelt's fishing reel to avoid admitting something far more serious? Yes, I decided. It explained why she'd appeared surprised when I declared she had nothing to feel guilty about.

"There's something you're not telling me, Loretta," I said.

"Next, you'll be accusing me of a crime," she responded, "or of sleeping with a married man—as if *you've* got room to talk."

Now I was very suspicious. Never before had she tried to bait me by alluding to a love affair she had kept secret for years—but that's what she was now attempting.

I knelt by the recliner again and asked for the third time, "Tell you the truth about *what*, Loretta? You were afraid I found something when I was at Mrs. Helms's house. What are you hiding from me?"

Right away, from the sad, sincere look my mother gave me, I knew what came next was a lie or another small truth meant to throw me off the track. "It's about that membership form you found at Pinky's," she said, meaning the Fisherfolk pamphlet. "I think you'll be proud when I explain about our family history's being preserved. But, Hannah darlin'? You're the one who never used Teddy Roosevelt's fishing reel or the rest of that junk, so please don't get mad when I do."

FUMING ONCE AGAIN, I let the porch door bang close and was almost to the dock when I noticed that Levi Thurloe was across the street, standing in the mangroves, watching me. Not hiding, exactly . . . Or maybe the strange man *was* hiding because he backed deeper into the bushes as I approached the road. Never in my life had Levi frightened me, but he did now—a silent presence dressed in coveralls who looked huge in the shadows and was holding something, a tool or a broken branch, in his hand.

I had to make a decision. If I crossed the road, as I'd intended, the path to the dock would take me within a few yards of Levi. Turn right, the road curved along the bay toward the marina and the row of rickety docks and cottages we called Munchkinville. Because of what Loretta had just told me, I had a reason to go there. I wanted to knock on every door and ask owners if they, too, had donated some of their property, or even all of it, to a non-profit organization that was collecting for a museum that, for all Loretta knew, existed only in the mind of some architect she's never met. Even if Joel Ransler hadn't offered me the job, it was a task I would have undertaken because that's exactly what my mother had done—signed over some of her property, how much I was still uncertain.

"It'll save me taxes!" was the only explanation she would offer.

I thought for a moment, then turned right to avoid Levi but took only a few strides before my spineless behavior angered me enough to reconsider. No one, especially a poor, brain-damaged man I'd known since childhood, was going to scare me away from my own boat. So I did an about-face and crossed the road, calling, "Come out of those bushes, Levi, before mosquitoes eat you alive!"

Instead of doing it, though, the man crouched lower as if unconvinced I could see him. It was a strange reaction even for Walkin' Levi, which should have stopped me in my tracks but only made me more determined. "You come out of there and talk to me or I'll come in and get you!"

Several slow steps the man took, his weight crunching branches, before he appeared in the shadows next to a buttonwood tree. A hammer—that's what he was holding in his right hand.

"I don't know nothing," he mumbled, responding to a question I hadn't asked. Then lifted his head enough to look at me, which was unusual and didn't last long but enough to notice that his eyes appeared as glazed and cold as glass. His earbuds were still missing, too, so maybe the absence of music had left the man alone in his head. Or had his expression *always* been so empty? He avoided eye contact, so I couldn't be sure, but I had an uneasy feeling that something inside Levi Thurloe had changed.

The boldness in me vanished. "I'm . . . sorry, Levi, I shouldn't have raised my voice like that."

The man's chin dropped to his chest. He looked at his muddy boots, looked at the hammer, then picked a leaf off his coveralls, which he rolled between his fingers.

Now what should I do? *Leave him alone,* a voice in me said. *Keep moving and pretend this never happened.* But we were here, only a few yards apart, and there could be no avoiding a handyman who worked next door. So I pushed ahead, saying, "Loretta told me you used the truck to deliver a box to Mrs. Helms. That she *asked* you to do it and you had permission. I shouldn't have doubted you the other day. You forgive me?"

A shrug was my reply. Levi began tapping the hammer against his thigh—hopefully because he was eager for me to be gone and not because he was agitated. What I wanted to ask was *Why were you so frightened on Pay Day Road?* but couldn't summon the courage. So I kept my tone chatty and stuck to a subject that had to be addressed. "I'm sure you took great care of the truck, no need to discuss that. But the thing is, Levi—"

He sensed a rebuke, and the man's nostrils widened to gather air, which caused me to pause, before I continued, "The thing about using the truck is, you probably shouldn't drive unless you have a license. See . . . my mother's not as fussy as some when it comes to breaking the law or going to jail. But if the police pulled you over, and if they checked your—"

I stopped talking because, for the second time in my life, Walkin' Levi risked eye contact, and what I saw scared me. *The police*—my choice of subjects could not have been more thought-less. It *was* the source of the problem between us. Because of me, Levi had been questioned by Billy, the tough detective, and he was still mad. I had no idea why anger had motivated him to spy on me from the mangroves, but now was not the time to discuss the police or even to hint that Levi might be arrested.

I took a step back and fumbled to change the subject. "On the other hand, the worst thing for an old truck is not to be used—so let's just forget it . . . okay?"

Was it my imagination or were Walkin' Levi's knuckles whit-ening as he gripped the hammer tighter? The man didn't respond, so I asked, "How's your new job going? You probably heard the news about Mrs. Candor's little dog."

That, at least, got a response. Levi's big head swiveled toward the oaks at the top of the mound behind the cement house. "Yeah . . . *she* hunts at night," he said, meaning the great horned owl, not Alice Candor, I felt certain, which would have made no sense. Then his head swiveled back, dodging eye contact, and offered me further reassurance by repeating what he'd told me in the truck, "But *you're* nice."

"Thank you, Levi," I said, "I think you're nice, too," which struck me as a hypocritical thing to say to a man who was bouncing a hammer against his thigh. Thankfully, I was spared additional awkwardness when a voice summoned me from the road.

"Hey, Missus Smith . . . *Hannah?* You got a minute to talk?"

Because she wasn't in uniform, it took a moment to recognize this petite woman wearing shorts and an amber blouse that turned her red hair to ginger. It was the sheriff's deputy from Boston who had an interest in archaeology.

I would soon learn her unusual first name: *Liberty.*

ELEVEN

When Liberty Tupplemeyer, the off-duty deputy, said, "I don't envy you putting up with that woman," she motioned so vaguely I assumed she meant Loretta, not Dr. Alice Candor, as was intended, which almost caused a fight, then got us into a confusing discussion about parents.

"If you met my mom, you wouldn't believe we're related," the redhead said. "She still bakes hash cookies—Christ, tried to get me to eat one on my sixteenth birthday. Said it would calm me down. 'Make me comatose, you mean,' I told her. Or wear peasant blouses and camp at Dead concerts with Dad and her pals from the old commune. Sing 'Rocky Mountain High' around the campfire; talk God and astrology. No thanks."

"Parents sometimes become childlike," I agreed, leading the woman onto the dock while also keeping an eye on Levi. When Tupplemeyer had appeared, he'd slipped back into the mangroves, then returned to work by crossing the road to the Candor property. Ten minutes, I'd been conversing with the deputy, who was chatty now that she was out of uniform, but I had yet to hear the sound of a nail being driven, or anything similar, to explain why Levi was carrying a hammer while he spied on me.

Something else that hadn't happened was hearing why Tupplemeyer, on her day off, had returned to Sulfur Wells. The delay was caused by my defensiveness when she'd seemed to criticize my mother, but, in fact, had meant Alice Candor.

"No one's asking you to put up with her!" I had countered with some heat. "Mind your own business—and walk yourself off our property while you're at it!"

Like two dogs who mistakenly snap at each other, we were now eager to make peace. For Liberty Tupplemeyer, that seemed to require proving her mother was even crazier than Loretta, who she'd yet to meet so had no idea how stiff the competition was.

Mrs. Tupplemeyer, however—who came from money, according to her daughter—was making a strong showing.

"My mom sees a mountain stream, particularly if it's a sunny day, she wants to go skinny-dipping. Doesn't matter who's around, can you imagine? Sixty-four years old—*skinny-dipping*. When I told her I was leaving BU for the police academy, you'd have thought I was marching off to join the Nazi Party. Know what she tells her friends? God forbid she gave birth to a cop, so she tells them, 'Bertie has gone into public service.' You know, like I married a Kennedy and I'm now devoting my life to flood victims."

"We've got to keep those two apart," I smiled but was becoming increasingly confused. BU, I knew, stood for Boston University, but what did our mothers have to do with the deputy's return to Sulfur Wells? "You were studying archaeology before that?" I asked, hoping to get the conversation on track.

The redhead nodded while she enjoyed the view from the dock. "In a way, my mom got me interested. Especially the way she behaves around her old hippie friends. Tribal, you know?"

I was lost. "Interested in archaeology, you mean? Or having the power to arrest people?"

"Pre-Columbian history," she replied. "Spend a day with Mom's friends, it's hard to believe space aliens didn't come down and impregnate half our parents' generation. You ever read *Chariots of the Gods*? Or look at satellite photos of the Plains of Nazca in Peru? The theory's been dismissed as bullshit, but it's interesting, you know? Their fascination with astronomy . . . geometry, advanced stuff. In high school, I got college credit volunteering on digs in Guatemala and Copán. You can't believe the vibe of those places, unless . . ." Tupplemeyer let the sentence trail off as her eyes focused on an island two miles away. "That's the western pyramid you mentioned, right?"

"Cushing Key," I said. "On this coast, whenever you see a high stand of trees, there's always a shell mound."

"I know that name. *Cushing* . . . Yeah, I saw his sketches on the Internet. He was sent here by the Smithsonian and collected artifacts in the eighteen hundreds. An ethnologist, right? Kind of a strange guy, but you were right about the mounds being pyramids. No doubt from his drawings."

I felt I should know more about Frank Hamilton Cushing but could only answer, "In the eighteen nineties, I'm pretty sure. You've done some reading since Friday."

"Everything I could find. And made some phone calls, too—an archaeologist in Tallahassee, and finally got the zoning department this morning. The guy wouldn't say shit, but it's a start." The deputy looked at me to see if I was interested or, possibly, impressed. I was both.

She continued, "Everything you told me is pretty accurate—an ancient, complex civilization, the remains are right here. What you told me about Dr. Candor is true, too. That she and her husband somehow got around all the restrictions and destroyed that Indian mound." The deputy turned and motioned toward the concrete mansion. "Sorry you thought I was talking about your mother, but I couldn't wait to get away from that bitch. You ever been inside her place?"

At last, I understood the confusion. "You were in Alice Candor's house? Just now?"

Yes. Tupplemeyer had actually passed the man with the camera as he was on his way out and she didn't care that he'd recognized her.

"Off duty, I'm still an officer of the court, but my time's my own," she explained. "I wanted to ask Candor face-to-face where they'd sent those dump trunks. And why the hell won't she tell the archaeologists? They could at least sift for artifacts, which would be a contextual mess, but, you know, valuable. I was more polite than the way I just put it. Trouble was, I couldn't pretend it was police business. The woman's too savvy. She's used to bullying people and getting what she wants. She wouldn't tell me where they dumped the stuff, of course. In fact, she said she'd call the sheriff personally if I kept asking questions."

"*Threatened* you," I said. "You've got a lot of nerve to even try."

Tupplemeyer flipped her hair back in a way that told me she

had some actress in her as well. "No, I'm just pissed off—and I don't have the financial worries most people do, so, you know, screw her if she wants to get tough. Over the weekend, I used a department computer to start putting the pieces together and also . . . Well, I'll just tell you—I ran background checks on the local players." She paused to give me a meaningful look before continuing. "There's not much I could do in two days. If Candor actually calls the sheriff, my sergeant could restrict my computer privileges. I don't want to lose my job, but I'll be damned if I'm going to let those assholes get away with destroying a shell pyramid. That's why I'm talking to you."

It was the second time that day a person had all but admitted to prying into my personal history. I decided to overlook the intrusion, however, until I understood the woman's motives. I said, "When I first realized it was you—you look so different out of uniform—I thought you'd come about my mother's garden. The attorney I called said don't touch it until she makes some calls. So if that's on your mind—"

Tupplemeyer had a lot of nervous energy and it showed. She stopped me by interrupting, "I get shitty assignments sometimes. That was one of them, so just drop it, okay? There's something going on around here that stinks, that's what I'm telling you."

"Just the Indian mound or Sulfur Wells?" I asked.

"Definitely one," she said, "maybe both."

"That wouldn't surprise me," I replied, which kept me neutral but willing to listen. I did.

"Do you have any idea how many agencies had to look the other way when the Candors dug up that mound? Either that or people in charge weren't paying attention. There's a long list, including that dweeb who came about your mom's garden. Plus county zoning and planning departments—the woman in charge of historical sites has a reputation for being an incompetent ditz. She'd be useless if I went to her." Tupplemeyer made a fluttering sound of frustration while her eyes flitted around as if she was eager to get moving.

"Are you saying the Candors paid bribes?"

The deputy read my tone correctly. "I know, I know, I don't believe it either. I work for county government, and it would be damn near impossible—too many people involved—to keep something like that quiet. But the Candors have money, and they know how bureaucracies work. They had a big health care business in Ohio. Bought two rehab clinics that were in trouble, then four hospitals in Indiana, and kept expanding until they screwed up and had to move out of the state."

You're shitting me? I nearly said but caught myself in time to ask, "That's *why* they came to Florida?"

The redhead shared the details she'd uncovered. Within a few years after buying the rehab clinics, the Candors had created the largest private, for-profit health care company in the Midwest. Dr. Alice Candor had the medical background and the brains. Her husband was a CPA, but she was the one who had been chairman of the board. Four years ago, their company had owned more than a hundred hospitals, but then it had all fallen apart. Investigators from the FBI and the Department of Health and Human Services had served search warrants at their main office. An investigation followed, during which the Candors struck a deal. They pled guilty to fourteen charges, all felonies, after admitting their employees had fraudulently billed Medicare and other state and federal programs. They also admitted to giving doctors partnerships in their hospitals as a kickback for referring patients. The kickbacks included free rent, fully furnished offices, and free drugs from hospital pharmacies. After plea bargaining, the company had paid out more than a million dollars in fines, but the Candors walked away free.

"My lord," I said, "most people would have gone to prison."

"Read up on Florida's governor, if you believe that," the deputy replied, then looked at the house again. "You've never been inside that place? What do you call it?"

I was still pondering her remark about the current governor when she pursued the question, saying, "Tasteless architecture is usually given a nickname by locals. You know, like McMansion, Garage Mahal. A name like that."

"Oh," I said. "The Bunker, for a while. Walmart, early on, but nothing really stuck."

The deputy, unimpressed, shaking her head, tried a few others—Bondo Condo, Slab-a-Lot, Plaster Disaster—but couldn't quite nail it, so she got back to her point about what it was like to be inside with the couple who had built the house.

"Creepy," Tupplemeyer said. "They're like two mushrooms who live in artificial lighting. Lots of pink tropical décor, Christ, even some replicas of wooden masks the Indians wore, but it's all fake."

"Instant Floridians," I said. "I didn't know for sure she really was a doctor. Neither one of them comes outside much."

"What they did was change the name of their company and moved here after they bought out a chain of rehab clinics—Tampa, Arcadia, Belle Glade—all low income areas with a lot of traffic. I'm guessing the clinics have a contract with the state or they bill Medicaid, but I'm not sure. She's licensed to practice in Florida, and makes rounds at some of the clinics, but doesn't actually practice, I don't think. There's a lot to find out."

"What kind of doctor is she?"

Alice Candor was a specialist in psychiatric medicine, Tupplemeyer said. When she added that Dr. Candor had done psychiatric research as well, I felt a chill. At the same instant, Levi Thurloe appeared from behind the cement house, pushing a wheelbarrow, his coveralls sweat-soaked. When he saw me, Walkin' Levi bowed his head to avoid eye contact but nonetheless watched me as he plodded toward the road.

"Let's go somewhere else to talk," I said to the deputy. "On my phone, I've got video I shot of them bulldozing the mound. They used a backhoe, too, for the landscaping. Want to see it?"

"Those pompous, destructive assholes," the redhead muttered, meaning *Yes, she did.*

WE WERE SITTING on my skiff, drinking diet RC Cola, which was getting hard to find and which the off-duty deputy had never tried before, while she explained why she had run a background check on me after checking out the Candors and a few other locals, too.

"How else would I know you can help?" she said, referring to the reason she had returned to Sulfur Wells. The former archaeology major was determined to find the tons of earth, shells, and artifacts that had been hauled away by trucks. Seeing my video of a bulldozer and backhoe destroying what had once been a pyramid had only fired her resolve.

"What sold me, Hannah, is you're licensed to knock on doors, ask nosy questions, the whole private detective deal. *And* collect information on civil matters." The woman paused and took a sip of her drink. "It is Hannah, right? Or do your friends call you something else? Like me, Liberty is so bullshit and butterfly sounding, I go by Bert or Bertie—but I hate Libby, so don't call me that."

I wondered if I had misheard. "Birdy as in bird?" I asked. It was a name that fit a skinny woman who wasn't pretty in the typical way but who had an interesting face and was in good shape.

"Sure, that's fine, too. But back to what I was saying . . . If we find human bones in the fill they hauled away, there's a state law against transporting human remains, even antiquities. You think that's possible?"

"That we'll find bones, you mean?"

The woman's impatient expression told me *Of course that's what I mean!*

"In a shell mound, well . . . Yeah, it's possible," I said. "Last year, Loretta gave permission, and a group from the University of Florida found the teeth and jaw of a young girl near our carport, just eighteen inches under the surface." I pointed to the house, which was yellow clapboard with a chimney poking out of the tin roof.

"Just to the left of the porch—I'll show you later. They carbon-dated one of the teeth, then put the bones back and left everything just they way they found it. That ended the dig, of course."

Fascinated, Birdy Tupplemeyer listened a while longer, then said, "You're shitting me!" when I told her the girl had probably died in her teens and had been buried more than eight hundred years ago. Then glared at the cement three-story again. "Okay, human bones, that's the part I wasn't sure about. See . . . even if they didn't destroy an actual burial mound, there could still be burials in the stuff they hauled away. Once we locate it, we can dig around and see what's there—contextually, the fill's ruined anyway. If we do find bones, you can file suit, or get someone else to file, but the thing is"—the woman became thoughtful and lowered her voice—"we've got to leave the archaeologists out of it—for now. Even if you know some of them personally." She looked at me. "Do you?"

"Four, probably more, they've been coming here for years," I said. "I trust them. Two drove down from Gainesville when they heard about the bulldozer. And Dr. Caren—you'll meet her, she's great—Caren cried like a baby, she was so upset. But there was nothing they could do to stop the digging."

The redhead camouflaged her cop cynicism with an open-minded shrug, then tested my naïvety by asking, "Did you know the Candors donated ten grand to the archaeology foundation that funds research here? That was *before* they started construction. Friends of The First People, that's the foundation's name."

I felt my face coloring because I don't like to be tested. "You did your homework, I'll give you that," I said, "but don't get tricky. If you researched the foundation, you saw my name on the members' list. Sure, I know they donated money. But hindsight is a hundred percent, and I guarantee you the board and archaeologists are embarrassed about it after what happened to the mound."

"Just a silly mistake," the redhead said, as if she was being dense.

"I don't appreciate sarcasm either," I told her. "The Candors saw it as a bribe, I don't doubt that. But you don't know the archaeologists. I do. The foundation's screwup was not knowing that people like the Candors exist."

Tupplemeyer's expression changed. "You've got a temper."

"I'll introduce you to Dr. Williams," I replied. "He's the head guy. Dr. Caren, too. You've never met finer people, but judge for yourself."

The deputy seemed temporarily convinced but said again, "You still can't say a word about what we're doing. One of the reasons I switched to law enforcement is because archaeology is so damn dependent on public funding. A ten-thousand-dollar donation? Yeah, of course they took it, I can understand that. But"—she paused to warn me about what came next—"don't get mad again, okay?"

I replied, "If I get mad, you'll *know* it . . . Birdy," using her nickname to see how it felt and it felt okay once I'd said it.

"I'm convinced," she said. "What you don't know about academics is that making waves is the fastest way to lose funding. But, as a cop, I can actually do something—but not until someone files a complaint."

Now she was getting down to what was actually on her mind.

"I have the name of the trucking company written somewhere," I said, "unless you already know where they dumped the fill."

Tupplemeyer did the thing with her hair again, but this time in a more natural way that didn't quite fit her sly expression. "I knew you'd come through. You should have seen your face when you first told me about them bulldozing that mound. Damn, you were mad. Yeah, I've got it narrowed down to four or five dump spots, but, when we search, it has to be at night. Three are county-owned landfills, and my ass would be in a sling if we get caught."

I liked the woman's spunk but finally had to say, "Tell me something. Talking about your mother was a way of softening me up, wasn't it?"

"No," she replied, offended, "I did it because my mom drives me insane. It was nice to vent to someone who . . . Well, I don't have many female friends. And why would the guys I work with care?"

That seemed honest enough, although I was still suspicious—but about something else now. Birdy Tupplemeyer was feminine in her mannerisms and dress, but she also wore pants five days a week and carried a gun. I wanted to make my own interests clear. "I don't have many women friends myself," I began. "Not close anyway. The man I'm dating keeps me busy most nights. He's a marine biologist, but he's out of town this week. That's probably why I'm a little on edge."

"Really," Birdy replied, the cop cynicism fresh in her voice. "How long you been dating?"

Three days, officially, but that wouldn't have gotten my message across. "Awhile," I responded, then told her a little about my late husband, who had been drunk when he stepped into traffic but omitted the fact we had spent only one night together before he was shipped overseas. As final proof, I alluded to a gift certificate from Saks and suggested we do some shopping on her next day off.

The redhead found that all very amusing for some reason and gave a snorting sort of laugh. "Relax, for christ's sake. I'm not gay. I'm not even bi."

"Who cares if you are?" I shot back.

"*I* care, and I get that question a lot. You probably get it even more." She eyed me, sizing me up. "What are you, five-ten, six-foot? Blue's a good color for you, and I like the cargo shorts, but a woman your size who wears tools on her belt?" She was still chuckling.

"They're *fishing pliers*," I replied, showing her. "I had a charter this morning, but my client canceled." I slipped the pliers back. "Your personal life is none of my business. It never crossed my mind that you're—"

"Oh, *stop* it." Birdy made a shushing motion, already tired of the topic, then patted the steering console of my skiff. "You've got the day off, huh? If I pay for the fuel, how about you take me out there?" She pointed toward the island where the remains of a western pyramid was elevated by trees.

"I've got to pick up clients at one and it's nearly noon now," I said, which was true but also a way of dodging her request— working for free is no way to run a charter business and it was the sort of offer I get a lot. Instead, I offered to show her the Marlow cruiser and explain the work needed to make the boat livable. By the time we'd finished the tour, I'd changed my mind. I liked Birdy Tupplemeyer, appreciated her high-energy way of dealing with awkward matters, so I suggested she come back tomorrow.

"I'm booked for the morning," I explained, "but I can show you around in the afternoon. Are you off?"

She shook her head. "I'm new, so it's Mondays/Thursdays off. But I could use a personal day."

I rechecked my watch. "Okay, then. We'll split the fuel. In return, maybe you can give me your opinion on a case I might be starting. It has to do with my mother, and maybe a bogus charity. Oh, and there's something else—"

Sitting on the flybridge of the cruiser—a boat that was soon to be my home—I told the deputy what had happened to me at the Helms place and the little I knew about the murder of Dwight Helms. Despite Tupplemeyer's energy and impatience, she was a thoughtful woman, and I soon felt comfortable enough to also share my fears about Levi Thurloe, too.

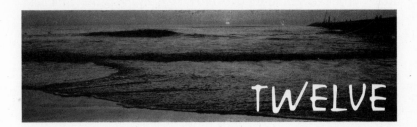

TWELVE

That night, when Loretta called in tears, claiming there was a man watching her from the yard, I was at the computer in my Uncle Jake's office, a two-room CBS that adjoins a strip mall off Pondella Road. Lots of traffic and neon glare; cars with subwoofers that rattle the windows. For the last three years, I'd been living here alone and had done my best to convert the place into a homey apartment, even though I knew it would never feel like home.

Loretta called around ten. I had finished my charter at seven and arrived at the office thirty minutes later. My routine when entering the place seldom varied. I locked the door behind me and put the teakettle on while I showered. Changed into jeans and a clean blouse, then settled myself at the desk to work. Tonight, my routine changed slightly because the first thing I did was check e-mails—but still no word from Ford. More disappointing was that the two cheerful notes I'd sent him hadn't been opened, possibly not even received in the remote Venezuelan village where he'd said he would be working.

"*Shit!*" Birdy Tupplemeyer's affection for profanity was rubbing off on me because that was my reaction. I got up, rechecked the door lock, then fussed with the heavy curtains that shielded me from outside noise and the eyes of loiterers in the parking lot next door.

Stop fretting, I told myself, and returned to the computer, carrying a mug of mango tea. Joel Ransler had postponed our charter to investigate what he said was a murder scene. It didn't take me long to find the few facts available. An eighty-two-year-old man, Clayton Edwards, had died of "multiple wounds" in a Sematee County mobile home park and his trailer had been ransacked. Murder-robbery was suspected.

The name Edwards is mentioned often in Florida history, so I spent another fifteen minutes searching for more information, then gave up. I had a lot to do: Fisherfolk Inc., the nonprofit organization based in Carnicero, had to have a founder, possibly even a board. What were their names? There were newspaper articles I needed to read about the Dwight Helms murder, and I also wanted to confirm what Birdy had told me about the Candors.

What kind of psychiatric research had Dr. Alice Candor conducted? Birdy hadn't had time at the sheriff's department to find out, or it was possible that medical journals were kept locked to all but subscribers. I also wanted to run a background check on Joel Ransler, who had confirmed by text he was meeting me at the dock in the morning. Everything about the man seemed genuine and likable, so why did I distrust him? No . . . that wasn't fair. Truth was, I didn't *want* to trust him because . . . *why?* Was it because I found Ransler attractive, was flattered by his interest, even though I was already in love with a good man?

Nothing wrong with that, my conscience insisted. *Finish with the computer, then go to bed. You won't have to sleep in an office much longer.*

It was never easy for me to be alone in this building at night. Living next to a strip mall was like waiting for a traffic light to change or for a bus to arrive—some sudden transitional signal that would thrust me forward into my future. Finally, it was happening. The beautiful little Marlow cruising boat would soon be my home, which is why most of my things were already packed in boxes. The office was becoming an office again, but that didn't change the emptiness I felt as I sat alone, trying to ignore the headlights and rumble of passing cars, the voices of faceless strangers who parked outside to use the fitness center or to buy beer at the Shop N Go.

Soon, the search engines, which debit our agency monthly, began to produce information I could not have found on my laptop, and the noise outside was silenced. One by one, I created folders labeled *Fisherfolk, Candors,* and *Helms Murder,* then dragged files into them as they appeared. I wanted to arrange the files chronologically before I began my reading. Because I dreaded what I might discover about the murder of Dwight Helms, I also wanted to save it for last.

I opened the Candor file first, even before the search engines had completed their work. Everything Birdy told me about the couple was true, but her words hadn't had the impact of seeing the mug shots of Dr. Alice Candor and her husband glowering at me from clippings in the *Toledo Blade* and Cleveland *Plain Dealer.* The charges made against their company, Firelands Physicians Regional Health Care, had made headlines. Something Birdy hadn't mentioned was their company had also managed rehab clinics for the state penal system. It was a lucrative contract that had been canceled when six inmate patients followed through on a suicide pact that, supposedly, didn't include a note explaining why they'd killed themselves. During the scandal that followed, letters to the editor about the Candors were so venomous, it was no wonder they had fled to Florida—a state where the best of people, and the worst, come to reinvent their lives.

Raymond—I now knew the husband's name. I had seen him from a distance and hadn't noticed his graying mustache or his pale, nervous eyes. A dog that fears his master's voice and hand— the expression on the husband's face was similar. Alice Candor's credentials—degrees from Oberlin, Ohio State, and Johns Hopkins—suggested that she, the overachiever, was the dominant of the two. She had done research at a psychiatric hospital prior to going into private practice, then chairing Firelands Health Care, but had published in only two journals. As feared, access to both was restricted, then further restricted when I attempted to subscribe: licensed physicians, medical students, and authorized clinicians only.

Even so, I found an abstract of Dr. Candor's first research paper, which produced a familiar chill because it suggested the doctor had done research using prison inmates as subjects:

Effects of Benzedrine on Violent Habitual Offenders
Unresponsive to Standard Protocols
A two-year study that suggests clinicians can assert surrogate
influence on habitually violent and criminal behavior after

administering Benzedrine in dosages that avoid addiction (but exceed the accepted maximum) via media that manipulate the subject's frontal lobes.

In high school, I got A's in physiology and chemistry but now couldn't remember what Benzedrine was for or remember the role our frontal lobe plays in the human brain. I knew what *assert surrogate influence* and *manipulate* meant, though, and it scared me. In this case, the assertive surrogate was Alice Candor. How she had manipulated the brains of her inmate patients, the abstract didn't say, but she'd readied them by administering a drug in large dosages. Could *assertive influence* also be translated as *control?* Was that why six prison inmates had committed suicide?

I looked up *Human brain, frontal lobes* and found too much to digest in one night. Basically, the frontal lobe is two sections of brain that presses against our foreheads. Combined, they are responsible for our behavior, our ability to learn, and all of our voluntary movements.

Voluntary movements—I wondered if the distinction was significant. To a man or woman in prison, I had no doubt that it was.

As I puzzled over the wording, my phone buzzed, which caused me to jump. I stood, checked the time—9:20 p.m.—then opened a text from Birdy Tupplemeyer, which read *Just leaving. Place closest me no luck. Can't call now. How long U up?*

Using two fast thumbs, I replied, *Late as you want, get out of there, be careful!* because her note could only mean one thing: she had gone alone to a dump site near her condo in South Fort Myers, one of the places we'd discussed earlier. It was a county landfill that was gated and guarded after hours but a common destination for trucks loaded with raw earth to unload.

"Crazy woman," I muttered but had to smile. I often meet people who talk bravely about their intentions, but Birdy, by god, was a doer, not just a talker. My respect for her had just climbed several notches.

As an afterthought, I sent a second text: *Don't go alone again! Mean it!* And I did. I had agreed to help the redhead, why hadn't she waited for another night? I walked around the office, expecting a response that didn't come. After five minutes had passed, I was worried enough to consider sending a third text, but decided Tupplemeyer—a cop—didn't need a babysitter, so I went to the bathroom, used the toilet, and washed my face to collect myself.

Assert surrogate influence. I couldn't get the phrase out of my head. Levi Thurloe, a huge man with a child's brain, was working for the Candors. Had Alice, the research psychiatrist, been giving Levi drugs and then . . . what? Issuing hypnotic commands? Whispering into his ear during lunch breaks, then sending him out to intimidate people she considered to be enemies? Or even ordering them killed with an axe? It sounded like ridiculous science fiction. But the couple now owned several small Florida clinics, according to Birdy. Dr. Alice was still licensed to practice, she had worked with violent criminals in the past, and the woman still had access to lord knows what types of drugs. Maybe the scenario wasn't so silly after all.

Enough with the Candors! Finish up and get to bed!

I returned to the computer but couldn't make myself sit in the chair. The three new folders were the same size, but the label *Helms Murder* seemed to leap off the screen at me, so I took another thoughtful lap around the room, pausing at the door to the storage closet. My Uncle Jake hadn't been a tidy man, so, after his death, it had taken me two weeks to sort through his personal files and belongings, which I had stored inside on shelves. Only yesterday I had unlocked this door, then traced my memory of Hoppe's Gun Oil to Jake's holster—an oddity that didn't mesh with my knowledge of the bookish Dr. Marion Ford.

I stood there for a moment, telling myself my fears were imaginary, but unlocked the door and flicked on the light anyway. Two single overhead bulbs showed stacks of boxes and plastic containers, all labeled. There was also a gun safe bolted to the back wall, the inexpensive type made of sheet metal, painted brown. My fears might be imaginary, but the man who had chased me with an axe had been as real as real can be. It seemed reasonable to protect myself if it ever happened again.

I got the key to the gun safe and opened it. Jake's empty shoulder holster was on the shelf above his old Mossberg shotgun and a .22 rifle, the first weapon I'd learned to shoot. I feel no warmth for firearms—who would?—but the memory of the days I'd spent with my sweet uncle, hiking the Everglades as a girl, created a brief nostalgia in me. But that vanished when I reached behind the holster and pulled out what appeared to be a large leather-bound book. It was the size of a family Bible and heavy; the holster made the pleasant sound of creaking leather when I looped it over my shoulder. There was a box of 9mm ammunition on the shelf, and I took that, too. I carried all three items to the desk, returned to lock the gun safe and the closet, then sat at the computer, my attention focused on the book.

NEGOTIATORS. The title was embossed in gold on the cover. A place marker made of red ribbon added to the illusion that this was just an old book. It wasn't. I flipped open the cover. Inside, nested in black velvet, was a small, stainless semiauto pistol, its transparent handgrip showing it contained no magazine. That didn't prove the chamber was empty, but I found myself reluctant when I reached to check. Months ago, this pistol had saved my life, yet the sight of it now caused a feeling of revulsion inside me—revulsion not for the pistol but for events associated with it. Joel Ransler had dropped a couple of hints, but Birdy Tupplemeyer hadn't mentioned reading about the man I'd shot and wounded, although she surely knew—a courtesy I appreciated because even though the man had brutalized other women and would have probably killed me, shooting him wasn't something I was proud of. I had blocked the details from that awful day, but now here I was, reaching for the same pistol again, a box of 9mm hollow-points nearby, ready to be loaded and do the job they were designed to do, which was kill.

I withdrew my hand and thought about it. Did I really want to carry a gun?

No . . . I did not. I had enjoyed target shooting as a girl, but putting a bullet through the hip of a human being, then witnessing my attacker's rage and pain, had replaced my naïve notions with the ugly reality that a bullet scars from both ends. Never again did I want to shoot another human being, so why carry a gun?

I closed the cover of the phony book, pushed it aside, and positioned the computer screen closer. To prove my resolve, I opened the folder I most dreaded and found fifteen documents related to the murder of Dwight Helms. The most repellent had been labeled by the Sematee County Sheriff's Department *Homicide; Helms, D. W., Crime Scene Photos*, followed by the date and the status, which was *Active*. In my current mood, it seemed required that I start there and I did.

It was a multiple PDF file. When I clicked it, sheets of thumbnail images appeared, then opened in such rapid-fire succession that I could only sit there dazed as the photographs stacked themselves on the screen. Old black-and-white shots that had been scanned into the system, each so graphic that my constant wincing soon mimicked the rhythm of a punching bag. The body of Dwight Helms had been found at night. Flashbulbs added a glossiness to the photos, turning pools of blood to silver, casting shadows that magnified each small, grisly detail.

Finally, I regained control of my eyes and managed to turn away. I stood, took a deep breath to stem my queasiness, then started toward the bathroom just in case. That's when the phone rang. It would have been a relief to hear the voice of Birdy Tupplemeyer, so I grabbed for it but heard Loretta's panicked voice instead.

"I called nine-one-one, but he's still out there and I'm scared!" she began, then told me she'd seen a man outside, his shadow in the moonlight, moving from window to window.

I asked just enough questions to convince myself my mother wasn't stoned or dreaming, and that she really had called police, before saying, "Make sure the doors are locked, I'm on my way."

In a rush, I shut down the computer and threw a few things in a bag. At the door, though, I hesitated, my hand on the light switch, while I stared at the leather-bound book on the desk.

NEGOTIATORS.

Such a strange title for a box that contained a deadly weapon— a pistol that had already saved my life once and might save me again if a man armed with an axe was on our property. If the crime scene photos hadn't been so fresh in my mind, I probably wouldn't have reconsidered, but I did because of the terrible way Dwight Helms had died.

As I drove toward Sulfur Well, the book was on the seat next to me but slightly heavier. Along with the pistol, it now contained a loaded magazine.

THIRTEEN

The nice sheriff's deputy, who said he'd seen Liberty Tupplemeyer but had never spoken to her, pulled away just before midnight. He had searched the area with a flashlight while I stayed inside and comforted my mother. Something else I'd done was use the house phone to fire the night sitter, who, Loretta claimed, had been drunk or high on crack, then pretended to be called away by a family emergency.

"I wouldn't trust that girl with a potato peeler, let alone my life," Loretta had sputtered. "Who hired her anyway? You should have better judgment, Hannah!"

"I just left a message for the agency," I replied with patience. "You don't have to worry about seeing her again."

"Seeing that tramp's not what I'm worried about. A man who peeps in windows isn't after a woman's money, if you know what I'm saying."

I asked, "Are you sure you saw someone in the yard? Mullet fishermen break down late sometimes and have to walk to the marina."

"Not just the yard," Loretta insisted, "he was going from window to window. Didn't I just say that? He wanted to get a look at me with my clothes off before he broke down the door. So don't lecture me about not taking a bath! If you had any sense, you'd be finding us winter coats to wear instead of worrying about mullet fishermen and broke-down engines."

I hadn't mentioned bathing, but I had asked why Joel Ransler's name and cell number were scribbled on the pad next to the phone. Now, once again, I asked for an explanation.

"I don't pry into your personal business," Loretta fired back, her gray eyes flaring. "At least there's one person in this world who cares what happens to me. And he's good-looking, too! Rance," she added, using the special prosecutor's nickname, "that's who I should've called after nine-one-one. He'd know how to deal with a rapist."

For too many minutes, we went back and forth like that before my mother finally conceded that Ransler had called that afternoon to see how she was getting along, and also with more questions about the late Rosanna Helms. The special prosecutor had covered more ground than that, though, I could tell by Loretta's evasive manner.

"Did he ask about me, or how much you donated to that charity, Fisherfolk?" I pressed, which only caused more turmoil, so I gave up and waited on the porch until the deputy was finished searching.

"I didn't see anyone, didn't find any tracks, nothing," the deputy said but wrote his cell number on a card. We talked for a while longer, then he returned to his car.

I got Loretta in bed, checked to make sure the doors were

locked behind me, then walked to the dock, undecided about what to do next. It was midnight. Should I wait until mother had quieted, then return to my office apartment? I dreaded the thought of that, but the option of sleeping in my old bedroom was even less inviting. I hadn't had what you'd call an *unhappy* childhood, but my years in Loretta's house hadn't allowed me much freedom, nor had I enjoyed the confidence I now felt. At night, my old room brought back memories of self-doubt and nervousness I didn't care to revisit. On the other hand, I had to be up before sunrise to catch bait for my charter. Only six hours between then and now.

On the dock, shepherd's-crook lamps cast yellow pools along the decking and showed the silhouette of the boat that would be my new home. I had yet to spend a night in the snug little cabin. My first night aboard, I had decided, should be a celebration of sorts, so I wanted all the work to be finished, everything clean and tidy, and my personal things stored where they belonged. Tonight, however, it seemed okay to postpone the celebration and get some sleep. I found a sleeping bag in the house, a toothbrush, a robe and a towel, and carried all that, plus my bag, down to the boat. The Marlow had no running water, but there was a hose on the dock and an extension cord for electrical power from shore.

I was below in the cabin, getting the V-berth ready, when I remembered I hadn't received a reply from Birdy. It was twelve-fifteen, but I sent a text anyway: *Make it home?* I finished making the bed, brushed my teeth, then switched off the dock lights, yet my phone remained silent.

143

————

THIRTY MINUTES LATER, I was still awake, fretting about my new friend among other things, when I heard what sounded like footsteps on the dock. I sat up in the darkness and listened. Uncle Jake had built the dock as solid as stone, but all decking vibrates beneath the weight of an adult even if that adult is taking slow, methodical steps, and that's what I was hearing—no, what I was *feeling*. The steady *thump-thump-thump* of what might be someone walking toward me, being extra careful because the moon was covered by clouds and the deck was hard to see. From the mild vibration, I guessed it was either an average person already close to my boat or a large person who had just mounted the dock from the mangroves.

Dear lord, what if it was Levi, carrying a hammer—or worse!

I grabbed my robe and put it on while continuing to listen. The wind had freshened, and I began to wonder if the steady thumping might be caused by a bumper or a floating log banging against a piling. Or raccoons—they loved ambushing crabs from the dock at night. Whatever or whoever it was, I wasn't going to sit there like a tethered goat and wait for something to happen. I had to unlock the cabin door and take a look.

Rather than alert my visitor, I left the lights off and felt my way soundlessly toward the companionway steps. I'd done so much sanding, painting, and buffing inside the cabin, my feet knew the interior from memory. What I'd forgotten was a box of heavy plumbing hardware that was sticking out of the entrance to the shower. In midstride, I kicked the thing and stubbed my toe so hard that I wanted to cry. When the box banged off my other foot, I threw out my hands to catch myself but pulled down a tray of tools instead. Wrenches and ratchet heads made a thunderous clatter when they hit the teak deck below.

Shit! Son of a bitch! I couldn't help myself from saying it because my toe was throbbing, and I had also probably damaged my polished flooring, too. No point in trying to surprise anyone now, not after so much noise. So I limped over and switched on the cabin lights, then the aft deck lights. Scattered near my bleeding toenail was a host of tools to choose from as a weapon. I selected a small pry bar, then unlocked the door and poked my head out, calling, "Who's there!"

I'd been wrong about raccoons and floating logs. It was a person, a person walking toward me: a tall gray shape in the moonlight. It slowed when I called out, then stopped midway between the shore and my boat. I felt my breath catch. The person's head was cloaked in something—a sun mask, possibly—and he was tall enough to convince me it was either Levi or the man who had come at me with an axe—or one in the same.

I yelled, "I've got a gun!" then ducked back into the cabin, intending to lock the door and arm the pistol before calling for help on my cell. I'd been uneasy about bringing the weapon aboard but was glad I had it now . . . or was until I heard the person reply.

"Redneck trash with a gun. Why am I not surprised?" It was a woman's voice; a deep voice with an edge that threatened hysteria or rage, both extremes within easy reach if needed. It was Alice Candor, who then demanded, "Come out of there! I knew this was going to happen!"

I had been so scared, it took me a moment to stop hyperventilating and to understand the situation. My brain spun through the details, then latched onto the most important: a woman I had never met, trespassing on *my* dock *after* midnight, was calling *me* names and yelling orders as if I was some lowlife peon or one of her prison inmate patients.

I wasn't scared now. I was *mad*. So mad, in fact, I didn't trust myself with a pry bar, so I left it on the counter before I pushed open the cabin door and stepped out onto the deck. It wasn't easy to disguise my limp, but I tried.

Candor was still yelling, "This area is trashy enough without people on boats polluting my view. This is the last warning you're going to get!"

She had come a few steps closer, weaving a little as if drunk. The cloudy blue moon was above us, but I could see she was wearing one of her flowing caftans, plus a scarf or hood on this cool spring night—a woman who was as tall or taller than me, so it was no wonder I had feared the worst. I was furious but managed to sound in control when I replied, "Is this the way you behaved before they ran you out of Ohio? No wonder! If you're going to call names, have the courage to do it face-to-face."

"Ran me out of—?" The woman caught herself, stunned for a moment, but rallied fast. "Why, you pathetic little bitch! You don't know what you're talking about and you're not smart enough to understand. I'll tell you this, though: spread rumors about me, my attorneys will have you in court so fast, I'll own that goddamn boat before you know what hit you. Then I'll—"

"Making threats from a distance is as trashy as it gets," I tried to interrupt, but Alice Candor talked over me, her voice suddenly shrill.

"Don't you threaten me! I'll take that shack your mother calls a house, too! The whole goddamn area needs to be leveled, that's what I think. And I'll start with you!"

I was losing control. "Get out of here. You're trespassing!"

"Not for long!" the woman laughed. "You'll see! Call the police, go ahead. It's illegal to live on a boat. Once they radio in, you're the one who's leaving, not me. I've *already* filed papers against your mother—the old bitch needs to be committed. Dementia, senility, a threat to the public good—classic symptoms. A colleague of mine is willing to sign the papers. I know how the system works, sweetie!"

Why hadn't I put on jeans and a blouse? Because of the robe, I couldn't hop onto the dock in a way that was imposing. I had to use one hand to keep myself covered—way too dainty—but I got out of the boat and faced the woman. "Lady, unless you're a good swimmer, I suggest you be on your way. You're either drunk or just plain mean."

"Mean?" Dr. Alice Candor was shaking her head in disbelief but already backing away. "You're the people who butchered my dog! You just threatened me with a gun! I'll have your *head* for that."

Her tone was so suddenly theatrical, I wondered if she had an audience and was attempting to justify her behavior. I was right. A second person was approaching from the road. A man . . . her husband, I realized, when he called, "Alice, what are you doing out here?"

The woman lowered her voice, hoping only I could hear, and proved just how vicious she could be. "Your mother should be on psychotropic meds, sweetie, and I can make that happen. So don't fuck with me!"

Raymond Candor had good ears or had been through similar confrontations. Seconds later, he was on the dock, trying to get an arm around a wife who was twice his size while also apologizing. "She had a couple of drinks tonight. No harm intended. I'm sure you understand." Then whispered to his wife, "Alice, please don't make *another* scene. Do you remember what happened last time?"

The woman shoved him away so forcefully, she nearly went into the water, but the man caught her. Even so, she yelled, "Go to hell, Ray! Get your hands off me, you . . ." Then she used a terrible word.

Dr. Candor wasn't done. She continued to berate her husband as he led her away, calling him names so foul that I guessed he was either immune to the abuse or afraid of his own wife. The arguing didn't stop until the heavy front door of their house banged shut, sealing off their voices with the abruptness of a stone slab.

SLAB-A-LOT—Birdy had suggested it as a name for the concrete house. It rhymed with Camelot, which struck me as a little too cute, so I experimented with others: the *Dipped Crypt . . . Psycho Place . . . Mount Stucco*.

No . . . naming a house wasn't enough to keep my mind busy, so I gave up.

It was one-thirty in the morning. I was so upset, I was shaking.

The untainted silence of stars and cloudy moonlight flooded down on me while I sat on the aft deck and tried to recover. It was too late for tea, too early for coffee, so I did what I always do when I can't sleep: went looking for something to read. Because I hadn't moved my things aboard, all the cabin contained were manuals on plumbing and wiring. During my search, the deceptive leather book fooled my eyes often enough that I carried it to the settee booth and switched on the lamp. It was a distraction, at least, and gave me something to think about.

NEGOTIATORS

I had puzzled over the title more than once; had even looked up the word: *An agent who brokers conflicts between two or more parties, often through compromise but sometimes by issuing an ultimate ruling.*

How had my Uncle Jake come to own such a weapon? It was such an ironic combination: violence in a benign case that was specially constructed to deceive. I had already done an Internet search, but there wasn't much to find. Twenty-some years ago, a master gunsmith had produced a concealment weapon for a State Department agency, the name of which was still classified. Less than two hundred had been made. The gun was a shortened Smith & Wesson with a hooked trigger guard, a sleek fluted barrel, plus some other tweaks for fast shooting. On the transparent window grips, in red, was stamped *DEVEL*, which was an archaic Scottish word, a noun.

I sat looking at the pistol while my mind drifted back to Uncle

Jake. Prior to his death, he had entrusted the weapon to a fishing client (who I had inherited), but the man knew nothing about Devel—didn't even know what the book contained. The strange ensemble wasn't something I could discuss with friends, either, even Ford—and why would I? They weren't experts on weapons. Like Uncle Jake, who was a sweet man but also shielded in his ways, the book and its contents remained private and a mystery.

Finally, I took the pistol from the case and checked the chamber. It was empty. Two magazines, one loaded, lay secure in their places—and that's where they would remain for the night.

Still restless, I closed the book, then returned to the deck in hopes of more comfort from the stars. Nearby, a school of mullet spooked; a family of dolphins sliced the moonlight, their blowholes *ploof*ing like snorkels. Then, from the mound behind my childhood home, came the baritone *boom-boom-boom* of a great horned owl, who watched from the high shadows of an oak.

I stood, a silly attempt to feel the owl's resonance on my face. When I did, for an instant—a single blink of my eyelids—I imagined the silhouette of a man standing near the tree. A large man with wide, familiar shoulders. One blink of the eyes later, though, the man was gone . . . or the illusion I had just experienced.

You're upset and you're lovesick, I reminded myself.

After watching the trees for another ten minutes, I went to bed.

FOURTEEN

With so many prime fishing spots between Sanibel Island and Punta Gorda, I'd had no need to make the tricky turns and cuts required to find the Helmses' property by water until Joel Ransler arrived the next morning. He was ten minutes late and dressed for fishing but also carrying a briefcase in one hand, a small cooler in the other.

The first thing I asked was if there was any news from the medical examiner about Rosanna Helms.

"Heart attack," he said, giving me a close look after he had stepped aboard my skiff. We talked about the woman awhile before he added, "You look tired. Up late?" Then offered a look of concern to assure me it wasn't an insult.

"You're the one who's been investigating a murder," I replied. Rather than mentioning I had read about the victim, the elderly man named Clayton Edwards, I asked, "Anything unusual?"

"I'm in an ugly line of work," Joel said, "nothing I haven't seen before. But on a morning like this"—his eyes were taking in a lucent April sky; the bay, which was glassy—"I'd rather talk about you. Tired or not, Hannah, you look incredible. And a perfect day to be on the water, huh?"

The special prosecutor sounded so cheerful and caring, I felt a twinge of guilt. I hadn't slept much, it was true, and part of my wakeful night had been spent wondering why Joel hadn't come right out and told me the truth about Dwight Helms. It had provided me with a solid reason not to trust the man.

I wasn't going to admit I'd seen the crime scene photos either. Ransler was my client. If he wanted to discuss the subject, that was up to him. Did he have that kind of honesty in him? Even if he did, why should I care?

"It's supposed to be calm all morning," I replied. "Do you want to fish first? I found a school of reds off Hemp Key—that's on the way."

No, the special prosecutor wanted to go straight to Deer Stop Bay, which was linked by tidal creeks to the cove where the late Dwight Helms had built his dock during the peak of the pot-hauling trade. It was also where Helms had been chased down by a person or persons unknown who, after wounding him badly, had finally finished the job. All night long, awake and in my dreams, those photos had hounded me and forced me to imagine the terrible sequence of events. To murder a human being was bad enough, but the way Mr. Helms had died was hideous.

Pretending to enjoy the twenty-minute boat ride to the old dock wasn't easy. Even when my full attention was required by shoal water and oyster bars, I remained subdued. Maybe Ransler sensed it, because he complimented me when I dropped the skiff off plane, saying, "Even with a chart, most people couldn't have found this place. A couple of deputies tried over the weekend but radioed in it was too shallow."

"It is too shallow," I replied, nudging the throttle back, "unless you know where the deep water is." Which might have sounded smug, so I added, "The channel isn't marked. Local fishermen always tear down the markers if someone tries."

"The deputies said their boat was too big."

"Oh?"

"A twenty-four-foot Grady White, I think. Bigger than this boat."

I didn't want to sound critical, but I also wasn't going to lie. "Back when they were hauling pot, I heard they ran small shrimp boats in here. A thirty-footer wouldn't have a problem if the tide's right and if the mangroves were trimmed—but maybe this place is harder to find from Sematee County."

Joel had a nice easy way of laughing that made it hard not to like him. "The marine division should follow my lead and hire you," he said. "They ran aground, that's exactly what happened— who knows where—and it took the guys something like three hours to get back." Then he did a slow circle with his eyes, seeing walls of green all around—mangroves fifty feet tall on the shoreward side. To the west, mangrove ledges trimmed by hurricanes, where pelicans and white wading birds were perched, warming themselves in sunlight. Shards of limestone rock, too, that pierced the shallows like teeth; sometimes a limestone outcropping that angled from tree roots into the water.

"This is Deer Stop Bay?" he asked.

"No, that was the first bay we came through. I don't think this place has a name."

"Prehistoric," the man responded, his voice softer.

"How long have you lived in Florida?" I asked, because he behaved like a person who was experiencing something for the first time.

"I was born right here in Sematee County," he answered and grinned at my surprise before explaining, "but I grew up in the Midwest. I spent spring breaks here when I was going to Valparaiso, then moved down after law school. That was four years ago, almost five." His eyes returned to a shoal area of limestone and water. "Are those oysters or rocks?"

I told him what he was seeing, then explained, "A geologist told me a limestone ridge angles northwest from the mainland but doesn't break the surface often. Not wide, either, where it branches off. A section runs across Pine Island. There's another off Sulfur Wells. I know spots in only six or eight feet of water where you can catch grouper because of the rock ledges. Spiny lobster, too—I used to dive for them when I was a girl."

It was the sort of thing fishing guides are expected to say, and my client liked it, but his eyes were busy. "I don't see the dock—am I missing something?"

"Around that point," I said, "unless I got us lost, too."

Joel took it as a joke and made one of his own by hinting he wouldn't mind being stranded alone in a boat with me. Or maybe he wasn't joking, because he nudged the little cooler he'd brought and said, "I made a thermos of margaritas—you've earned a drink. Or we can be proper about it and wait until noon."

I smiled but was thinking, *Don't let him get too familiar.* Which is why I answered, "I don't drink when I'm working, but clients can make themselves at home." Then nodded as we rounded the point and asked, "Is it the way you pictured it?"

The loading platform Dwight Helms had built was supported by a double span of sixteen-foot stringers on telephone pole pilings that had been jettied deep. The planking was thick enough to hold a pickup truck or two plus a metal derrick. The derrick was still there but leaning badly because the wood had rotted. The diesel engine next to it appeared to be frozen in brown rust.

"Quite an operation," Joel said, and moved forward. Because he was wearing shorts and a blue polo, he looked like a tennis player from where I stood, with his long tan legs and golden body hair. He placed his hands on the casting platform while he studied the dock, then said, "It looked smaller from the satellite photos."

"From space, it probably would," I replied.

The man glanced back. "I can usually read sarcasm. Not with you, though."

Now I actually did smile. "Sorry. I don't think making fun of people is funny, so don't worry. What I meant is, the dock *was* bigger—the way I remember it anyway. So of course it would be smaller from high up."

Ransler was interested. "*Oh.* You saw it back in the days when it was . . ."

"Operational?" I said, helping him out. "Yeah, I did. My Uncle

Jake brought me in here once or twice when I was a little girl. Not because of the dock, we came here to fish, but I saw it." Then I told the prosecutor what I remembered, which, possibly, had been colored by what I'd heard in later years. Dwight Helms, and others in the pot-smuggling trade, had rigged a shrimp net in the trees like an awning to camouflage the dock from DEA planes passing overhead.

"It was like a gigantic tent," I said, "covered with tree branches and leaves. I remember thinking it was even bigger than a tent. You know, impressive to a girl only seven or eight years old. My mother didn't believe me when I described it—she was so sure I was exaggerating, I remember getting mad. My uncle said it was a good lesson for me."

Ransler looked over his shoulder again. "The lesson being?"

I had to think for a moment. "Something about *It's easier for a stranger to trick us because they've yet to be caught in a lie.* Or maybe he said *to con us*, I forget. Loretta—my mother—she would have believed a stranger, that's what he was telling me."

"You've mentioned him a couple of times. You must have been close."

"Jake?" I said. "He was a lot more fun than Barbie dolls and dress-up parties. Probably because he treated me like a friend, not his precious little niece."

Joel hadn't asked about my father, which was a relief but made me suspicious. He had telephoned Loretta with questions about Rosanna Helms, that much she had already admitted. But had she strayed—or been led—on to other topics? Before her stroke, my mother had avoided embarrassing topics. Now there wasn't any word or subject too tasteless for her to share with the postman or even with passing strangers while out shopping. Worse, she had begun to confuse me with my late aunts, Hannah Two and Hannah Three, whose bad judgment and love of men had brought both of their lives to a violent end. Trying to avoid my late aunts' errors was complicated enough without the fear of Loretta telling a stranger that *To get Hannah's panties down, just tap her on the head*. I had heard her say those exact words to Christian, our good-looking UPS man, and so now began to wonder if Joel Ransler's flattery was based on misinformation provided by my addled mother.

No way of knowing because Ransler stuck to the subject of my late uncle.

"Did he help support you two? She told me how hard up for money she was—a single woman raising a little girl. It had to be tough . . . on *both* of you."

The man sounded sympathetic, but I didn't like the direction the conversation was going. There was no guessing what else Loretta had said about me. One thing I felt sure she *hadn't* mentioned while discussing money was her long affair with a married man— something she has never admitted and I've never brought up. No reason to embarrass her needlessly, plus it was a secret comfort to have the ammunition ready if Loretta ever pushed me too far. Her lover had been a wealthy man—although the source of his income was a mystery—who she had never brought to the house, but I had heard them talking on the phone often enough to know his name was Arnie-something. Thanks to Arnie, Loretta had had a nice car and money enough for shopping, which she loved. There had been a few hard times financially, but that was after Arnie or

Loretta—both, possibly—had found religion, which had ended their affair. Joel's gentle way of asking questions, however, made me feel obligated to be conversational because there was still water between us and the dock.

"Jake helped out when he could, I suppose, but most of his income went to alimony. Loretta always managed to get by, and I give her full credit for that. I didn't have to go to work until I was a sophomore in high school, which was late in the game compared to a lot of kids on the islands."

"You worked in your uncle's detective agency," Ransler said. "At least you're listed as an employee in state records. Hope you don't mind that I checked."

"It was better than waiting tables," I responded. "I wasn't crazy about being in an office, but I learned how to keep books, and I did the computer searches, too. So, no, checking on me, I understand that it's part of your job."

"Office work beats what some of your neighbors did to make a living," the special prosecutor said, his eyes on the derrick that had hoisted unknown tons of drugs.

His meaning was obvious and his tone had a hint of superiority, which was irritating.

I turned, opened a hatch, and got out the stern line, before saying, "One thing you might not understand is why people here starting running marijuana. Used their mullet boats to meet bigger boats offshore, then off-loaded the bales in places like this because the Marine Patrol and Coast Guard didn't know the local waters."

"Money," he replied. "Isn't it always about money? Then they'd truck the drugs to Miami, sometimes Atlanta, right? Poor men became millionaires in a few months. Hannah, I *have* done a fair amount of research on the subject. For a while, the DEA kept active files on more than half the adult population of Sematee County *and* Sulfur Wells—did you know that?" The man looked at me in an odd way, which put me on the defensive.

"You're skipping over something important," I countered. "The state put a lot of commercial fishermen out of business in those days. More and more regulations, then a net ban. Families that had been fishing for five or six generations were suddenly out of work and they didn't know any other kind of work." I nodded to indicate the dock we were approaching. "If you had a mortgage to pay and children to feed, do you think you might have chosen pot hauling to losing your home?"

"Maybe," he said. "But not cocaine and crack hauling, which made some of those same guys even richer. Or, at least, I'd like to believe I wouldn't."

Joel had a point, but he'd oversimplified the dilemma fishing families had faced during two decades that had all but eliminated their working heritage. I knew from local gossip that pot hauling had turned ugly when smuggling cocaine became a more lucrative option. It brought professional criminals and crime syndicates into the area. It also got some of the locals and their children hooked on the product. Cocaine was the division line between ethical and unethical behavior in the minds of many fishermen and those who refused to do it were soon forced out of business.

As I explained this, the special prosecutor swung around to

face me from the casting platform and was nodding before I'd finished. "I'm not making moral judgments. You want to know why I'm so interested?"

"Let me finish," I said. "What I'm saying is, sometimes a new law can make criminals out of people who've never broken a law in their life. But my Uncle Jake wasn't among them and I get the feeling you believe he was. Isn't that why you keep asking about him? Half the population of Sulfur Wells was being investigated, you said. That's only about a hundred people, not counting kids."

Ransler shrugged in a way that suggested he was open to all possibilities. "It crossed my mind, but so what? Your uncle's dead, plus the statute of limitations ran out years ago—on smuggling, at any rate."

Had the special prosecutor just implied something?

To communicate disapproval, I cleared my throat before saying, "If you did background checks, you know Jake was a highly decorated detective, Tampa police force. Wounded while saving the lives of at least two other deputies, maybe more. If you're asking questions because you suspect Jake of murdering Mr. Helms, you couldn't be more wrong."

Joel Ransler flexed his jaw and smiled at the same time, giving me his handsome Sundance Kid look. "No, *you're* wrong. The reason I'm interested in your family is because"—he laced his hands together and flexed his jaw again—"well, there are a couple of reasons, and I'll just be up front. You're an unusual woman. I find you attractive, Hannah. Didn't I already say that?"

"It wouldn't matter if you had," I replied, trying not to sound flustered. "I'm in a serious relationship. If that's why you offered to hire me as an investigator, though—"

"Hold on a second," he said. "I'm trying to explain something." He stopped, reconsidered, then switched gears. "Does that mean you decided to take the job?"

"If someone's trying to rob my mother and some of her friends, sure, I'd like the chance. But not if it's because you're interested in me personally."

"Two entirely separate things," he responded. "But I do *like* you. You're not glib, you don't chatter, and you don't act like you have to prove yourself. Something in your background made you different. So I'm curious about the people who raised you—on a personal level. But my interest is professional, too. Is that so offensive?"

No, but neither could I respond sensibly, so I blocked the subject by asking, "Do you want to tie up or is this close enough?" I had swung my skiff parallel to the dock and shifted to neutral.

"Let's get out and look around," Ransler said, amused. "Want me to take the bowline?"

I seldom accept help docking but the man had proven he was competent, so I replied, "When you step out, watch that decking. It looks bad."

JOEL WAS GOING through his briefcase while I roamed the dock, checking the shallows for fish, but also imagining the murder that had occurred here. As he searched folders, he surprised me by asking, "Are you mad at me for some reason? Something's bothering you."

I wasn't going to bring up the crime scene photos, so I reminded him, "I was attacked by dogs and someone with an axe not a hundred yards from here. And Mrs. Helms died somewhere over there"—I motioned toward the trail—"a woman I knew my whole life. You can't blame me for thinking the place is a little spooky."

Ransler glanced around us, willing to be supportive. "Yeah . . . it is, isn't it?" Then tested his heel on the dock but not hard because the planks were rotten. "And her husband died where we're standing. Drug smuggling and violence. There is a weird vibe, I agree."

"That's another thing," I said. "I still don't know why you wanted to come here. Are you looking for new evidence about the murder? Or . . ." What I wanted to ask was *Or a quiet place to drink margaritas, just the two of us?* but didn't. Couldn't bring myself to be mean to a man who, thus far, had only been thoughtful and complimentary.

Joel was perceptive, though. He got the message and became more businesslike. "A twenty-year-old murder isn't the reason. Not the main reason anyway. I wanted to confirm something." He looked at the bay for emphasis. "You just proved that if your attacker came by boat, he has to be a local. And not just any local, he's probably a commercial fisherman—or someone who learned the channel smuggling drugs. Make sense?"

Not entirely. I had already told him and the detectives about the old horse trail that led through the mangroves to Sulfur Wells but mentioned it again.

"I'd like to see it," Joel said.

"We'll need more mosquito spray," I told him, "and we should have brought a machete."

"I don't mind bugs. But first, there's something you should know. I wanted to be sure of the details before I said anything."

In his hand was a crime scene map. Finally, the special prosecutor told me that Dwight Helms had been murdered with an axe. Then asked a question my Internet research hadn't prepared me for.

"You ever hear any rumors about who found Helms's body? The department never released the names to the public."

I remembered a newspaper story crediting *an unnamed informant*, but that's all, so I shook my head.

Ransler was serious now. "There were actually two people who reported the body, both men. Do you remember anyone around named Arnold?—that was his first name. The dispatcher either didn't get his last name or he refused to give it."

"Arnold," I repeated. "We were taught to call adults by their last names, mister or missus, so I seldom knew an adult's whole name." I mulled it over. "*Arnold*. It sounds familiar, but I'm not sure why. So far, no one comes to mind."

"That was a long time ago, I know—more than twenty years, but there's a reason I'm asking, Hannah." He paused. "Or . . . maybe you *know* the reason."

The way Joel said it put me on guard. I sensed a trap. "If you have something to say, say it," I told him. Then stared at him for a moment before taking a guess. "Was my Uncle Jake one of the men who found Mr. Helms?"

"Yes," Joel said. "He was the first to call it in—a little after midnight, according to the report. I assumed you knew."

"Jake?"

"Captain Jacob Hansen Smith. That's him, right? I was hoping you could help me with the name of the second man."

When I turned away to collect myself, Joel reached as if to put a hand on my shoulder but stopped when he saw me flinch. "Your uncle was never a suspect, I wasn't lying about that. He still isn't, as far as I'm concerned."

"Jake never said a word about finding a body—but I was only eight or nine at the time, so—"

"That's right," Ransler cut in as if he hadn't thought it through. "You were only a kid. Of course he wouldn't have said anything. Even later, why bring it up? I'm such an idiot sometimes."

The special prosecutor shook his head, disappointed with himself, and continued to apologize. My mind was already on something else. I was picturing how it had been for my uncle the night he found the body, used my eyes to match crime scene photos with the area around the dock.

Twenty feet away was a huge buttonwood. Dwight Helms had lost part of his hand near the base of a large tree—possibly the same tree. They had found his ankle and foot, his boot still tied, near the diesel engine that was now red with rust, but, on a night twenty years ago, had glistened beneath flashbulbs. Helms had curled himself in a fetal position beneath the derrick. He had died there, his head crushed by several blows. Jake, or a man named Arnold, had been the first to find the carnage—the first to report it, anyway, which gave the murder a new importance.

Arnold . . . Arnold. The name continued to bounce around in my head. It *was* familiar, I felt sure of it, yet my memory couldn't attach the name to an adult who had lived on the island.

Then it hit me. Arnold—or *Arnie* for short! It was the name of Loretta's secret lover. I had never discovered the man's last name because I didn't *want* to know it. A nickname didn't prove her old boyfriend was a murderer, of course, or even that he was the same Arnie, but it was a startling connection. Suddenly, I wanted to know more about Arnie—especially now that the reputation of my late uncle might be involved through association.

"Hannah . . . are you okay? I wasn't trying to be graphic." Joel was touching my elbow, I realized. It took me a moment to understand I had missed something he'd said, something important, apparently.

I took a full breath and forced a smile. "Fine, fine—my attention wanders sometimes. What were you saying?"

The special prosecutor had been easing into the facts about the murder. "The way Helms died was so brutal, I see only three possible options. I'm not going to bother you with details. I'm projecting from the killer's point of view."

"Options?" I asked.

"Motives, I mean. It was a crime of passion or a revenge killing or . . . a message, like a warning to other smugglers. That's my read. The murder was so brutal, it scared people, so they avoided the subject by telling outsiders that Helms had been shot. After a while, the lie became accepted as fact. We both know that a lot of islanders went into drug running. If the killer was sending a message, it worked in one way: the murder scared them. The question is, what was the message the killer—or *killers*—was sending?"

I nodded as if I agreed but was trying to recall more about Loretta's lover. The relationship had gone on for a decade. I suspected I had seen the man on more than one occasion—in church, most likely—yet had no idea who he was or what he'd looked like. Loretta had guarded the secret carefully, but it was my own distaste for the truth that had provided the strongest shield.

Now Joel was saying, "I didn't come here to trap you. More than anything, I was trying to help. The way Helms was killed isn't related to what happened to you Friday night. My theory hasn't changed. You surprised a burglar—some local crackhead, most likely—hoping to find money or drugs. He probably heard the dogs, too, and grabbed the first weapon he saw—an axe. It was a *coincidence*." The man sighed. "Instead of making you feel better, I screwed up by assuming you knew more than you did. Sorry, Hannah. Like I said, I'm in an ugly business. Sometimes I forget there are still people you can be open and honest with."

This time I let the prosecutor place a hand on my shoulder— but as a comfort to him, not to me. His regret seemed genuine, and I soften easily when touched by the upset of others. "Joel," I said, "I believe you, okay? So let's drop the subject."

"Rance," he corrected, then squared himself so both hands were on my shoulders, holding me as if to reassure me of his support. He had done the same thing the night I was attacked.

"Rance," I conceded, then joked, "I usually don't tolerate pushy clients."

Sundance Kid from the movie, yes, Joel had the same jaw-flexing smile as we stood face-to-face, joined by the warmth of his hands. Smart gray eyes, too, with a glint—boyish, but in a devilish way. For a moment, I felt comfortable standing close to this good-looking attorney who was trying so hard to win my approval . . . but then the look in his eyes struck me as more devilish than boyish and I began to doubt my own judgment. Two of my aunts had died because they had misread the intentions of charming men. I knew nothing about Joel Ransler, had yet to even run a background check, yet here we were alone, just the two of us.

"Hang on a second," I said, then ducked under his arms and walked toward my skiff.

"Where you going?" He sounded hopeful when he added, "The thermos of margaritas in the cooler—we could probably both use a drink."

I replied, "I'm getting bug spray. If you want to see the horse trail, we need to go. I've got to be back by noon and the tide's falling fast."

"Noon?"

"I have an afternoon charter," I told him.

Birdy Tupplemeyer wasn't paying me, but that didn't make my excuse any less true.

FIFTEEN

After an hour with the redheaded deputy, I was beginning to agree with her mother that a hash cookie or two was just what the doctor ordered for a girl whose mind never stopped working and who wanted to be everywhere at once, especially any island with a beach or high ground, even if it meant trespassing, or wading through swamp.

Birdy's willingness to trespass had almost gotten her into trouble the previous night. She had slipped under the gate of a landfill, only a mile from the condo where she lived, and was hiking among the piles of raw earth and asphalt when a security guard in a golf cart had appeared out of nowhere.

"He was pretty good, had his lights off," she explained. "I don't know if he saw me or not, but I went over the back fence anyway. I'm trying to borrow a night vision unit from a friend. If he doesn't come through, our next visit will have to wait for a night or two."

Something else that had to wait was our trip to Cushing Key, but that was because of low tide, not our lack of equipment. When we left the dock at one, the flats resembled green meadows, the bay was so shallow, so I drove us straight through Captiva Pass and into the Gulf of Mexico.

"That's the most beautiful beach I've ever seen," the redhead grinned, then asked, "What's the name of the island?" We were running along the outside in water that was turquoise, wind-streaked. To our right floated a strand of silver beach, miles long, with coconut palms that leaned westward.

"Cayo Costa," I told her, then explained that some locals still called it *La Costa*. "Years ago, Cuban fishermen kept fish ranches there—*rancheros*. They caught mullet but made most of their money smuggling rum."

"Some things never change," the off-duty deputy replied.

I wasn't sure how to take that, so I continued to tell her about the island. "At the north end, there's a tiny cemetery and a park where you can camp. Next time, bring a swimsuit. We'll anchor off a patch of rocks that's good for snorkeling—fire coral and a lot of fish to see. I'll bring a speargun."

"I've got a bra and panties," Birdy replied. "There's nobody around. Plus, I'm so flat-chested, who's gonna notice?"

"Up to you," I said, then anchored near the rocks and waited while she splashed around, using my mask and fins. I was playing tour guide, which wasn't as interesting as fishing but fun and more relaxed, even though the redhead fired question after question at me. For the last hour, too many of her questions had been about Joel Ransler, so it was a relief to get a break while her mouth was plugged with a snorkel.

Fifteen minutes later, wearing clothes but hair still wet, she was lecturing, "It happens every time, Smithie, I swear to Christ. I'll go months without a date, then finally meet a decent guy. Moment we start sleeping together, you can count on it, an even better-looking guy appears out of the blue. Total stranger. Would I like to go to dinner, maybe fly to Paris for the weekend? That actually *happened* to me, by the way."

"How'd you like Paris?" I asked, giving it an edge.

"Didn't go, smartass. I should've—I'm not dating anyone now, so see where it got me? When God needs a laugh, He hauls out His list of single women and tacks it to a dartboard. Keep your options open, Smithie, that's all I'm saying."

Smithie, that's what she had decided to call me, which was okay. I had made a mistake by describing the special prosecutor as "handsome," then mentioning the name of the movie star he favored. This was after telling her I had accepted Ransler's job offer, but I hadn't gotten around yet to the more unpleasant topics of Alice Candor's behavior last night or the unsolved murder. Nor had I told her much about Marion Ford, but it was time, I decided, to set her straight.

"Once you meet Marion," I said, "you'll understand why I'm not interested in Joel, even if he is an attorney—or any other good-looking man." I had my hand on the throttle when I realized how clumsily I'd spoken. Birdy, with her sharp sense of humor, couldn't resist.

"You prefer guys who aren't good-looking, huh?" she asked. "Smithie, you need to think this over."

"You need to hang on," I replied, and shoved the throttle forward. The redhead gave a startled whoop, and we were both laughing while I made a slow turn, then pointed my skiff south.

At South Seas Resort, I cut through Redfish Pass, dropped off plain and was soon idling along the back side of Captiva Island. To keep the off-duty deputy quiet, I pointed out houses owned by people I knew—multimillionaires, many of them, and some my clients—before I killed the engine and got off the first question, asking, "Remember the fishing reel missing from the attic?"

"That charity, nonprofit thing," she said. "I'm glad you took the job. You'll get to know your hot attorney better. Plus, I can help you if the bastards turn out to be con men."

"I was talking about Teddy Roosevelt," I said. "This is where he anchored his houseboat. Nineteen seventeen."

"No kidding?" Birdy swiveled her head as if expecting to see a brass plaque.

"Maybe not the exact spot but close," I said. We were drifting between Buck Key and Captiva, the gas dock at Jensen's Marina to our right, several skiffs anchored off the pool bar at 'Tween Waters just ahead.

"Do people still harpoon giant stingrays? That reel must be worth a ton of money. Sounds to me like your grandfather must've been Teddy's favorite fishing guide."

The woman seldom asked one question at a time, but I was getting used to it. "Manta rays," I corrected, "and it was my *great*-grandfather. But he was too young to captain a boat."

"Teddy must have liked him, though. Vom Hofe, was he a famous reel maker? Quite a present to give a boy—or was he a teenager?"

I replied, "There was a local girl the president made friends with, too. She was younger, only nine or ten, but they say he liked people with spirit. He gave her a pair of boots. If I find the book he wrote—or maybe the library has a copy—there are photos of the manta rays they harpooned. Huge animals, the size of cars."

"Teddy Roosevelt slept here," Birdy said, smiling, her eyes taking in the scenery.

I told her the boat the president had lived on was a one-room house built on a barge that was fifty-some feet long. "For a while, it was anchored behind Castaway's—that's a nice place to stay when you get some time off. Years later, a storm pushed it way back in the mangroves. One day, if you want, we'll try to find what's left."

In reply, Tupplemeyer asked several questions nonstop, which I didn't have to answer because a friend of mine, Nathan Pace, appeared on a dock not far from where we were drifting. Nate had been skinny in high school but was now a bodybuilder and good-looking, despite a crooked tooth and his shyness.

"Damn, who's the hunk?" Tupplemeyer whispered as we idled over to say hello. "I like guys with muscles. He's gotta have money, too, if he lives there."

No, but the famous photographer Nate sometimes slept with was wealthy—a nice man named Darren. I didn't explain all this to Birdy, though, until we were a mile or two from Captiva. The tide had risen, and we soon had the mounds of Cushing Key in sight.

AS WE MUCKED our way toward the island's interior, Deputy Tupplemeyer, who oozed confidence but who knew nothing about swamps, sounded uneasy when she asked, "Any snakes around here?"

By then, we were friendly enough to have traded several more barbs, so I was tempted to reply, *No—alligators eat them all*. I might have said it, too, if I thought she would have slowed her pace. Now that we were on land, following Birdy was like being pulled along by a propeller that had been revved too high or a generator that discharged currency into the ground. The woman's energy seeped in through my feet, my ears, and was beginning to short-circuit my own more careful method of thinking.

Normally, I wouldn't have put up with such a person. In fact, when she had latched onto the subject of Joel Ransler, I had come close to inventing an excuse to end the trip early. But I didn't, and was glad. I admired the woman's spirit. She was curious and enthusiastic about . . . well, *everything*, and her positive attitude was seeping into me as well. Plus, she was funny—often crude, true, but at least she came out and spoke her mind.

"I'd bet my ass there are snakes galore," Birdy insisted, finally stopping for a breather. She used a tree limb to steady herself, looked to the left, then the right, seeing muck, spiderwebs glistening in the shadows, and a tangle of mangrove jungle where prop roots hung like bars in a cave. "Nothing else would live in a place like this."

"Except for mosquitoes," I said, then couldn't help saying with a straight face, "Gators eat the snakes. No need to worry about them."

Automatically, the deputy's hand moved toward the holster she wasn't wearing. "*Alligators!* You serious?"

"We get an occasional saltwater croc, too," I replied.

"Shit, *now* she tells me. I should have brought my Glock."

"They're a protected species," I reminded her.

"I'm a protected species, too, when I'm carrying a Glock," the deputy answered. "Screw the law, how big?"

I was losing control, so walked ahead of her and didn't look back. "Ten, sometimes twelve feet long. I've never seen a *really* big one. Not on this side of the island anyway."

"*This* side of the island! Jesus Christ, I pity the poor guy you're dating—what do you consider big?"

Now my chest was shaking, couldn't help myself, so I kept walking.

She called after me, "Maybe we should head back to the boat. Hannah . . . where you going? Hey . . . *Jungle Jane*! Goddamn it, I'm talking to you!"

I stopped and turned and let my laughter go. When Birdy realized I was joking, she gave me a fierce look and hissed, "Asshole!" but soon was laughing, too, then tried to imitate a Southern accent. "Yep, big-ass gators'll eat you city folk. Diddle you up the be-hind, too, if rattlers and rednecks turn scarce. Ya'll gotta be *mindful*." Her voice returned to normal. "*Shit!* Can't believe I just got taken in by some rube chick."

Now I was tearing up, I was laughing so hard. "Sorry . . . sorry," I croaked. "The look on your face when I said *gators* . . . My lord!"

"Paybacks are hell, Smithie," she fired back, then plucked a foot out of the muck and inspected her shoe. Almost new Reeboks—Tupplemeyer had gotten hooked on jogging while at the police academy and had shown me the soles to prove she ran three to five miles daily but had a pronation problem, or possibly the term was *supination*—she wasn't sure but had promised to look it up when we got back.

"Those shoes are ruined," I said. "At least I told you the truth about that."

"Okay, okay, you were right, so stop harping," she said, pulling her other foot out of the mud. "How much farther?" To the Indian mounds, she meant.

I was wearing cheap white rubber boots I always keep on the boat and was secretly pleased by her admission. "We'll hose those down and throw them in the washer later," I suggested. "You can meet Loretta."

"Your mom? I'd like that. The poor woman has to be a saint to raise a daughter like you. Did you hear what I just asked?"

"Weird," I smiled. "I've been thinking the same thing about *your* mother." I continued walking before answering, "Not far. Once we get on the mounds, there really could be rattlesnakes. Pygmy rattlers, mostly—I'm serious this time. But they're not aggressive, so don't worry."

"Not aggressive," she says, "my ass. *You* go first. I'll follow from now on."

Near the center of Cushing Key were two shell mounds that rose abruptly out of the swamp like miniature volcanoes but cloaked by trees, Spanish bayonet plants, and cactus. We saw no snakes but used cell phones to photograph shards of pottery and tools made from big whelk and conch shells. Artifacts everywhere.

"It's pronounced *konk*, not *cawnsh*," I corrected Tupplemeyer for the second time. She had summoned me to the western edge of the highest mound where she'd found a wall of conch shells embedded like bricks, the sharp ends pointed outward.

"A defense against invaders," the former archaeology major told me. "I read about this. There's no rock around here to quarry—that's what the Maya and Aztec did. So they used shells. All four sides of the pyramid covered with shell spikes except for one path to the top. Smart, huh? These things would cut the hell out of someone."

She was referencing the sketches she'd seen by Frank Cushing— the island's namesake—who the Smithsonian had sent to Florida in the 1890s.

The redhead knelt and took more photos but had yet to so much as touch a shell or a piece of pottery—shards of baked clay, yellow-orange, that had accumulated over the thousands of years people had hunted and cooked and lived their lives here. I was impressed by the respect she was showing for the state that was her new home.

"*Whoa* . . . look at this!" Birdy called after pulling foliage away. Then began snapping more photos while I squatted beside her. She had found a large conch horn, its point sawed off as a mouth-piece, and part of a bowl with a triangular pattern etched around the rim. It was so simple and eloquent, I tried to imagine the artist—a woman, no doubt—who had lived on this island and who had done her work with extra care.

The redhead, apparently, felt a connection, too, because she stood, tilted her nose up, and said, "Does the air seem . . . heavier here to you? In Tikal, it was *exactly* the same."

"That's in Guatemala?" I asked.

The deputy nodded while she rearranged leaves to cover the pottery shard. "Some jerk will cart this off if he finds it. I don't know why I'm so attracted to places like this, but . . . they give me the weirdest feeling. *Powerful*, you know?" She looked up, her expression intense, a tinge of anger showing, too. "We've got to find those artifacts that bitch had hauled away. You still up for it?"

I replied, "I've got a story about Dr. Candor. She's an alcoholic, I think. Or crazy. Maybe both. One thing I know for sure is, she's trying to run the locals out of Sulfur Wells, Loretta and me included. That woman's vindictive, and I don't want you to lose your job." I described last night's scene on the dock, then started to share what I'd uncovered about the couple, but no need—Tupplemeyer knew more about the Candors than I realized.

"They're both dirty," Birdy said. "This morning, I figured out where they sent those dump trucks—and it wasn't to a public landfill. They filed for a zoning variance on some wetlands near one of their rehab clinics. Documents that were dated Monday, but they've owned the property for more than a year. The application claims the land's actually above the floodplain." Tupplemeyer's tone emphasized the importance of the time lag.

"Where?" I asked.

"Inland, near some little town in Sematee County. About an hour's drive."

"That's Joel Ransler's area," I said. "He's got a friend who works in the planning department, Delmont Chatham, an older man. He's been on my boat. Is *planning department* the same as *zoning*?" I was thinking that Mr. Chatham, a charter client, might be willing to speak with me.

The off-duty deputy shrugged. "Ask your handsome attorney. I guarantee he knows who the Candors are—or, at least, about their clinic. It's one of those revolving-door rehab facilities that targets public funding. Just like they did in Ohio—prescribe meds, then treat the very same patients when they get hooked. That's why the Candors are still rich. They know how the system works."

Dr. Alice Candor had told me the same thing, bragging about it.

I asked, "Is the property near the clinic? If it is, security's going to be more than just one guard driving around in a golf cart."

"Stop worrying! Where I think they dumped the stuff is half a mile from the actual facility—you know, the buildings where they keep patients." Birdy paused to look at me as if gauging my courage, then asked, "Do you have anything planned for tonight?"

She's leading you into trouble, a voice warned, which is why I replied, "You know I do." As we'd left Sulfur Wells, I had pointed to the cabins known as Munchkinville and explained I was going to question the owners about their charity donations. But I hadn't said *tonight*.

"How about we do this," the deputy suggested. "We'll split up the cabins and go door-to-door—" She stopped in midsentence, a woman who was easily distracted, and tilted her nose again. "Smell that? You know what I mean about the air?"

No, but I was happy to switch subjects. "The mounds have a different smell to them, that's true. It could be the trees—gumbo-limbos and key lime trees, and one called white stopper—it's got an unusual smell. They made a medicine out of the leaves to stop diarrhea."

Birdy shook her head in a way that told me I wasn't close, which gave me an idea. "I've got a friend you should meet," I said. "You two are opposites in most ways, but he'd understand. And he's fun. Tomlinson's his name."

"A mystic, huh?" the redhead said, either not interested or she didn't believe me. But several minutes later, as we hiked back to the boat, she asked, "Is this guy another one of your gay buddies or is he married?"

That made me smile. "Keeping your bra snapped is the only problem women have with Tomlinson. He lives on a sailboat in Dinkin's Bay—that's Sanibel."

"Is it on the way home?" she asked.

Dinkin's Bay was three miles southwest, but it was safer than sneaking around rehab clinics after dark. I replied, "It can be."

"Great. But if we stay late, we'll drive up there and search tomorrow. My shift ends at six, so we can leave around seven. Okay?"

When I asked, "Where's this place again?" she picked up her phone and told me, "I'll send you the link."

HOURS LATER, I was alone in Marion Ford's lab, waiting for Birdy to return from Tomlinson's sailboat, when impatience caused me to open my phone. Instead of dialing Birdy, I sat down, surprised, because I saw the link for the first time.

Sematee Evaluation and Treatment Clinic, Carnicero, Florida
The clinic had a different box number, but it used the same little Carnicero post office as the charity Fisherfolk of South Florida Inc.

Rather than calling my new friend, I texted, *How much longer? We need to talk.*

It took awhile, but the off-duty deputy finally replied, *Float on, Smithie* ☺, which told me I would have to wait until morning—but only because she added the smiley face.

SIXTEEN

In the morning, at my office, after tracing three familiar names to the origins of Fisherfolk Incorporated, a headline in the news caught my attention.

VENEZUELAN LEADER MISSING;
GUERRILLAS VOW RIOTS, "REVENGE"

I couldn't help but read the story. A revolutionary group known as FARC had been attending peace talks in Caracas and their chairman had disappeared while swimming near a beach resort. No body had been found, but FARC members insisted he had either been abducted or murdered. They were blaming U.S. "covert gangsters" and warned North Americans to stay out of the streets during the protest march they were organizing. The Venezuelan president said he anticipated rioting if the FARC leader was not returned unharmed. Police, he said, had detained several U.S. citizens for questioning.

That alone was enough to worry me, so I hunted around for a

more detailed account. The only facts I could add, though, were that late yesterday afternoon the FARC leader had told friends he was going snorkel diving, not swimming, and he was supposedly an experienced diver. An unnamed FARC member was quoted as saying, "We know who did this and will soon have him."

Once again, I checked e-mails, hoping for a note from Marion or, at the very least, that he had read the e-mails I had sent. There were three now, one for every day he'd been gone, but none had been opened.

I brought up Google Earth and studied Venezuela's coastline, eight hundred miles along the Caribbean sea, much of it jungle and isolated islands.

That, at least, was comforting. Ford had said the aquaculture company that had hired him was in a remote place. He had also mentioned something about access to clean seawater away from cities. Good! If people were going to protest and riot, they would do it in a place where there were streets, not raw jungle. And police certainly wouldn't bother with a marine biologist who was in the country to work, not cause trouble.

Ford's safe, I reassured myself. Even so, I sent him a fourth e-mail that included a link to the story. At the bottom, I wrote, "Get yourself home in one piece!" I was tempted to add a smiley face to prove I wasn't worried but didn't.

Thinking about it reminded me that I hadn't heard from Birdy Tupplemeyer. Her car had been gone when I'd stopped to check on Loretta, so I assumed she'd gotten home okay. I sent her a text, asking, *You make it to work?* then got back to my own work, which was nearly done—the computer search portion, that is.

In Florida, a nonprofit corporation has to name at least three primary officers. They don't have to live in Florida, but their street addresses have to be included in the formal documents. I had had to peel through a dozen layers of bureaucracy but had laid the truth bare—a partial truth anyway. It was no wonder the late Rosanna Helms was collecting donations from her friends. Her children, Crystal and Mica, were listed as directors of Fisherfolk Inc. It was the name of the third officer, however, that convinced me a broader truth existed—a truth that would be much harder to unveil, I suspected.

I called Joel Ransler, who listened in silence, then confirmed my fears, saying, "Wow, that's not going to be easy to prove, Hannah. You know . . . it might be wiser to gather complaints from people you know, locals who've made donations, and create a media stink—see what I'm saying? Stop what they're doing from the bottom rather than going after power people at the top. The results will be the same, and it's a hell of a lot safer."

Joel, for the first time, sounded nervous. It made me curious. "Power *people?*" I said. "I only mentioned one name."

"I was speaking generally," he said. "In county infrastructure, all businesses are linked. Which wouldn't bother me a bit if there's a provable crime. Look"—a smile came into his voice—"collect all the information you can. Give it to me when you're ready, then we'll have dinner together and discuss it."

Dinner? I had just shared details about a transparent donation scam. The charity was providing elderly "fisherfolk" with the forms necessary to donate their homes, savings accounts and valuables in return for "tax benefits" and the promise to preserve their "heritage" by displaying family heirlooms and photos in a museum that didn't exist.

"Am I missing something here?" I asked. "You hired me to investigate and that's what I'm doing."

"No, you're guessing," Joel replied. "It's not illegal for two convicted felons to be on the board of a nonprofit. That's all you can prove, right?"

My disappointment in Ransler was turning into frustration. "Can't you see who's really behind this? If it wasn't wrong, they wouldn't target people like my mother; older people who can't think straight."

The man asked a few questions—Did Loretta have receipts for our missing property? Had I questioned other donors?—before reminding me, "*Wrong* isn't the same as *illegal*. I believe what you're telling me, Hannah, but you haven't given me anything I can work with. You can't accuse someone of complicity without proof—not by name anyway. Especially if they have enough money to turn their attorneys loose on you *and* me."

"Power people," I muttered.

"Money is power, dear. It's the way the world works."

"In Sematee County, apparently," I responded.

Instead of getting angry, the special prosecutor became more understanding. "Come on, now, Captain Smith, don't get sullen. Things have gotten a lot better up here in the last few years. There are still a few good ol' boys with clout from the local pot-hauling days, I admit it, but—"

"They're not *my* pot-hauling days," I interrupted.

"You know what I mean. It frustrates the hell out of me, too, sometimes. But we have to touch all the bases before I can seat a grand jury—or even subpoena the owners of a prominent business."

"Can I at least talk to Mica and Crystal Helms?" I asked. "You don't consider *them* power people?"

Joel started to reply, but then was distracted by someone who came into his office. Seconds later, he said, "I've got a meeting. Just be careful, okay? Text me an address before you interview anyone—especially those two. It's a safety thing."

"Any chance you can get hold of their medical records?" I asked. "If Crystal spent time in rehab or a psych ward, maybe Mica did, too."

"We'll see—just keep me in the loop," he replied, and hung up.

I texted Joel the only valid street address I had for Fisher-folk Inc., then went out the door, still convinced that Walkin' Levi Thurloe—who had been listed as the organization's third director—was the pawn of his employer . . . and maybe Dr. Alice Candor's patient, too.

AS I LEFT the parking lot headed for Sematee County, it dawned on me that I should talk to people who'd actually donated to Fisherfolk before trying to interview Mica or Crystal Helms. To ask hard questions, I needed hard facts to supplement my list, which, so far, included only a book and a rare fishing reel. Sulfur Wells was only a few miles out of my way, so I detoured west and parked beyond the curve so Loretta wouldn't notice my SUV. Across the street was Munchkinville, with its white fence and communal parking area with enough trucks and rusting cars to indicate to me most of the inhabitants were home.

I got out carrying a leather organizer, prepared to do a couple of quick interviews, then I'd be on my way. Of the dozen cottages squeezed along the bay, eight were lived in by people I had known since childhood—nine, counting the late Rosanna Helms—so I figured I'd have damning evidence enough within an hour, probably less.

I couldn't have been more wrong.

Going door-to-door, I spoke to Mrs. Morgan and the House sisters, then tried the dilapidated cabin where old Captain Elmer Joiner was mending nets beneath a tree. The results were the same. My old neighbors were happy to see me, happy to discuss the weather and Mrs. Helms's funeral or to inquire about Loretta's health, but when I mentioned Fisherfolk, our friendships vaporized, then a wary chill followed me out the door. Same when I asked for the name of the person who had approached them about donating, and even when I said, "I think you and my mother are being robbed!"

Didn't matter. Their behavior was more than just strange, it was revealing. People who donate to a good cause are usually happy to discuss their generosity, so the few responses I did get hinted at a larger truth, a truth my old neighbors refused to share.

"What's the difference between paying taxes and robbery?" Mrs. Padilla, a widow, asked me. She had always been a spirited woman but sounded nervous, not angry, when I suggested that she was being cheated. Prior to knocking on her door, it had been my secret hope that Mrs. Padilla might also be willing to gossip about my mother's secret lover—she and Loretta had never gotten along—but I gave up when she told me, "Just because I played organ at your recital doesn't give you the right to nose into my affairs!"

Which was true, I had to admit it. But I couldn't resist asking Mrs. Padilla why she, a woman on Social Security, was worried about taxes. Loretta had mentioned taxes, too, which was consistent, at least, and hinted that the benefits of donating to Fisherfolk had been misrepresented.

Mrs. Padilla's response was more of a threat than an explanation. "Around here, Hannah, you pry open the wrong box, something might jump out and bite you." Then asked, "You're goin' to Pinky's funeral, aren't you?" saying it as if there was a connection.

I replied, "Thursday afternoon, of course. Are you telling me Mrs. Helms was murdered?"

The woman shrugged, but there was a knowing look on her face as if she had made her point. End of conversation. End of my visit to the cottages of Munchkinville.

As I returned to my SUV, Captain Joiner looked up from his mending long enough to wave, but he didn't smile.

SEVENTEEN

Mica Helms's "home address" turned out to be a junkyard in Glades City, which I thought was an intentional error until I saw the dog. It was a brindle-yellow pit bull, the same alpha female that had attacked me Friday, minus her pack mate whose head had been found in a freezer.

By the time I saw the dog, it was too late.

I had parked and walked to the fence, which was chain-link, eight feet high, with razor wire at the top. Inside, among rows of wrecked cars, was a trailer that looked lived in, but a sign on the door read *Office*. There was also a gravel path that seemed to invite business. I tried hollering to get attention but a machine—a wood shredder, it sounded like—made so much noise, I couldn't hear my own voice. The noise came at me in waves and was piercing, so I covered my ears as I walked to the gate. It was a sliding gate, not open but slightly ajar. I looked around and tried hollering again. Pointless. There was a *Keep Out* sign, but no warnings about a dog, so I slipped through the gate and walked toward the trailer.

Midway between the door and the fence, someone switched off

the shredder, creating an explosion of silence that was so abrupt, I actually stopped and blinked my eyes. That's when I heard a softer sound, a warning familiar from my nightmare, the low rumble of a dog.

I turned. The female pit bull appeared from behind a stack of tires, her dark eyes black in the afternoon sunlight. Because of the shredding machine, she was momentarily surprised to see a trespasser only a few yards from where she'd been dozing. The dog stiffened, as if in recognition, and bared her teeth, while her body hunkered lower for traction. I was already backing away when she roared at me and charged.

Attached to the pit bull's collar was a galvanized chain. But how long? Was the chain anchored? The questions were displaced by panic. I turned and ran. The shock waves of the dog's barking hammered at my ankles and pushed me faster. Then pushed me high into the air. Before I could understand what had happened, I was crouched on the hood of a car, my eyes affixed to the eyes of the pit bull as she hurled herself at me, her teeth inches from my face.

I threw up an arm and dived toward the roof of the car. When I looked, the dog was still at face level, jaws gnashing, but then she dropped from sight. An instant later, the animal reappeared, bug-eyed with frustration because the chain had stopped her just short of the car. She was jumping, her claws scrabbling against metal, trying to snatch a piece of me before gravity yanked her back to the ground.

I was atop a wrecked car, I realized. Its windshield was shattered, its metal so traumatized by collision, its roof creaked beneath my weight when I got to my knees, then my feet. I looked around, trying to understand what had just happened, while the pit bull barked and leaped and slathered itself into a frenzy. For now, though, I was safe—unless the chain broke. But was there a way to get back to my SUV? Still in shock, I had to think it through methodically.

Yes, there was a way to escape . . . if I scampered off the trunk of the car and stayed close to the trailer. But the chain's perimeter circled perilously close to the gate. I was gauging the distance when I remembered the leather organizer I had been carrying. It contained my ID, a pad to take notes, plus a fine Kate Spade bill-fold that had been given to me by a friend. And . . . my cell phone!

Damn it. I couldn't leave all that behind!

I got down on my knees and infuriated the alpha female even more by peering over the side, where I saw weeds and a crumpled Marlboro carton but no leather organizer. That's when I remembered something else that had been displaced by panic during the last few seconds: someone had switched off the shredding machine . . . and the gate wasn't locked.

Where were the people who worked here?

"Hello!" I called tentatively at first, then yelled over the barking of the pit bull, "Who owns this dog?"

I didn't expect an answer but I got it.

"Same person who owns the goddamn property you're tres-passin' on!" A bully's voice that came from the back of the lot. Then the man laughed, "By god, woman, you got some legs on you! You can run, I'll give you that. But you just cost me ten bucks!"

I stood and searched the junkyard until I found two men, not one, at the back of the lot. Both tall, one skinny, the other man huge, with a massive face beneath a ZZ Top beard of gray and a belly that gave shape to his coveralls. The men had hands on hips and both were chuckling as if they'd shared some private joke while standing near a hill of tires and a machine, the words *Moline Industrial Shredder* stenciled on a yellow feeding hopper.

I hollered back, "Your dog almost bit me!"

"Good! That's what she's paid to do!" It was the bully gray-beard. He was lumbering toward me and still laughing as he said to his partner, "Goddamn, most folks'll jump up on that Chevy every time. Leave it to a woman to choose a Lincoln!"

Hilarious—both men roared.

What were they talking about? I looked around until I understood. Junked cars had been jammed tight into the lot. I could have chosen a rusting Chevy Malibu as refuge, but I had climbed onto the car next to it because it had looked bigger, higher off the ground—a Lincoln, apparently.

I felt my ears warming. "You let a dog attack people, then bet on where they run? *You're* the animals!" I yelled.

I was so mad, it must have startled the younger man because he stopped. He stood staring at me for a moment, but then proved it wasn't my anger that had given him pause. "Hannah . . . ?" he asked, his voice familiar. "God A'mighty, it is you—Hannah Smith! Harris, I know this girl!" The skinny man clapped his hands together, delighted, but then got serious and called to the pit bull, "Vixxy! Get your ass back in the kennel!"

The dog continued leaping at me but finally obeyed when graybeard, the ZZ Top giant, grabbed a chunk of pipe.

When it was safe, I climbed down and said to the skinny man, "Sorry to hear about your mother," because, despite what had just happened, it was the right thing to say to Mica Helms.

MICA HAD BEEN a tall boy in school but was now six-five, six-six—even he wasn't sure—but looked taller because his body, instead of filling out, had only stretched longer as he grew, his skin tight on a boney frame that looked to be all elbows and ribs, but with a gaunt face and a set of shoulders that could have made him handsome were it not for the tattoos and the chemical sparking of his eyes.

Crack or meth? I wondered. *Oxycodone, painkillers . . . or something new?*

Mica's nervous chattering, his barks of pointless laughter, made it evident that he was using again. The name of the chemical didn't matter. His brain was starving. It made him a hunter, his glittering eyes always on the alert for a new source—or a new threat. Those eyes were studying me now as he said, "What if I told you donations to the museum were being kept right here? There's a building out back—nothing fancy, but it's safe. Would you keep your mouth shut? New donors might not like their family treasures bein' stored in a junkyard—just temporary, of course."

For ten minutes, we had been circling the subject of Fisherfolk Incorporated and I was getting impatient. "Would I tell the police, you mean?"

"The *po-lice?*" Mica said, making it a two-syllable word. "Why the hell you do that? Honey, I'm on probation. Last thing I'm gonna do is break the law. I don't remember seeing your old fishing reels, but if your mamma's stuff is there, I'll find it." He paused, patted the shredding machine affectionately, then smiled down at me. "But Harris runs this place. He didn't like it when those cops come around asking questions about me . . . when was that, Saturday? He'd like it even less if he knew you was the reason."

I didn't care for Mica's threatening tone. "From the way that dog minded Harris but ignored you," I said, "maybe they should come back and ask him some questions, too. Is that what you're making me do? Call police?"

Mica straightened as if insulted, then lowered his voice to say, "Hannah, you always was the world's most pigheaded girl. Watch what you say around Harris Spooner! My first six months at Raiford, that man showed me how to jail. Baby, you don't wanna mess with—" He glanced at the trailer where graybeard, in his coveralls, stood watching from the doorway, then gave up, saying, "Hell, you wouldn't understand. Better to show you." Mica waved me closer to the shredding machine. "Watch this," he said, then hit a switch.

I stepped back, not closer, and covered my ears because of the noise. The shredding machine was built on a trailer so it could be towed and had a conveyor belt that led to a rectangular hopper at the top, a yellow box the size of a bathtub. Nothing I could do but stand there while Mica rolled a tire onto the conveyor and then wince when the tire dropped down into the chute. An auger inside the chute rotated the tire like a corkscrew while gradually devouring the thing. The noise, already horrendous, became an ascending scream. Beneath the chute were steel teeth on spindles that rotated in a blur and never slowed while streamers of black rubber, suddenly as light as ribbons, were vented into a metal container. Soon the tire disappeared.

Mica watched me, not the shredder, and his glittering eyes warned *It could happen to you.*

"Shut it off!" I ordered.

Instead of hitting the switch, he peeked at the ZZ Top giant again, his manner suddenly secretive, then signaled for me to follow as if he didn't want Spooner to know. So I followed.

Anything was better than standing near that awful machine—or so I believed until I was told how the man with the gray beard, Harris Spooner, had disposed of his late wife.

EIGHTEEN

Mica led me behind tires and through more wreckage that screened us from graybeard's view. In the far corner of the property was a metal building where weeds sprouted along the fencing. The building was to our right, but we turned left and didn't stop until we were among a row of vehicles that had crashed so violently, they resembled bread loaves all blackened by rust and fire. In red paint on a windshield, someone had scrawled *Death Cars*, as if designating the area a theme park.

"How'd you like to have been in that van?" Mica asked me, taking out his lighter and cigarettes. "Cops had that towed in last week. Still some flies around it—see 'em?" He leaned his head, exhaled smoke, then offered the pack to me. "Menthol? I got used to 'em in the joint."

Out here, the noise of the shredder wasn't so bad and there was more sunlight. I could see that Mica's skin was pale and that his teeth were blackening at the roots. I had read somewhere that decay was common in meth addicts because their mouths stopped producing saliva. I wouldn't have made the connection if Mica hadn't grinned at me, but he did.

"I didn't come here to provide entertainment," I said. I had retrieved my organizer and was taking out my cell phone.

"Just explaining why you shouldn't piss off my Uncle Harris."

"Your *uncle?*"

"Grandma's little brother," he said, and pointed toward the van wreckage. "I'd rather been riding shotgun in that mess than have ol' Harris stuff me in a shredder. Hell, he'd do it, too! That boy'd still be in Raiford if they could'a found more than a piece or two of his wife. Harris, he might look messy, but when it comes to his work, that boy's goddamn tidy!" Mica took a long drag of his cigarette, his message sent, then asked, "How many years it been since we seen each other, Hannah-han?"

Hannah-han. As a toddler, Mica had been unable to pronounce my name, and the nickname had stuck with the Helms children. Which might have been endearing, but Mica was still grinning while his eyes ogled the contours of my blouse.

"I was hoping we could talk like adults," I replied, concentrating on my phone. The mention of Harris Spooner's wife being found in pieces had made my stomach roll, and I didn't want to show he'd upset me.

"Go right ahead, I'm enjoying the scenery. By god, you've filled out, girl!" Apparently, Mica expected me to smile at the compliment. I didn't, which offended him enough to trigger his temper. I was scrolling through recent calls when he added, "A body like a Q-tip, that's the way I remember you looking. No . . . what was it kids called you? Oh! Pizza on a stick 'cause of them pimples! One thing that hasn't changed is your shitty sense of humor. Honey . . . you need to loosen up."

Even as a boy, Mica had had a viper's tongue and the brains to hit his target where it hurt most. His words stung, but the girl he was taunting was long, long gone. I remained calm. "There's nothing funny about stealing from old folks, people you've known all your life," I said. "But I'll admit that someone played a pretty good joke when they listed you on the board of directors."

I had shown him the Fisherfolk membership form but hadn't mentioned that I had been hired to investigate the organization. It was unprofessional of me, no doubt, but mentioning his directorship now wiped the grin off Mica's face. He had been lounging against the fence but stepped away. "Who told you that?"

I said, "I don't know what all Loretta gave you, but the items I mentioned belong to our family, not her. I've got a right to know the thief's name, don't I? So I checked public records. Crystal's name's there, too, but I can't imagine her being involved in something like this."

Mica did a vaudevillian take, the one where the comedian's cheeks bulge instead of spitting water, then sputtered, "You sure as hell ain't spoke with Crystal in a while, have you?"

"I plan to see her next," I said.

"The hell you are!"

"Before the funeral, if you wouldn't mind giving me an address. Is she doing okay?"

Mica played along. "Well, let's put it this way: Crystal got religion long enough to gain a hundred pounds—but I imagine she's improving since Mamma died."

"That's a terrible way to speak!" I told him.

"Don't care if it is. It's true—those two hated each other. If you want Crystal's address, check with the loony ward or call her probation officer."

I let that go by saying, "The funeral's tomorrow, Mica. I expect I'll see her."

The man had lost track of the days, though. I could tell by the blank look on his face. "Tomorrow's Thursday," I reminded him. "Services are at Kirby Funeral Home, then burial's at the cemetery on Pine Island Road. I'm sure Crystal will be there, but maybe you have other plans."

He pointed a finger and stepped toward me. "You stop your damn nagging! And stay away from my sister!"

"What I'm going to do is call a sheriff," I said, concentrating on my phone, "and get all your threats down on paper."

That made him even madder, but Mica was too smart to put his freedom and his starving brain at risk. "Hold on a sec . . . *please*?" He waited until he had my attention, then the meth addict tried to become a salesman. "For one thing, Fisherfolk is a legal nonprofit, so no one's stealing nothin'. If you checked the records, you know that's true. Give me a chance and I'll prove what a good deal it is for the folks around here."

"Someone filled out all the right forms," I countered, "which means it wasn't you. Was it a doctor named Alice Candor? Or maybe a company she and her husband own. I'll find out anyway, so you might as well tell me."

Mica recognized the name, I could tell by the thoughtful look he affected, but seemed unaware of a connection. "Some doctor's name's listed in the records? Show me, I'd like to see if it's true."

"I didn't say that. But if that's who you're working for, be careful. She's a psychiatrist, Dr. Alice Candor. She treated prison inmates before she came to Florida. And if she's treating Crystal, there's something Crystal should know. This woman did experiments on her patients. The paper she published is on the Internet."

What kind of experiments? I could see the question forming in Mica's eyes, but he couldn't ask without conceding that he knew the woman.

"It's the truth," I pressed. "This was in Ohio, but she's here now. Is that how you got involved? There's no shame in going to a rehab clinic, Mica, but Dr. Candor is a dangerous choice."

The man was becoming agitated and tried to regain control by saying, "She don't have anything to do with what we're doing—and what we're doing is legal."

"Doesn't mean it's right," I said, which was Joel Ransler's line but seemed appropriate.

"Right?" Mica snorted, then turned to me with a wild look in his eyes. "Name me one time this state treated people like us right. Think about it, girl! Families like ours—there was just a handful who settled this state. They put up with the 'skeeters and heat and snakes long enough to turn this shithole swamp into prime real estate. Our people put fish and citrus on the tables of Yankees who treated us like redneck trash. Then how'd they thank us? Soon as there was enough Ohioans, they voted the net fishermen out of business."

He began to pace, using his boney hands to gesture. "They closed our co-ops but sold commercial licenses to any asshole from

'Bama or Georgia who plunked down seventy-five bucks. Japs and Cubans, too, running factory ships twelve miles off Marco Island—shit, I seen it, girl! Then taxed us out of our houses, and said, 'Oh, by the way, you can't net no more mullet or trout or pompano, neither!'" He snapped his cigarette away. "If there's anyone who should understand why our people deserve a museum, it's you, Hannah Smith."

I looked at my phone again. Birdy Tupplemeyer, Joel Ransler, and Tomlinson had all left phone messages, but it was Birdy's number that I had selected. My thumb had remained poised, though, while Mica talked. The question I was asking myself was *Is he exploiting the truth or does he believe what he's saying?* because much of what he had said was true.

Exploiting, I decided. It didn't take long to make up my mind.

MICA HAD GOTTEN some coaching. It showed when he went into his sales pitch, telling me, "Picture a whole room showing what the Smith family did for Florida. Old photos of your Aunt Hannahs, your grandfolks, all the famous Smiths." He used his hands to create a wall for me to imagine. "Your granddaddy's fishing gear, that would look good up there, too, wouldn't it? Same thing for my family—a place where tourists could enjoy our family's pictures and antiques."

I wondered if he'd practiced these lines on Mrs. Padilla and the others while he continued, "Then you got your Browns and Weeks families. The Padillas, the Hamiltons, and Joiners—you know all the names. Hell, the Woodrings alone should have a whole room. Same with the Chatham family and the Colliers—don't matter they're rich or poor," Mica smiled while his eyes sought my approval.

"The Chathams, huh?" I said, suddenly more interested. "Are they paying to have this museum built?"

"Everybody's got to chip in. It wouldn't be fair otherwise." Mica stood straighter, his smile broadened.

I had to smile, too, when he said that. "You were never known for fairness, Mica Helms. Tell me the truth. How much you charging Loretta and the others to get into this museum of yours?"

Before he answered, he studied me, his manner now asking *Can I trust you?* It was his reluctance that told me my suspicions were accurate.

"What you're really doing," I said, "is tricking old people into signing over their property, *aren't you?* Especially waterfront. That's why your mother moved out of Munchkinville, I'd bet. She signed over her cottage, then you got her preaching to her friends and handing out donation forms. Mica"—I tried to stop myself but couldn't—"Mica, did it ever cross your mind that your mother might still be alive if she'd lived closer to her friends? I'm not going to let that happen to Loretta!"

He glared a glassy warning, then tried to settle himself by lighting another cigarette. He smoked and paced in a circle, but he was too mad, and too mean, not to punish me for guessing the truth. Finally, he stopped and faced me. "You always did act like Miss High-and-Mighty. Well, let me tell you something, girl. You're just mangrove trash, no better than the rest of us."

I deflected the insult by replying, "If that's true, maybe I'd understand why you're stealing from your own people."

Mica pretended to give that some serious thought, then seemed to drop his guard a little. "Well, honey, truth is, I ain't the dumb little kid you remember. I figured something out. Back in the day, folks around here made money. I'm talking piles of cash. Now that they're old, most of 'em are happy to donate to a place that will show off their family history. Plus it helps ease the *guilt* they feel—which I'm sure you already know." He let that sink in before adding, "Mamma was tickled pink to help spread the word about Fisherfolk. Same with your own sweet Loretta. So I don't see it as stealing."

What was that supposed to mean? I told him, "I didn't hear you mention any pot haulers on your list of names."

"Didn't I?" he said, and gave me a look that asked *How can you be so damn naïve?* At last, I understood. He was hinting that Rosanna Helms and Loretta had both been involved in smuggling drugs.

"That's cruel, even for you," I said. "Your mother's not even in the ground yet, and Loretta hated boats. Still does! Show some respect!"

Mica laughed that away while a silky wink came into his tone. "Instead of fighting me, you could be helping collect donations. I wouldn't expect you to work for free. You'd be paid on a percentage basis—like all charities do it. Hannah-han"—he spoke my name as if I was already a conspirator—"some of our people had so much cash lying around, they didn't know what to do with it. You think they put it in banks? You think they paid income tax on that money? Hell no! They *hid* it—and killed more than one man to protect what they were doing."

"You're talking about your father," I said.

"Goddamn right I am! Didn't you hear me say folks around here got reasons to feel guilty? Daddy was a mean sonuvabitch, but he wasn't dumb. Think how much you could sock away if you made ten, twenty million cash, and didn't pay the IRS? If I'm right, someone owes us both. Think of this as collecting your inheritance, 'cause that's the way I see it."

Once again, taxes had been mentioned, but that ended the conversation as far as I was concerned—and also explained why Mica Helms might have ransacked his own mother's house. Hunting for cash, hunting for *something*. I started toward the gate while tapping numbers on my phone.

"Hey . . . hey! Who you calling?" Mica followed, the cigarette clinched between his teeth.

"That sheriff's deputy," I replied. "I'm less tolerant of bullying since Friday when you chased me with an axe. Or was it him?" I looked toward the trailer, but Spooner had vanished from the steps.

"You're crazy!" Mica hollered, but then surrendered in a rush by promising to return Loretta's donations if I hung up the phone.

Too late. Birdy answered, saying, "You better not be backing out. My friend loaned me his night vision dealie." She was talking about the plans we'd made for tonight.

I remained formal. "Deputy Tupplemeyer, you said I should call if I had any problems at the junkyard."

Mica groaned and spun away while the redhead became all business. "If you're in trouble, give me a landmark, I'm on my way.

In danger, say something about—shit, I don't know—say your watch broke, that's why you're late. Then pretend to hang up—but *don't*."

Looking at Mica, I said, "No trouble so far, but you asked me to check in. Can I call you back in twenty?"

"Is this about that charity scam?"

"Seems so."

"You're trying to scare some asshole," Birdy guessed. "No problem. I'll call *you* back in five. Put your phone on *Speaker* before you answer."

I replied, "Well, if you're already in Glades City, that's fine," and hung up.

Mica was lighting another cigarette, his nerves and starving brain on overload. "Shit, that's just dandy. I give you a chance to make some real money, but you go crying to the cops anyway!"

I pointed to the metal building and said, "Not if we find Loretta's things in there. Otherwise, the deputy and I are just meeting for lunch."

"Lunch! With a *cop*?" Mica studied me, suddenly suspicious. "You stay away from that storage barn. Hear me? It's up to Harris whether he gives us the keys or not."

For the first time, I took a real look at the building: corrugated roof and siding, with sliding doors like a garage but bigger, and they were padlocked. Against an outside wall was a stack of car batteries and piles of trash that included metal cans—the kind that hold paint thinner. I sniffed the air and suddenly understood why the area had a nasty chemical smell. The building was probably a meth lab.

"Don't get any stupid ideas," Mica warned softly.

I was moving away from him when Birdy, whose internal clock runs fast, called back. I touched *Speaker* and turned the volume loud so Mica wouldn't miss a word.

"Ms. Smith? Deputy Tupplemeyer here. We've got a couple of K-nine units in the area, and I know how much you like dogs. Mind if we stop and say hello?"

When my eyes shifted to Mica, he was waving his hands to focus my attention and mouthing the words *Okay! . . . Okay!* meaning he would open the storage barn, answer my questions, anything I wanted. I didn't believe him but the K-9 unit was a fiction, too, so I went along with it, telling Birdy I would call back in a few minutes.

Mica was lying, as expected. But it gave Harris Spooner time to appear, the ZZ Top giant who moved methodically despite the pit bull that was pulling him along by its leash.

"I'm betting on that Chevy again!" he called to us, grinning. "Or she can pay me twenty bucks and walk out like a lady. Her choice."

The man had added an extra ten as interest, apparently, but it was actually extortion because I was terrified of the dog, which he could read in my reaction. It caused Spooner's grin to broaden, a grin so wide and wild it spread his beard like a curtain and laid his teeth bare on a face that was the size of a yeti and just as hairy.

I didn't freeze but didn't argue back either. Just stood there numbly while Harris knelt to slap the dog's neck while saying to Mica, "You talk too much, dickweed."

Mica feigned indignation. "You know I wouldn't do that!"

"I *heard* you, boy. Piles of money and unpaid taxes. You didn't say that?" Harris's head pivoted slowly until his eyes found Mica. "You ever bring another stranger back here, keep flapping your lips way you do, I'll turn you into something Vixxy can lap from a bowl."

Mica's expression became glassy, but he tried to save face by saying, "This girl, she's almost like family. You knew her people!"

Spooner nailed him with another look that read *I'll deal with you later,* then got back to me and his wager, saying, "I don't see no money in your hand, girl, so you must be real proud of those legs of yours. Well, if that's the way you want it." He reached to unsnap the dog's collar. "You get a five-second head start. Damn it, girl, better run!"

The threat shocked me out of my daze and I replied with a threat of my own. "Mister, I've got a sheriff's deputy waiting outside—ask Mica, if you don't believe me. A whole team, plus a K-nine unit!"

It was the wildest of lies but didn't matter. Before Spooner could respond, a familiar voice stopped everything by hollering, "Leave her alone, Harris! Mica, back away, and let me see your hands! I'll shoot that damn dog, if I have to."

Joel Ransler was there when I turned, a pistol in his left hand and ready but pointed at the ground. Then proved he could bully both men—possibly showing off for my benefit—by asking, "What's the problem, you fellas miss showering at Raiford? Or just the strip searches?"

A few minutes later, in the parking lot, I told Joel, "Thank god you made me text the address!" which I had to yell out because Mica had resumed shredding tires.

The special prosecutor responded by asking me to lunch, then leading me to his Audi, which was a new A6, it turned out.

Best of all, the car was quiet inside.

NINETEEN

That evening, just after sunset, I parked my SUV at the Lowe's on Pine Island Road, and Birdy drove us inland toward Carnicero, a trip that took less than an hour but seemed longer because the woman enjoyed showing off her driving skills and the speed of her BMW convertible.

"We'll keep the top down until we're closer," she told me, then pretended to respect traffic laws until we were on Route 17, a country road I didn't remember as curvy, but it *was* curvy with Birdy Tupplemeyer at the wheel. As she drove, she questioned me about what had happened at the junkyard—especially Joel Ransler's role—but often interrupted my answers to demonstrate driving advice, such as, "The trick is to maintain speed into a curve . . . *then* accelerate." And, "You never want to surprise a drunk from behind, so I'll flash my high beams before passing that asshole. Then downshift . . . always check your mirrors . . . then *floor* it!"

Finally, I had to ask, "Are we in a hurry? I thought the later we searched that field, the better."

I was referring to our destination. It was a rectangular lot between the rehab clinic and a church the deputy had located on Google Earth. She had printed out copies for both of us. The photos suggested that cypress trees screened the field from the clinic, which made me more optimistic about trespassing on property owned by Dr. Alice Candor but no less nervous.

"I'd hardly call it a field," Birdy said. "It's less than a quarter acre. We hop out of the car, take a quick look, then we're out of there. This far inland, even a few big conch shells will tell us we found the right place. After that, we'll get serious."

When I didn't reply, she laughed, "You are so uptight! Next time Rance the Lance asks you out for dinner, you'd better say yes before you explode."

Apparently, assigning nicknames to people she'd never met was something else the woman enjoyed. Even with the top down, the BMW was fairly quiet, but I still had to raise my voice to ask, "How'd you come up with that?"

"From the look on your face when you talk about him. He shows up out of nowhere, like a knight in shining armor, and saves your butt. Rance the Lance, see? Admit it. You've got the hots for the guy."

"Oh," I said, "*that* kind of lance. No . . . all we did was stop at Denny's for iced tea. We talked, it was fun, sure. I figured I owed him at least that."

"At the very least," she scolded. "You said he scared the hell out of those rednecks. So he must be a pretty big guy, a hardass but classy, you said. The guy knows how to dress, how to behave around women, but you turned him down anyway. How many times you think he'll ask before saying to hell with you?"

I said, "He's tall, but not big compared to Harris Spooner. You'd have to see Spooner to understand. That man's got something missing in his brain, and he's a bully, too—until Joel showed up. I haven't figured that part out yet."

"One of the rednecks, yeah," Birdy said. "That's my point. The guy's intimidating when he needs to be. But also an attorney, a man who's made something of himself."

I was reviewing the scene in my head, trying to understand why Mica and his uncle had reacted so meekly. "Joel didn't wave the gun around or threaten to have them arrested. He even cracked a joke about them taking showers together—you know, after he sends them back to prison. I grew up around hard cases like Harris Spooner and I've never met a one who would tolerate being called a homosexual."

"They just stood there and took it, huh?"

"Hardly said a word until Joel made them apologize."

"Apologize?" Birdy slapped the steering wheel, delighted. "I've got to meet this Rance the Lance."

"You mind not calling him that?" I said. "It wasn't until we were at Denny's that I mentioned there might be a meth lab on the property. Oh, and that Spooner supposedly cut his wife into pieces."

"What?"

I said it again, and added, "Or put her in a tire shredder—I didn't want the details."

"You don't really believe that?" she said.

"Maybe. I hope Mica was just trying to scare me, but Harris's wife disappeared, that much is true. Joel told me a little bit, and I checked the records, too. Seven, almost eight years ago, Spooner went to prison for attempted murder, but it was a totally unrelated case. Hopefully, I'll find out more when I get back to the office."

"Thank god you've got this guy Rance looking out for you."

"He's good at his job," I conceded. "That's why I think he asked me out to dinner—you know, so I could give him more details. He's especially interested in what Mica said about older property owners not paying taxes. You know, on illegal income, money they earned hauling marijuana. But I'd already made plans with you for tonight. And Marion's dog arrives tomorrow, so I'll be busy."

Birdy smiled and said, "Pot hauling," amused by the term, which I had used earlier. Then got serious. "What's wrong with you? Turn down a dinner date to babysit a dog?"

"I'm already in a relationship," I said patiently. "Even if I weren't, Joel's not my type."

Birdy kept pushing, but in a friendly way that was more like a game. We traded a few barbs before she said, "You think Tomlinson is *my* type? It didn't stop us from having a fun night, though, did it? Haven't you noticed how much more relaxed I am?"

"Not from your driving," I replied.

"You know what I mean. Basic female physiology, particularly in women our age—it's total puritanical bullshit to deny ourselves. You're not even engaged, right? So why act like you're married?"

"The subject of marriage hasn't come up," I answered. "It's more of an understanding." I felt no obligation to add that I'd had only two dates with Ford unless counting the times we'd gone jogging together, which I *did*—apparently because I was full of puritanical bullshit. Why else would my conscience demand it?

Birdy said, "It's *your* understanding, not his, Smithie, that's what I'm telling you! If you meet a good-looking guy who's single and not some kind of psych job or an ego freak, there's no harm in having fun. Psychologically, it's healthy. Tomlinson happens to agree, by the way."

"Bless his philandering heart," I said. "The man's finally coming out of his shell."

My deputy friend thought that was funny and called me smart-ass but kept her eyes focused on the road. "I'll tell you a secret," she offered, then proceeded to share information about Tomlinson that was in poor taste and much too personal, but I listened to every word. While I was laughing, I tilted my head up to enjoy the odor of a citrus grove we were traveling through. Rows of trees, their canopies black, streamed by, while, above, a waxing moon floated on a bubble of pollen-scented air. We drove in silence for a few minutes before Birdy added, "God, the scariest thing is, my mother would *love* Tomlinson. Talk about not my type. But he's so sweet and perceptive, I wouldn't mind getting to know him better. It's not just about the sex."

"Weird how it works," I said. "I don't know much about Ford, either—and it doesn't matter. But Joel, I don't know anything about him and it *does* matter. That's what's strange."

As I spoke, the gray asphalt road changed, becoming black and uneven. At the same instant, the BMW's headlights sparked off a sign that read *Welcome to Sematee County*.

"I know a clerk who works for the sheriff's department,"

Birdy said, referring to the sign. "We both went to BU—a total coincidence—but she's a lot of fun and smart when it comes to men. If you want, I'll call her right now and find out what she knows about Rance the"—she caught herself—"about Joel."

"I couldn't ask you to do that," I said.

"You didn't ask, I'm offering," Birdy replied, meaning she was going to call her friend anyway.

My eyes moved to the car's GPS screen. To make finding the spot easier, Tupplemeyer had entered the address of the rehab clinic as our destination, and I could see that we had only seven miles to go.

Birdy's busy brain jumped ahead of me. "You're right. We should pull over and put the top up before anyone sees us. Then I'll call."

PHONE TO HER EAR, Birdy turned north onto County Road 731, which skirted Glades City and the Brighton Indian Reservation, while I listened to a one-sided conversation with her friend Gail. The BMW smelled new, it had hands-free calling, but she had opted to keep the call private. Why?

I wasn't going to interrupt to ask.

"Gailstrom, it's me, Bertie!" she exclaimed when her friend answered. She had to say it twice due to the poor reception, enunciating so clearly I realized I'd been calling Tupplemeyer by the wrong nickname. Maybe I made a wincing noise because she covered the phone long enough to whisper, "Would you *stop*? Birdy's cool!" then went back to Gail, first discussing a college friend, then Gail's recent breakup, Birdy Tupplemeyer offering comfort by saying, "You just dodged the big Loser Bullet, sister. And Loser Bullets aren't made out of silver, trust me."

It provided the opening she needed to ask about single men and then mention Joel by name. A moment later, an *Oh my god* look appeared on her face and she included me in the conversation long enough to say, "That's what they call him!"

Rance the Lance, I assumed she meant but didn't want to provide another distraction—not at sixty-five on a bad two-lane road. Birdy returned to the phone, still grinning in the dash lights, but the grin faded as she listened and said things like, "Small towns, yeah, of course you do . . . Gail, I *understand*. Sure, sure . . . so when can we get together? Yes, I'm curious as hell now."

Several seconds after Birdy had put away the phone, I broke the silence, saying, "Is something wrong? Your friend probably has sense enough not to gossip about people she works with."

The deputy shook her head. "That was the excuse she used. But it wasn't the reason."

"What did she say?"

Tupplemeyer slowed to fifty and touched the *Cruise Control* button while her mind worked at something. Finally, she answered, "I think Gail's scared."

"Of Joel?"

"Maybe not him, exactly, but she's afraid her phone's bugged. I'd bet on it. And she's a tough girl—grew up in some tenement shit factory with pimps and ghetto monsters. I wouldn't think the local cowboys could scratch the paint on a girl like her."

Maybe she's doing something illegal. That's what I was thinking.

"You said Ransler made those two rednecks apologize?" Birdy asked. "Were those his actual words? I mean, was it a suggestion or did he say, 'You assholes, apologize,' more like an order?"

The question jogged the memory of the way Joel had spoken to Delmont Chatham on my boat, telling an older man, and a member of a wealthy family, *Del, you're going to apologize to Captain Smith*. Not loud or bossy, but saying it in a way that left no doubt it was going to happen.

"He didn't call them assholes," I said. "But he was firm."

"Two tough ex-cons," she said, still puzzled, then had an idea. "What about the pit bull? Why didn't Ransler call animal control and have the damn thing taken away?"

"First thing in the morning, that's what's going to happen," I said. "Joel's going to have the sheriff's department check on the meth lab, too. Because I was trespassing, who knows what animal control will do? But Joel's taking care of it. I believe him. Why wouldn't I?"

While she thought about that, I decided to add, "Maybe there's another reason Gail thinks someone is listening to her conversations. How much do you know about her?"

We had come to a flashing yellow light, a plywood fruit stand on one corner, a Hess station straight ahead. The windows and gas pumps created a circle of neon in an area where citrus grew on both sides of the road, no streetlights for miles in either direction.

"The local hangout," Birdy said, referring to a couple of men talking across the bed of a pickup and kids sitting beneath a *Florida Lottery* sign, their bikes parked near a coil of air hose. She downshifted and turned east before answering, "I think Gail's too smart to be dealing in bad shit when she's working for the same people who would arrest her."

The GPS prompted me to say, "Maybe that's something you should think about before we do any trespassing." Our destination was less than a mile away, and it was only eight-thirty. Traffic was spotty—trucks hauling sugarcane and citrus, mostly—but still there were people around who might notice two women in a sporty white Beamer.

The deputy was unfazed. "She sure clammed up when I mentioned Ransler's name. Said we'd have to talk in private. You know . . . very careful about her wording. Scared? Yeah, I really think she is."

"But nothing bad about Joel personally," I said.

Tupplemeyer liked energy drinks—Lord knows why she would add fuel to the fire but she did—and had opened a fresh can when we'd stopped to put the car's top up. She took a gulp now and glanced at me, her expression serious. "The dumbest thing two friends can do is pass along third-party information—especially when it comes from a mutual friend. It's the sort of bullshit I hate."

I replied, "After you've told me what's on your mind, we should discuss your caffeine intake." The way the woman's attention bounced around, I had no idea what she was talking about.

Birdy took another drink and muttered, *"Damn it,"* as if chastising herself, then said, "There's a reason I was pushing you to date this guy Ransler. Not just him—I meant it generally speaking. You're not engaged, you should date. That's all I meant."

At that instant, I realized the obvious: Birdy and Tomlinson had discussed Marion Ford during her night at Dinkin's Bay yet she continued to dismiss him as if he were an object blocking my way to freedom. A warning light went off in my head. "Before we go any further," I told her, "how drunk or stoned was Tomlinson? And what, exactly, did he say?"

The deputy sighed. "Smithie, I'll never do this again. Seriously, I feel like we could be really good friends and I don't want that ruined because I stupidly—"

"Just tell me what he said," I interrupted. Unconsciously, I had stretched my legs out as if preparing myself for a crash.

The crash came, but it wasn't as bad as I feared.

"Tomlinson raved about your guy. Respect, integrity, smart, and he's nice to old ladies—all the things you want to hear about a man but almost never do, even from his friends. A little strait-laced, maybe, yet open-minded. But then he let something slip that I should have told you right off the bat. What Tomlinson said was, 'Doc will never settle down with one woman.' No . . ." Birdy touched a finger to her lips, trying to remember. "No, his almost exact words were, 'Doc won't let a woman get close enough to hurt herself. That's why he'll never settle down.' Tomlinson says he's got a bad case of Hannah fever. That's how we got on the subject."

"Tomlinson said *Doc's* got a bad case of me," I repeated, wanting to hear it again but also to be sure of her meaning.

"Of course. We're lying there naked, you think Tomlinson's going to ruin his shot at an encore by admitting he has a thing for another woman?"

I'd been holding my breath, I realized. I let it out. "That's *it*?"

"The man's best friend says he's never going to settle down

with one woman, how bad you want it to be? That's the reason I was hinting around you should go out for dinner if you're asked."

I felt around until I found the right button, lowered my window, then took Birdy's energy drink from its holder.

"Hey! What do you think you're doing?"

"Pouring it out," I said, and I did. When the window was closed, I placed the can behind the seat. "We can stop and have a glass of wine later, but no more speed drinks for you. Doc's been careful in his life about making a commitment? I don't consider that bad news. He cares about a woman's feelings. I think it's sweet."

"*Sweet?* Well, if you say so. Anyhow, I won't push you about the good-looking attorney—not after what Gail said."

I would have picked up on the remark, but was in the middle of explaining I'd expected her to say something shocking—that Ford had a terminal illness or he was living a secret life—when I saw a patch of cleared land flash by on our left. Was it the spot we had come to search? Yes, because ahead was a lighted sign so small, it encouraged anonymity rather than advertise the cluster of buildings inside the gate.

Sematee Evaluation and Treatment Clinic

"I didn't see the church, but we had to have passed it," Birdy said, checking the mirror. "We'll do a U-ee at the next road."

It gave me time to ask what *exactly* had her friend Gail said about Joel.

"What she told me was, 'Don't go out with the guy until you talk to me first.' I didn't get the impression it was because of his nickname. Something more serious. Doesn't sound good, does it?"

We had turned around and were passing the clinic again, but at seventy miles an hour the only notable details were a chain-link fence, an electronic gate, and security lights way back in the trees. Something else I noted was an eighteen-wheeler, its cab lit up like a Ferris wheel, coming from the opposite direction a quarter mile away.

I had started to reassure my friend by saying, "I wouldn't have gone out with Joel anyway unless—" And that's as far as I got. From the corner of my eye, I saw something leap from the ditch and try to sprint across the road but then freeze as if surprised by the dazzling glare of the BMW's headlights—or the headlights of the eighteen-wheeler.

It was a person, I realized . . . a *woman* dressed in yellow, her eyes huge behind the two pale arms that she threw up to protect herself.

Birdy jerked the wheel to the right, yelling, "Hang on!" then I felt a sickening thud as the woman hurled herself at the windshield and the car skidded off the asphalt.

TWENTY

My fishing clients are amused when I tell them I've never seen snow but plan to one day visit a mountain resort where people wear sweaters and sit by the fire when they are not skiing S-turns down a snowy slope.

Skiing down an asphalt straightaway—that was the sensation in my stomach when the BMW went into a skid after hitting loose gravel at the side of the road. I'm sure Birdy took her foot off the accelerator, yet the car seemed to go faster when she corrected the skid by yanking the wheel to the left, which only vaulted us into the path of the eighteen-wheeler. The truck protested with a diesel bellow and flooded our windshield with lights until Birdy fishtailed us to the right. We went off the road again and hit more gravel while the truck went speeding past, but Birdy didn't over-correct this time. She kept the steering wheel straight and allowed the shoulder of the road to punish the little sports car until we had banged to a stop.

"Jesus Christ, that was close!" Birdy whispered, then put her face in her hands.

I swung around in my seat and watched the eighteen-wheeler's brakes flare as the driver slowed, probably using his mirrors to confirm we hadn't crashed, and then went speeding on. To the west, a wafer of moon provided light, but all I saw was the truck and empty asphalt. No sign of the woman who had leaped in front of us.

"Did we hit her?"

"Jesus Christ!" Birdy said again, then sat up straight. "No. But, goddamn, that was close!"

"I felt *something*," I said. "Like a thud against the fender. Are you sure?"

"Yeah . . . *yes*, I'm sure. I got a glimpse of her in the mirror when we went off the road. That's what you heard, a sort of thump when we hit the berm. But I saw her. Standing there like a statue—what an idiot! Ran right out in front of us!"

I said, "Let's go back and check. What do you think?"

"Yeah, I guess. I didn't hit her, but she has to be in some sort of trouble. Or drunk. What was she wearing? A robe maybe. It wasn't yellow, but it looked yellow because of the lights."

"Are you okay to drive?" I asked.

"Stood there like a statue!" Birdy said again, then took a deep breath. "Probably some redneck who had a fight with her boyfriend, out here crazy drunk or high." She opened the glove box and took out a flashlight. "Let's go see."

We turned around on the empty road and retraced our path with the windows down, Birdy driving slowly, until we found the BMW's first skid marks. The night air was dense with April moisture and vibrated with cicadas and trilling frogs. We shared the flashlight. Ditches on both sides of the road were a tangle of weeds and beer cans, but no sign of the woman.

Ahead was the entrance to Sematee Evaluation and Treatment Clinic. I was already thinking it when Birdy said, "Hospital clothes, that's what she was wearing. Or scrubs, something like that." She looked toward the clinic's security lights, way back in the trees, which showed a wedge of empty parking lot and a couple of low buildings that reminded me of government housing. "Think we should go find someone?"

I still wasn't convinced we hadn't grazed the woman. What if she had wandered off into a field and was dying? "Let's park and search on foot," I said. "We need to make sure she's okay before we waste time talking to people."

"I just got this car," Birdy replied in a way that told me she wanted to check for damage, too. "Let's find that church, we'll get out."

We turned around again.

THE REASON we hadn't noticed the church was because it wasn't there. The building had collapsed beneath the weight of its own rotting frame or had been intentionally demolished—a tiny structure the size of a schoolhouse, if photographed from a satellite, that lay a quarter mile west of the clinic.

We didn't see the cemetery, either, until Birdy babied the BMW into the drive and hit her brights. That's when the wreckage of the church appeared and headstones began emerging from the weeds, a dozen or fewer stones at the edge of the property where vines and cattails created a wall. From the satellite photos, I knew that a section of what might be swamp, and the lake that fed it, were nearby, then miles of sugarcane and citrus beyond that.

"At least no one will see the car," Birdy said, getting out, and I had to agree that the spot seemed hidden from the road. She inspected the Beamer for damage—there was none—then popped the trunk so I could get the flashlight and mosquito spray I'd brought. Soon she was telling me that her friend's night vision equipment didn't work the way she expected.

"Maybe weak batteries," Birdy said, holding a plastic scope to her eye. "It's one of the cheapies—can't see crap—but I'll bring it along anyway." She locked the car and listened to the chirring insects before saying, "Smithie, I'm sure I didn't hit that woman. Not even a scratch on my fenders."

"The poor thing's out here all by herself," I said. "How about we jog along the road? You take one side, I'll take the other." I turned and started away.

Birdy had the scope to her eye again and stopped me by saying, "What the hell's *that*?" She was looking in the direction of the area we had planned to search, the quarter-acre lot the Candors had changed from wetlands by hauling in fill. There was no way she could see anything, though, even if the scope had worked, because vines and cypress trees separated us from the clearing.

"You're wasting time," I said. "What if she's hurt?"

"Listen!" The woman deputy appeared to crouch into a shooting stance and began backing away.

"What's wrong?"

"Someone's coming!" she said, and motioned for me to return to the car.

I didn't see or hear anything, so I switched on my flashlight—a small Fenix LED that Ford had given me. The light was blinding, and I used its beam to paint gravestones white as I probed among the weeds. Finally, the light spooked something. Bushes moved, branches crackled. I searched until I found the source: an armor-plated animal that made a squealing noise when the light found it, then bounced away in retreat.

"Armadillo," I said, smiling. "Good thing you didn't bring your gun."

Birdy was explaining that animals sometimes *sound* like footsteps when a distant howl silenced her and caused the back of my neck to tingle. The howl climbed in pitch and became a shriek— the scream of a woman who was terrified or in pain.

"It's her!" I said, and took off running toward the road but then stopped because the screaming stopped. I hadn't had time to pinpoint the woman's location but Birdy had. She was already zigzagging through the cemetery, using her flashlight to take what she thought was a shorter route through the trees.

"That might be swamp!" I yelled, but she kept going. So I followed. The cemetery had once been enclosed by a wrought-iron fence that had fallen and was hidden by weeds. Birdy stumbled over a section and went sprawling. It gave me time to catch up.

"Are you okay?"

"Shit," she said, shining her light on a tombstone. The stone had been worn smooth by decades, and she looked at it for a second. "My ass just landed on someone's grave. Good thing I'm not superstitious."

I said, "Check your clothes for fire ants," because what her ass had almost landed on was an ant nest, a sandy mound the size of a pumpkin. Fire ants like rough ground and attack in mass when their nest is disturbed. The bites burn like hot coals, so I was making a thorough search of my friend's clothes when we heard a woman scream again and then men shouting. The voices came from the other side of the trees.

"Are they hurting her or trying to help?" I whispered.

"Before I call my dispatcher, let's make sure," Birdy said, then motioned for me to take the lead and I did.

WHAT I HAD FEARED would be swamp was actually the remains of a cypress strand that had been drained by a pond. The ground was soft but not mushy, and the pond appeared in the beam of my flashlight as a sheen of black that was dotted with lily pads and stars. When we were closer, though, pairs of glowing red eyes floated to the surface.

"Gators," I told Birdy. "Keep moving."

She did. It took us only a minute or two to cross the strand, but the screaming had stopped by the time we exited the trees. We were at the edge of the clearing we had come to search, a building lot that had been elevated with fill, then tamped flat by heavy equipment. Beyond that were more trees, then the lights of the medical clinic—but no woman dressed in a hospital gown, no sign of the men we had heard yelling.

"Sound plays tricks at night," I said. "Maybe they're up on the road."

Birdy switched off her flashlight and told me to do the same. "Even if they aren't," she said, putting the nightscope to her eye, "I'm not walking past that damn pond again. Gators, my ass!" A moment later, she handed the scope to me, saying, "This thing's useless," and stepped up onto the rectangle of packed earth, her short attention span now back on the subject of artifacts.

Looking through the night vision scope was like trying to see through a green marble. I fiddled with the focus without success but did decipher something moving near the highway. I lowered the scope and was about to use my flashlight when another eighteen-wheeler zoomed past and illuminated what I was seeing. It was a person running—a woman, which became apparent when she paused to catch her breath only fifty yards away. I called out, "Are you okay?"

It startled her—and startled Birdy, too, whose attention was elsewhere. "I'm not deaf!" she snapped, and switched on her flashlight. She was kicking at something on the ground.

"I'm going to talk to *her*," I said.

"Who?"

"The woman we almost hit," I said. She was jogging toward us now, attracted by our voices or the light. Didn't say a word until her last few wobbly strides, but then spoke to us in a rush, saying, "I need to use your phone! You gotta help me." The accent was Caribbean, a singsong rhythm that didn't fit her urgency.

Birdy swung the flashlight but was polite enough not to blind the woman. She was pale-skinned, tall, and so emaciated it suggested anorexia or illness. I also got the impression her arms were heavily tattooed, but that might have been an illusion. The harsh lighting had distorted the color of the scrubs she wore. They were prison orange, not yellow. Instantly, Birdy, the amateur archaeologist, became Deputy Liberty Tupplemeyer.

"Mind telling us your name?" Birdy switched off the flashlight to calm matters, but her hardass attitude scared the woman.

"Don't let 'em take me," she said. "Even if you're cops, don't let them no matter what they say. *Please*." Then backed away, taking nervous glances over her shoulder.

She was referring to the clinic, I assumed, or maybe she meant prison, but it didn't matter. Her pleading tone was heartbreaking. The woman was exhausted, near tears, and out here all alone. I said, "No one's taking you anywhere until we get this straightened out," then walked toward her, moving slowly as if approaching a creature that had been wounded.

"You mean it?"

I told her, "I'm not a cop, but I want to help. Why were you screaming?"

The woman was still edging away and worried about someone surprising her from the road, which is where she was looking. She started to explain, "You'd scream, too, if they—" But then her breath caught as if she'd seen something, and she whispered, "Dear god."

"What did those men do to you?" I asked. "We heard them yelling." Then I told Birdy, "Call nine-one-one."

The woman was focused on something in the distance and it took her a moment to react. "Not the police!" she said, then hurried toward me, pleading, "You have a car? Take me with you! At least let me use your phone!"

Birdy tried to get between us, saying, "Back off," but I handed the woman my phone anyway, which surprised them both. Birdy's body language showed disapproval but then softened when the woman hurried away to dial. "Poor thing looks half starved," Birdy said. "If someone hurt her, I'll have their ass."

I was trying to eavesdrop when two shadows materialized near the road and floated toward us—two men who had seen our light and were closing the distance. At the same instant, a police car rocketed past, blue lights spinning but no siren, then braked hard at the clinic gate. Birdy saw the car, too.

"Sheriff's department," she said. "Good. I wonder if that trucker called."

I listened to the woman say into the phone, "Answer, damn you," before I told Birdy, "We're not going to let those guys touch her. Are they orderlies, you think?"

Birdy turned to look. "Jesus, I didn't notice. You have any ID on you?"

We were about to be caught trespassing, I realized, which didn't worry me. Police would consider it a duty, not a crime, to check on the welfare of a pedestrian we'd almost killed, so I continued to eavesdrop, hearing the woman mutter a profanity when she got voice mail. Then she left a message, which I strained to hear, the woman saying, "It's me! You gotta get me out tonight. Crystal . . . pick up the phone!"

Crystal? I edged closer, but there was nothing else to hear because a spotlight came on, panned the field briefly, then froze the woman in its beam.

"Brenita!" a man yelled. "When you gonna stop this silliness and come eat your dinner?" His voice mimicked kindness but actually taunted her. The woman, Brenita, stood rigid for a moment, then dropped my phone and ran toward the cypress strand where the pond created an emptiness in the trees.

The man hollered, "I've got your meds in my pocket!" talking as if he would reward her with ice cream, but Brenita continued running, so he said, *"Shit!"* then listened to his partner ask, "Who the hell are those two?" Meaning us. And then a second spotlight blinded us.

I turned my face away, worried that Brenita was unaware of the pond and of the animals that fed there, while Birdy went into full-on cop mode. She hollered back, "After you take that goddamn light out of our eyes, I'll show you my badge! Then you can explain what you did to that woman—we heard her screaming, assholes!"

The lights went off, and I imagined the men stiffening to attention, before one of them replied, "How were we supposed to know you're a cop?"

A minute later, I had retrieved my phone and was telling Birdy, "I think that woman knows Crystal Helms. How many felons you've heard of named Crystal?" The area code was local, and I was debating on whether to memorize the number or risk sharing my childhood friend's number with police.

Birdy nodded, interested in the Helms connection, then added a link of her own. "The reason I didn't see those guys coming was I was looking for more of these." She switched on her flashlight and pointed it at a large conch shell nested in the earth.

"Look familiar?"

Yes, it did. The tip of the conch had been sawed cleanly, similar to the ceremonial shell horn we had found on Cushing Key.

Birdy had guessed right about where trucks had dumped the earth and artifacts taken from Sulfur Wells.

TWENTY-ONE

The next morning, from my SUV, I was about to dial what I hoped was Crystal Helms's number for the third time when Tomlinson called with news. Ford's retriever would be delivered by a van service around eight that evening, hopefully before sunset.

"Think you can handle the animal?" he asked.

Mindful of his comments to Birdy, I said, "As long as he doesn't get too attached—I'd hate to hurt anyone's feelings."

"Won't happen," Tomlinson said. "That dog's sensitivity chip wasn't installed, and I sorta wonder about the way his brain's wired, too. It's a match made in heaven, now that I think about it. Him and Doc, I mean—not you."

I had met the dog, who was a stubborn animal, but at least he didn't yap or hump, and I replied that I was looking forward to spending the next few nights at Dinkin's Bay. Then asked about Ford, saying, "Any news?"

Tomlinson replied with a *Ho ho ho* Santa laugh. "Doc never makes contact when he's traveling. Like a sort of a religious thing with him—he doesn't want to interrupt the flow of whatever bizarre experience he's enjoying. Different planes of existence with that dude . . . or moral boundaries. I've never been whacked enough to inquire. Or had the balls."

"There's fighting going on in Venezuela," I told him. "Almost a war, according to the Internet."

"*Perfect.* Then our boy's happy as a pig in clover. Probably shopping for a beach time-share, hoping the kimchi really hits the fan."

"It's nothing to joke about," I said.

Puzzled for a moment, Tomlinson replied, *"Huh?"* Then said, *"Oh.* Well . . . back to the dog. The owner dude from Atlanta, he called about the delivery time. After a few minutes listening to that cyborg, I've decided to change his name."

"Change the *dog's* name?" I said.

"Of course! It would take a court battle to change the owner's name. Where's your head today?"

I was still confused. Ford had found the retriever starved and half wild in the Everglades but hadn't named the animal during the week it took to locate the rightful owner, who lived in Atlanta. Tomlinson often said things that seemed absurd, however, so I listened patiently while he explained that the owner didn't really care about the dog—why else would he sell him to Ford?—so this was a fresh start in the retriever's life.

"What do you think about Largo?" he asked. "It came to me last night in a dream."

I replied, "It's a good name for an island, but shouldn't you leave that up to Marion?"

"Why? You think Rex is better? Or maybe Ranger?"

I was thinking that Ranger sounded pretty good but didn't say it because Tomlinson was implying that Ford and I both lacked creativity. Instead, I listened to him explain that the dog had been traveling south through the Everglades on his way to Florida Bay when he and Ford had interceded. "Next stop, Bogie and Bacall Land," Tomlinson said. "Key Largo."

I was on my way to Rosanna Helms's funeral and had just spoken with Joel, then Loretta, and didn't want to continue with a phone glued to my ear. So I tried to end the conversation, saying, "Lower Matecumbe might work just as well, then. Or Islamorada. How about we talk about it later when I get to Dinkin's Bay?"

"I considered Matecumbe," Tomlinson said, totally serious. "Cudjoe Key, too, which actually fits the dog's personality, but only because of the movie. This is a whole new karma deal we're trying to create, so the devil-dog thing's out. Islamorada, however . . . hum. Kinda feminine, nice—but, hey! What about Ramrod—as in Ramrod Key?"

Thankfully, his phone beeped. A moment later, he told me, "It's my pistol-packin' yarmulke calling. Gotta run."

Birdy Tupplemeyer, who had Mondays and Thursdays off, was spending the afternoon with Tomlinson but wasn't going to stay late, she had told me. We had spoken only briefly. She was relieved that, according to Joel, Brenita had been found before midnight and returned peacefully to the clinic, where she was being treated for addiction and bipolar disorder. Because her symptoms included bouts of paranoia, it wasn't surprising that we'd heard her screaming, although the two orderlies were still being questioned. For the same reason, the public defender had already asked the court to review Brenita's case, which included several assault charges, along with prostitution.

Birdy had remarked on how unsavory a job in law enforcement can be, then asked, "You didn't contact your archaeologist friends about last night, did you? When I go back there, if I find even a shard of human bone, the whole dynamic changes. That's when we take it public."

As I drove toward the cemetery, anything was better than thinking about the funeral, which I dreaded, so recent conversations pinged around in my head, vying for attention: Joel Ransler discussing Brenita and commenting on what Mica had said, telling me, *With few exceptions, there's no statute of limitations on federal income tax evasion.*

Same as murder. Joel didn't say it, but I knew it was true because of our conversation on the dock where Dwight Helms had died.

Loretta's voice, and her odd behavior, soon displaced Joel. She had sounded nervous on the phone earlier that morning, telling me, *The girls and me are taking the courtesy bus, so no reason for you to come to the services, sugar. Or even the cemetery. A woman's not dead until her last friend is buried, so Pinky's doing just fine.*

Strange. My demanding mother had excused me from an obligation—something she'd never done before. Clearly, she didn't want me at the funeral, and I shuffled through possible reasons but came up with only one: someone she didn't want me to see or meet might be there.

Crystal possibly? More likely Crystal *and* Mica. Loretta had to have known they were out of prison, yet she hadn't said a word to me.

Something else very odd was the comforting way she had said, *A woman's not dead until her last friend is buried, so Pinky's doing just fine.* What did that mean? Even before her stroke, my mother had chastened me with cryptic remarks, then reveled in my confusion, but now it was impossible to separate nonsense from wisdom, let alone an utterance that had the ring of divine insight.

On the other hand, maybe Loretta was just being sneaky again and laying a false trail.

I was thinking, *Maybe it's true what Mica said. Loretta really was involved with pot hauling . . . on the sales end, possibly. Yes . . . selling the stuff because she hates boats, and no one in their right mind would trust Loretta to drive a truck loaded with weed.*

But then I reminded myself that Loretta wouldn't have had to depend on her secret lover for a nice car and clothes if she'd had money. *Arnie,* she had called him.

I was mulling that over when something new shot into my mind: the oddity of Birdy Tupplemeyer saying, *When I go back there . . . if I find even a shard of bone.*

Why had she said *I,* not *we?*

Then I remembered her telling me she wasn't staying at Dinkin's Bay late enough to see me when I came to meet the dog. She hadn't explained why, but I now knew the reason . . . suspected anyway.

Immediately, I grabbed my cell and called. I got her voice mail and left a message. "Don't you dare go back there tonight alone," I said. "Call me as soon as you get this."

I hung up and tried Tomlinson's cell, which went immediately to his new voice mail recording: *I know why you're calling and your suspicions are correct. A message would only murk matters . . . BEEP!*

Talk about cryptic! I was so taken aback, I stumbled and stam-

mered but finally said, "Have Birdy call me, don't let her do anything stupid," which sounded nonsensical, but that was okay
because it was Tomlinson.

From the parking lot of Kirby Funeral Home, I tried Birdy's
number one more time, then turned off my phone and went
inside.

THE TWO DOZEN PEOPLE who had attended services for Rosanna
Helms were now reassembling at the cemetery, a modern place
designed to accommodate lawn mowers rather than celebrate the
dead who lay beneath plaques that didn't exceed the height of
the grass.

Dwight Helms was there, and I was careful to step over him
before taking my place next to Loretta and her three bingo-playing
friends. The ladies were dressed in their finest black and wore hats
with lace veils. They had been whispering back and forth until I
appeared, then went silent but for their sniffing. Loretta, however,
was cried out and had no trouble saying to me, "This place is
nothing but a strip mall for undertakers. Bury me here, I'll come
back and haunt you."

She wasn't trying to lighten the mood, my mother was serious.
To prove it, she lifted her veil and shook her head at the indignity
being forced upon Rosanna Helms. Her best friend's coffin was
elevated beneath a blue awning, fresh flowers around it that would
soon be replaced by plastic—cemetery rules.

"Don't worry," I said. "You're too ornery to die, and I wouldn't come back here if you did." Then I asked a question I couldn't ask during the service: "Who's that man?"

Loretta knew exactly who I meant: a tall man with wide shoulders who appeared to be in his eighties but still had a sheen of silver hair combed slick and wore a gray suit that was tailored to fit, a quarter inch of white sleeves showing and a blue hankie. Her veil couldn't hide the fact that she had traded looks with him more than once during the service. Now he was staring at her again . . . or at me, although that was unlikely.

"What man?" Loretta asked, then shushed me when I tried to answer, saying, "The preacher's ready, no talking, dear."

I stepped back and let my mother have her way. Watched her and her best friends join hands: Epsey Hendry, Becky Darwin, and Jody Summerlin, all from old fishing families. Together, they became a single unit, four women who had weathered a lot of life together and who were set apart by their unity even in a circle of people who had all known Rosanna Helms. At that instant, the remark *A woman's not dead until her last friend is buried* took on new meaning. I realized the three women knew my mother better than I ever would. They had shared their private lives together and knew Loretta's secrets, the things a mother can't tell a daughter. Pot hauling, selling weed was possibly one of those secrets, although I didn't believe it, but I had a strong suspicion they all knew the silver-haired man. He was Arnie, I suspected, Loretta's lover until one or both of them got religion and ended their affair—he was the real reason she had offered me an excuse not to attend.

I understood now. Surrounded by so much death, their past intimacy was—if I was right about the man—still important to Loretta and him, too, which no longer struck me as tawdry. To be loved and loving, whatever the circumstances, was worth the risk and more valuable than the wobbly tower that is morality. It caused me to feel softer toward my mother and reminded me to value my own friends and to revel in love while I could because the years were ticking past.

"Nice service. Are you staying to eat?"

The man had whispered the question, but I jumped anyway, unaware that someone had slipped up behind me. It was Joel Ransler, wearing a black sports coat and a tie that set off his eyes. He hadn't attended the earlier service, and I hadn't seen him arrive.

I shook my head *No* and touched a finger to my lips, which was unnecessary. The minister had finished praying and was making people laugh by telling anecdotes about "Pinky," so it seemed okay when Joel cupped my elbow and walked me to a spindly tree held straight by gardening wire. We could talk there if we kept our voices low.

"How's your mother holding up?"

"She baked two pies and a ham this morning, then threatened to haunt me if I buried her here," I said. "Why didn't you tell me you were coming?"

"Would you have baked something? I've never seen you dressed up before."

I was wearing a tan sleeveless dress from Chico's and black heels, which Joel's expression told me looked pretty good even at a funeral. I said, "Mica's over there—see him? But Crystal didn't show up. He told me she was sick, but I got the feeling he was lying."

"What's new?" Joel said. He was looking at Mica, who was dressed in a suit that might have fit when he was fifteen, standing opposite us at the back of the circle, but a foot taller than everyone but the silver-haired man, so they both stood out. Mica noticed Joel staring and used a handkerchief to wipe his face, the tattoos on Mica's forearms showing because his jacket was so short.

I said, "You make him nervous," then asked, "Who's the man next to him?" and prepared myself finally to hear the name of Loretta's lover.

"With the gray hair? That's Harold Chatham, the richest man in Sematee County, maybe the whole west coast. I don't know why I'm surprised to see him—he was big in politics for a while and knows just about everyone."

Not as surprised as I was. *"Harold?"* I said. "His name's not *Arnold?"*

Joel's jaws flexed in bemusement. "I get the feeling I just burst your bubble somehow. But you're pretty enough, he'd probably let you call him Arnold or Larry or anything else you wanted." The smile faded while Joel looked at the man and added, "Yeah, ol' Harney Chatham loved the ladies—until he found Christ. Supposedly. He owned a marina and car dealerships, then became lieutenant governor—not that anyone remembers lieutenant governors. That was years ago, but he still shakes hands."

This was Rance the Lance talking, I could have reminded myself, but my mind was busy translating Harold into the nickname *Harney*. As a child I had heard it as Arnie, so it was all making sense again. But then I had to stop and put it in perspective by thinking, *Loretta's lover was lieutenant governor of Florida? My lord, she must have been good-looking and very . . .*

Sexy was the word, but it made me wince to attach it to my own mother. The concept of her bedding a rich politician was tough enough to grasp.

The minister and attendees were singing "A Closer Walk with Thee" while my eyes found Loretta, a wrinkled bird of a woman who was now chirping out the chorus along with her friends. In old photos she was attractive enough, possibly even shapely— although it was hard to tell because Baptist women were partial to baggy clothes in those days. Even so, Loretta, my mother had suddenly become Loretta the *woman* in my eyes, and the perverse pride I felt was shameful, but in a delicious way that made me smile.

"What's going on in that head of yours? They're not singing that loud."

Joel, I realized, had said something important. "Sorry, I was thinking about my mother. I should get back to her, we've got things to discuss."

"Well, if it has anything to do with Fisherfolk, that's what I was just saying. Don't bother—not after what happened yesterday."

I was surprised. "You're firing me because of what someone else did?"

"Don't be silly. You gave me plenty to work with in no time at all, so you're my rising star. But you're done dealing with lowlifes like Mica and Harris Spooner." Joel moved close enough that I got a whiff of soap but no cologne, which was nice, while he continued, "Spooner is dangerous. Maybe psychotic, I don't know, but he's a killer—he killed his ex-wife, but they couldn't prove it. Might have killed Dwight Helms, too—I'm still working on a time line, but it seems to fit. And I think he's the guy who chased you. That's why I stopped by. I got a search warrant issued this morning, and our guys are going through Spooner's trailer right now. If they find the shark mask or the raincoat, or anything close, they're arresting him. I wanted to tell you in person."

"You move fast," I said.

"In some areas, maybe, but I'm way behind in others."

I pretended to be unaware of his meaning. "Maybe Mica knows," I said. "Don't look at him now, but see how fidgety he is?" Then said, "Hold it a second," because I had just remembered a point that Joel had missed. "You forgot that the pit bull minded Spooner but not Mica. I told you how it happened. Spooner's own dogs wouldn't have attacked him, and he sure wouldn't have killed one with an axe . . . would he?"

"*Psychotic*, a *sociopath*—there are so many terms, who knows? Look, Hannah"—Joel was checking his cell—"what I'm saying is, Spooner's dangerous. I want you to stay close to home because he's going to blame you. Guys like him, it's the way their minds work. If we arrest him, no problem. But if we don't, I don't want you anywhere near Sematee County, especially Glades City. Got it?" Then Joel said, "Damn, got to go," and pocketed his phone before giving me the kind of friendly hug people do at funerals, but he added an extra squeeze that squeezed the wind out of me, the man tall and unexpectedly powerful.

"You don't know your own strength," I told him, taking a step back.

Joel flashed his Sundance smile and became thoughtful. "Why don't we have dinner tonight, then I can follow you home to make sure you're safe."

I told him that I would be spending the next few nights at Dinkin's Bay, so the timing, as far as danger was concerned, couldn't be better.

Joel said, "With your boyfriend? I thought he was out of town."

Rance the Lance had been snooping again, and I didn't like it. "If you're pretending you heard that from me, keep walking. Or you can explain, but it better be good."

"Now, Hannah—"

"I never said a word about him being gone. Who told you?"

Joel raised his eyebrows to indicate Loretta, then shook his head the way boys do when they're ashamed. "What can I say? I gave her my cell number. Your mom gets scared sometimes and talkative—but I don't mind, she's fun when she gets on a roll. And she thinks the world of you, Hannah. You *do* know that?"

I couldn't reply because the minster had just said, "Let us pray," so I bowed my head, relieved that the funeral was about over. I couldn't be mad at Loretta, not after my recent revelation, nor Joel either—*if* he was telling the truth. When the minister had finished, I told Joel, "There's a dog where I'll be staying, so I won't need any extra protection."

"That temper of yours," Joel said, looking up from his phone. "I've got to watch what I say around you."

He had just sent a text and didn't seem so rushed, so I told him, "It's just that I'm careful about who I see and what I say. Sorry if I overreacted. The women in my family have a bad habit of trusting the wrong men."

"*Tell* me about it," Joel said, giving it an edge that empathized with my reasons, and I noticed that he glanced at Mica as he spoke.

It wasn't until I was crossing the parking lot, however, that I realized Joel might have been looking at the former lieutenant governor, not Mica. The thought came into my mind when I saw a black limo, the engine running, parked behind my SUV. Smiling at me from the backseat was Harold "Harney" Chatham.

"Hannah dear," he said as I approached. "Figure it's 'bout time we two met. You willing to go for a little ride so we can get acquainted?"

The music of a Southern man's voice can be bad acid rock or an alluring sonata, and Mr. Chatham spoke with the sweetness of cello strings.

When the chauffeur opened the door, I got in—but only after noting the car's license number.

TWENTY-TWO

I was texting the limo's license to Birdy, Tomlinson, and Marion Ford as Mr. Chatham told the chauffeur, "Swing us through Sulfur Wells, then we'll come straight back. Oh—you mind closin' that glass? The young lady and I want to talk private."

"Yes-sir-ee, Governor," the driver said, capitalizing the word to show respect, as he probably had for years, this tiny man in a sporty black cap and wearing driving gloves, always eager to please. Then the hum of an electric motor sealed the passenger cabin with a pane of dark Plexiglas thick enough to be soundproof.

"What year's that vehicle you're driving?" Mr. Chatham asked. He was opening a cabinet of wood veneer that, in fact, was a tiny fridge. "Ford Explorer, isn't it?"

I replied, "It's not that old, and I'm a fishing guide. I need something with a trailer hitch that's roomy and not too nice because I haul bait sometimes. Cast nets, too."

Chatham, who was familiar with marinas and fishing, enjoyed that. "How about something to drink? I've got liquor, Coke-Cola, some bottled tea that's not too bad, and fizzy water, too."

I accepted a bottle of Perrier while he talked and poured Scotch into a heavy glass. "How'd you like to get out of that old Ford and into a new Toyota 4Runner? Payments wouldn't be much. Or what about an Audi allroad? Plenty of room, still an SUV but a lot more stylish. A young woman pretty as you deserves stylish." The man gestured to indicate where we were sitting. "Feels nice, doesn't it? You look right at home riding in luxury. Not all women have the shoulders to handle it. *Grace*, I mean."

I had attended bachelorette parties and had been in limos before, but never one as tasteful as this. The cabin smelled of leather and wood and had a flat-screen TV that folded into the headliner and plush seats on both sides, so Mr. Chatham sat facing me but with plenty of legroom between us.

I said, "Did you invite me along to sell a car or was there something you wanted to discuss?"

The man chuckled to show he valued directness, which people often do but seldom mean. Maybe Chatham was an exception, though, because he said, "Rance told me you weren't shy about speaking your mind. I wouldn't have wasted my time otherwise." He leaned back, his eyes taking me in and seemed to approve of what he was seeing. "Sure you don't want something stronger than that fizzy water? No need to pretend properness around me."

"Mr. Chatham, I didn't know who you were until twenty minutes ago. And I didn't get the impression you and Joel Ransler are friends. Why in the world were you talking about me?"

The man had a friendly laugh, a sort of tympani rumble, his voice lower than most. "That's often the way," he said. "A lot of fathers and sons aren't friends, exactly, but they find ways to get along. Sorta like bulls in the same pasture. Rance, he's got himself a bad case of the Hannahs, so your name comes up. That boy's goin' places—you could do a lot worse. But it's your mamma I wanted to talk about."

I took a second to sort through what I'd just heard. "You mean Joel Ransler is *like* a son to you. He was born here, but his family moved to the Midwest. He told me that."

Chatham's expression said otherwise, then he explained, "Aside from Rance and me, you're the only one who knows. His mother, God rest her soul, never told her husband. She's where the boy got his good looks—that lady was *something*, I'll tell you. But I'd like to think he got his brains and knack for people from me."

Which sounded coldhearted, Chatham realized, so he tried to soften it by saying, "I suppose it was wrong for the husband not to know, but he wasn't much of a man. First sniff of trouble, he packed up the family and hightailed it north. Then ran off and left them both a year later. Even Rance doesn't know the reason they left Florida, so don't bother asking me."

I said, "Does he know you're telling me this?"

"About me being his father, you mean? Nope. Didn't decide to do it 'till just now after I'd sized you up." The man unfolded his bifocals and put them on for the first time, then looked at me as if to reaffirm his decision. It took a few seconds. "You don't favor your mamma, never did. But you've turned into a beautiful woman, Miss Hannah Smith. Remind me a lot more of your Aunt Hannah. And, by god, she was more than just *something*!"

I didn't know whether to be angry on Loretta's behalf or let it slide. What I did know was that men like Harney Chatham didn't share damaging secrets unless they already possessed leverage of equal power. He'd had an affair with my mother, but that wasn't exactly earth-shattering. Besides, the Chathams had money, so it was his reputation at stake, not Loretta's or mine. There was only one explanation.

"What do you want from me?" I asked.

"See there?" he said. "That's why I wouldn't a'wasted my time on some ditzy-headed girl who didn't have brains and a mind of her own. By god, Hannah, you do aim right for the heart, don't you?"

"Not yet," I said, giving him a look, "but I haven't heard your answer."

Chatham's laughter was a tympani drum solo, nothing fake about it. He was still laughing when he touched a button on the armrest and told the driver, "Reggie? I believe I've finally met my match, so use that gas pedal. We want to get Hannah back before the funeral food's gone or she'll be chewing off my leg next."

"Bound to happen one day, Governor!" the driver cackled, and didn't slow down until he had to brake for the first S-curve on the road to Sulfur Wells.

NOW WE WERE barely moving, idling past Munchkinville, the car's tinted windows up so as not to be recognized, but I could see the cottages just fine on this breezy late afternoon. Captain Elmer

Joiner was outside still mending nets, but the parking area was all but empty, most residents at the post-funeral potluck, which was being held at Judd Park off Pondella Road.

During the drive, Mr. Chatham had asked about Loretta's health, had shared a few more secrets, saying he had followed my progress over the years and had seen me several times—at church, usually, him sitting in the back row—and at my uncle's funeral, too, although I'd been too emotional for him to approach or to even notice his presence. Chatham had also spoken of his respect for Jake, but he admitted that my uncle had never warmed to him—said it as if he didn't blame Jake either, which, so far, was as close as he'd come to acknowledging his affair with my mother.

Now, as we watched the cabins of Munchkinville file by, he got down to business, saying, "I got word that idiot Mica Helms told you that folks here are guilty of income tax evasion. Scared to death of the IRS 'cause of what went on back in the pot-hauling days. Or had stacks of cash buried away—some such nonsense."

"It's not true?" I asked.

"Nah!" Chatham said it in a way that dismissed Mica and his claims as absurd, then pressed the button again and told the driver, "Park at the marina, Reggie. Back us in so Miz Hannah and me can enjoy the bay."

The man patted the seat next to him so I could look out the rear window, but I didn't move. Nonetheless, he returned to his thread, saying, "See . . . the few folks that actually made a pile on dope got arrested or net-worthed years ago. Besides, you ever known anyone rich enough or smart enough to hide cash money 'till it was safe? Hell no. Especially a bunch of poor fishermen! That boy Mica, he was trying to hustle you. Boy's desperate 'cause them drugs has shrunk his brain. There's a lesson for you, Hannah, when you start raising babies of your own. If them Helms children would'a spent more time in church and less time smokin' their daddy's dope, they might still have the sense the good Lord gave 'em." The man reflected for a moment before adding, "You and your mother still go to church? That's what I hear."

There was something I wanted to ask and tried to widen the opening he'd just given me. "Chapel By the Sea on Captiva," I said. "I missed last Sunday, but, most weeks, we're there. Loretta goes Wednesday nights, too, but we stopped attending Foursquare Pentecostal like before. Are you still a deacon there, Mr. Chatham?"

The man was wily, knew exactly where I was going with it, so he shared another secret as a preemptive. "You're right. Never was the good Christian I pretended to be—didn't I just admit that? We aren't perfect, Hannah, but we *are* forgiven. Or did you forget?"

I replied, "I hope you told me about Joel because you trust me. See . . . I'm not perfect either. I'm too suspicious sometimes and can't help thinking it might be because you have something on my family and me." I used my hand to stop him from interrupting. "I'd like to ask you something, Mr. Chatham. Were you involved with smuggling drugs? Normally, it would be none of my business, but it is my business because I know you and Loretta had an affair—ten years, it lasted, all during the pot-hauling days. She never said a word, but I knew. Now someone is blackmailing—

extorting's probably a better word—or bullying her and her friends and they're afraid. If you were involved, *she* was involved. See why I'm concerned? I'd like the truth, sir."

Chatham held up his Scotch, which he'd been nursing, savored the color, and took a sip. Through the limo's back window were the cabins of Munchkinville—Loretta's house, too—and coconut palms green against blue water. That's where his eyes were focused when he said, "They're being squeezed out. Accuse an older person of a crime, they'll believe it, 'cause everyone's guilty of something. Call it extortion or whatever you want, but it'll appear to be done legal—*if* it gets done. I'm not behind what's happening, though."

I felt my face warming, which happens when I am snubbed by an evasion. I said, "That's interesting, but you didn't answer my question."

The man continued talking as if I hadn't said a word. "See, the problem with those piddly old fish shacks is they're on lots too small to conform to code. One by itself is worthless. Even if three got blown down, you couldn't build a decent place. Put all twelve together, you've got a chunk of multimillion-dollar waterfront. Developers have tried to buy the whole kit 'n' caboodle, but folks here are too stubborn to sell. So someone come up with a smart way to get rid of them. At least *they* think it's smart."

I said, "Mr. Chatham, this morning I told Joel almost the exact same thing because that's what I suspect is happening. Maybe he told you, I don't know. What I asked was, did you involve my mother in drug trafficking?"

Chatham tilted the whisky glass, barely wetting his lips, which seemed to signal that I was being ignored again. That did it.

I said, "I'd rather walk than ride with a man who won't answer an honest question," then tried to open the door—a dramatic exit that was ruined because the door was locked. I tried several times before tapping on the Plexiglas to get the chauffeur's attention. Apparently, Reggie had been through these scenes before because he ignored me, too.

"Is this how you charmed Loretta?" I sputtered. "Joel's mother? I bet your wife was real proud of you!"

"No, my late wife tolerated me" was the reply. "She was a good woman. Deserved better than me, I'll admit that, too."

Now I was mad. "While you're in a confessing mood, why not tell *me* the truth?"

Chatham looked at me, his expression sharp for the first time, and so was his tone. "Young lady, if you ever ask a man to admit to a felony again, expect to be disappointed. If he doesn't answer, your blood pressure's gonna shoot up. If he does, you'll be conversing with a fool. Worse than that, you've given him a reason to do you harm. Maybe even kill you."

"Now you're *threatening* me?" I asked, and picked up my phone.

"I'm talking to you like you're my own daughter!" the man fired back, but it was the look of pain on his face that stopped me from dialing. "I would've never done anything to hurt you or your mother. I loved her, Hannah, and protected her as best I could. Always will." Chatham let me deal with that while he touched the button again and told Reggie, "Open Miz Hannah's door, please. She might want to stretch her legs."

Reggie was a cackler. "She got the legs to do it, Governor," and there was an electronic click that told me I was free to go. I didn't budge, though. Sat there blankly while a numbing possibility formed in my mind—Mr. Chatham saying he'd kept track of me, had viewed me from afar as I grew into adulthood, and now admitting that he had loved my mother.

Was it possible?

I did some rapid math.

Yes . . . it was possible.

TWENTY-THREE

Sitting in the backseat of a limo with my mother's ex-lover—and a former lieutenant governor of the state—it was suddenly difficult for me to form words let alone pose a question that might change my life forever. I finally did, although it sounded like a stranger's voice as the words left my mouth.

"Is this the way you handled it with Joel?" I asked. "Are you telling me that you're my—"

I couldn't finish. Didn't need to.

"Wish I could say it's true," Chatham interrupted. "I would have taken better care of you both." He cleared his throat, then pretended to sip his drink while he looked away, his eyes tearing possibly.

Because my own throat felt tight, I said, "It was stupid of me to think such a thing. I shouldn't have asked about smuggling drugs either. If Loretta wants to tell me, that's up to her."

"Your mother's not the same woman," Chatham reminded me, and, for the first time, the man sounded lost and old.

"You'd be surprised," I said, trying to boost his spirits for some reason. "Her head's clearer sometimes than she let's on. When's the last time you spoke?"

"Up until her stroke, we talked on the phone every week, usually more. Once she was out of the hospital, though, it caused her too much upset—Lorrie gets embarrassed when she can't remember something. You know what a proud woman she is."

Lorrie? I sat back to clear my head. "I had no idea!"

Mr. Chatham had been a good-looking man in his time and carried the genes required to smile while flexing his jaw. He did it now, saying, "All through your school years, Loretta couldn't wait to tell me when you'd done something special. *Hannah got all A's* or about your clarinet recital, then when you were on the swim team. If Lorrie didn't answer for a couple of days, I'd call Pinky and she'd catch me up on the news."

"Lorrie and Pinky," I whispered, thinking about it.

The man sensed the question forming in my mind. "No," he said gently, "I only phoned Pinky because they were best friends. No other reason. And she liked to gossip even more than Loretta."

I laughed and suddenly felt better about things, but Chatham remained lost in the past. "Poor, poor Pinky," he murmured. "It was a *nice* funeral, wasn't it?"

"Mrs. Helms had a lot of friends," I agreed.

"Strange how things go, Hannah. It's the rare person who meets their real partner before they make a mistake—Pinky told me that herself. She was in the hospital at the time 'cause Dwight beat her, but she wouldn't do anything about it. The man she married brought the Devil into her house and the ol' Devil doesn't leave until he's planted bad seed. The way her kids turned out about broke that woman's heart. By then, it was too late for her to start over."

I was reading between the lines. "Did he beat Mrs. Helms often?"

Chatham replied, "The rule for any woman should be *Once is your last stop on the way to jail*. But those were different times. People tended to look the other way. Women tolerated unhappiness for the sake of their children. Even when a better man come along."

I said, "It sounds like Mrs. Helms was in love with someone. If it wasn't you, who was it?"

"You'd have to ask Miz Helms," Chatham replied, an irony that closed the subject. He then pointed at something he could see through the rear window. "The Devil squirt his seed in that place, too. You ever seen an uglier pile of concrete in your life?"

He had to be talking about the Candor house. I craned around to look while he added, "Rance says you already guessed who's trying to squeeze your mamma and her friends out of Sulfur Wells. Only took you a couple of days. He was impressed."

"I didn't guess," I replied, which was true, but it was also a warning. I'd become vulnerable, I realized, charmed by the man's words and openness, but I wasn't going to be manipulated. "If you knew about it, why did Joel bother hiring me?"

"I try to help that boy when I can, but I don't tell him *everything* I know. Gotta let him sort things out on his own. One thing's for sure, young lady, you two would make sparks 'cause Rance has got a temper on him, too. That's another reason I seldom nose into his business."

I asked, "What about Delmont Chatham? You two have to be related. Is he your buffer?"

The man made a snorting noise of disgust but didn't answer, so I pressed him. "You and Joel don't get along, that's obvious. If there isn't a go-between, it means you didn't tell Joel you're his father until recently. He wouldn't have moved back to Florida. How long has Joel known?"

"Smart girl," Chatham said but again didn't answer my question. Instead, he removed his glasses to look out the window again at the concrete house. "You got all the information you need on Alice Candor, do you?"

It was maddening the way the man controlled the conversation. But I wanted to hear what he had to say, so I replied, "Tell me what you know."

"She and her husband have dodged some bullets, but their luck's about to run out. A couple'a doctors in Ohio—that's where the Candors come from—they tried to get her license pulled 'cause she's got a screw loose in her head. Not in those words, of course. And she's a drunk."

"I've met her," I said, meaning I'd yet to hear anything new.

"Don't underestimate your enemies, young lady. That pair's got a lot of money invested. What they want to do is tear down them little cottages and build a high-end drug rehab. Waterfront, rooms with a view. And something else—the woman *knows* you've been investigating her. Knows Mica told you his lies about income tax evasion, too. That's what they're using for leverage—you're right about that. Your testimony could help put them in jail. Keep it in mind."

Rather than asking who had told Alice Candor about me, I took a guess, saying, "You don't like Delmont, do you? What is he, your cousin? Your brother? He pretended it was just good luck when he chartered my boat."

The man was looking at me, interested, so I continued, "One thing I do know is, he collects antique fishing tackle, and my family is missing a Vom Hofe reel owned by Teddy Roosevelt. This isn't the first time it's crossed my mind."

"Good lord, a *Vom Hofe?*" Chatham said, impressed or feigning innocence, I couldn't be sure. That's how smooth he was. Then he made it harder, asking, "Poor Loretta donated it, I assume?"

"Joel took me off the case, but I want that reel back," I replied. "And there's a book President Roosevelt wrote, too. And some other things. You might pass that along to Delmont because I'll see the man arrested if we don't get our property back. I don't care if he is a Chatham or how he's related to you and Joel."

Mr. Chatham was studying me now, his face old but his eyes young enough to admire what he was seeing—possibly to even undress me—so I pulled my skirt farther below my knees. It seemed to snap him out of it because he gave a shake and said, "Delmont's a second cousin, which is the only reason he has a job. He got hooked on morphine in Vietnam and that's why he relies on Alice Candor. But don't worry, that woman has made two serious mistakes."

He left the statement hanging there until I finally said, "I have to ask?"

Chatham was already savoring what came next and answered in an old He-Coon sort of way. "'Member when I asked if you'd ever met a pot hauler rich and smart enough to hide a bundle of money away? Until it was safe, I mean—safe enough to blow trash out of the water and never leave a trace." He waited a moment, then smiled to inform me *I'm that man*.

"I knew it!" I said, but then backtracked, still on guard. "Why risk telling me this? Now you've got a hold on me and Loretta."

"Hannah, I'm eighty-six years old. If someone I trust comes along, I'm willing to show my cards just to speed up the game. Being rich is nice," he continued, "but having cash money that can't be tracked, well, honey . . . that's *power*. Your mother was never involved, though. And if she was, well"—he shrugged—"I would never admit it."

Now Chatham *was* feigning innocence, but it was okay. I was starting to enjoy our sparring, holding my own with a man who had lived a big life and who didn't waste his time on women not his equal—or so he had claimed—and I wanted to believe him.

"I'm surprised you weren't governor," I said, then remembered to ask, "What was Alice Candor's second mistake?"

Before answering, Chatham tapped the seat to his right— another invitation to join him.

This time, I did.

TWO HOURS LATER, I was still replaying Mr. Chatham's response in my head, smiling every time and sometimes laughing, because his tone had added a richer meaning and so allowed me to take liberties with his wording.

Me asking, "What was Dr. Candor's second mistake?" The former lieutenant governor replying, "What that silly bitch did was threaten your mamma's vegetable garden. Now her walls are going to come tumbling down. Lorrie would be lost without turnips to hoe. Where would she drink her coffee in the morning?"

He hadn't said *bitch*, of course—the man was too much of a gentleman—but profanity was the invisible wrapping on his response. And he had said *Loretta*, not *Lorrie*, but the endearment added intimacy and a caring touch that was communicated by his concern. Then Chatham had asked me about the garden, saying, "Did you show Loretta the cease and desist notice?" When I replied, "Didn't have the heart," the man had patted my knee, but in a fatherly way, and said, *"The acorn doesn't fall far from the tree."*

I was enjoying myself as I reviewed my encounter, sitting behind the wheel of my SUV on my way to Sanibel to take delivery of Marion Ford's dog and to spend a few nights. I had returned to check on Loretta, then showered, changed, and packed a small bag. Now it was 7:30 p.m., nearly sunset. Tim McGraw was on the radio but turned low so I could think while I drove, Tim— the handsomest man I've never seen—singing "Two Lanes of Freedom," which added a sweetness to the new freedom I felt. The lyrics also caused me to check my driver's-side mirror, which was cracked, and my thoughts soon shifted to the vehicle I was driving and the shimmy in my old SUV's steering wheel.

I can get you out of that wreck and into a new 4Runner for next to nothing, Harney Chatham had told me. Not his exact words, but, in my vacation frame of mind, I was free to remember events as I wanted. I had ridden in Toyotas but had never driven a 4Runner so tried to imagine how it would feel.

Then heard the cello strings of Mr. Chatham's voice ask, *Or what about an Audi allroad? A beautiful young woman deserves to ride in luxury.*

An Audi was more of a stretch for my imagination. When Joel had driven me to Denny's in his new A6, I had enjoyed the leather smell and was impressed by all the electronics but couldn't help thinking, *What a silly waste of money.* Audis were so expensive . . . But, on the other hand, what had Mr. Chatham meant by *next to nothing?*

Well . . . maybe he'd factored in part of the seven-plus million in cash he had stashed back when he owned a marina and had done some pot hauling on the side.

The man had been in a card-showing mood on our drive back to the cemetery and had shared that secret, too.

Seven million dollars? It was still difficult to grasp the amount, and the former lieutenant governor had made it no easier when he had added, "It would'a been twice that if I'd had the brains to learn better Spanish. There was a Perkins diesel giving me fits, too, so I missed a couple of trips."

Not cash, actually. Gradually, Chatham had converted the paper bills into silver dollars and gold coins. Never touched a penny of it, he had told me. Wasn't safe, the IRS would have net-worthed him. But a wealthy man could afford to wait for the right time.

Now, apparently, was the right time, because what made me

smile most was Mr. Chatham telling me, *A pinch of tainted money will buy a ton of honest testimony. Alice Candor won't know what hit her. With what's left, we'll make that lie about a Fisherfolk museum come true. That's where you come in, Hannah. I want you to help make it happen when the time comes.*

The museum, it turned out, had been Mr. Chatham's idea from the start. But he had shared it with the gossipy Rosanna Helms, whose children, while on parole, were mandated to make weekly visits to a rehab clinic. Dr. Alice Candor again.

My cell rang. It startled me. Then I became worried when I saw the caller ID.

Joel Ransler checking in.

Had Mr. Chatham told Joel about our conversation? If not, was I obligated to share some, or all, of what I'd learned?

I picked up the phone, saying, "How you doing, Joel?"

No need to ruminate. Mr. Chatham had been right about the special prosecutor's temper. Joel was furious.

TWENTY-FOUR

Because traffic was heavy and I wanted to concentrate on what I was hearing, I pulled into a Publix parking lot only a mile from the bridge to Sanibel Island. Joel had started the conversation by saying, "I hope you didn't believe anything that old son of a bitch told you!"

I was so taken aback, it wasn't safe to drive.

Now I was parked, the sunset a blur of tropic colors, an orange smear on Gulf Stream blue, while I listened to Joel explain, "You know why he told me I'm his son? Because I reopened the Dwight Helms case. I still think Harris Spooner is the murderer, but it's possible that Harney Chatham paid him to do it. Or paid money into a pool to have it done. I think he was heavy into drug trafficking but behind the scenes. He was too smart to get his hands dirty. Of course, that's something he wouldn't have admitted to you."

I don't shift allegiances easily so ducked the issue by replying, "He didn't say a word about paying anyone to do anything. Or about being behind the scenes during the pot-hauling years—I'd swear to that."

"See what I mean?" Joel said. "The old man plays the saint in front of women he wants to impress. He's charming, I'll admit that, but he's a ruthless son of a bitch. Money is all he cares about. I suppose he tried to sell you a car while he was at it."

I wasn't going to confirm it was true until I understood something. "Are you saying he lied about you being his son? There are DNA kits. You could prove you're not related in just a couple of days."

No . . . Mr. Chatham had told me the truth about Joel. It was in Joel's sigh of exasperation before he answered, "Why the hell bother? Point is, he didn't get around to telling me until he could use it to manipulate me. See, Hannah"—Joel sighed again and tried to collect himself—"let me explain something: Harney Chatham doesn't do anything unless it benefits Harney Chatham. He wants something from *you*, plain and simple. Same with the bullshit about him being my father—tells me out of the blue for no reason? I don't *think* so."

"It is strange," I admitted. "But he spoke so highly of you."

"No, it's self-serving," Joel said. "I'd bet the old man was somehow involved with that murder and drug running, too. That's what this is about. I think Dwight Helms was getting into the cocaine trade, working with outsiders. The locals didn't like it, so it makes sense they wanted to send a message. The other morning, on your boat, I had it all backward. Remember lecturing me about islanders smuggling pot but they drew the line at cocaine? If it hadn't been for you, I wouldn't have figured it out."

I wasn't convinced, but I was softening. "I didn't lecture, just told you the truth," I said.

Joel said, "That's what I'm getting at! You know more than you realize about what went on here twenty years ago. It scared him. Chatham was probably probing, afraid you know something important. Told you I was his son, like he was sharing a big secret, then expected you to confide in him in return. What else did you talk about?"

To give myself a second, I replied, "A lot of things," because I had been thinking about Chatham's friendship with Pinky Helms. If he'd had something to do with the murder, my feelings told me it wasn't just about cocaine. It was about Dwight Helms beating his wife so badly, she had been hospitalized. Mr. Chatham had also gotten teary-eyed when talking about Loretta—there was no faking that.

Maybe I wasn't softening.

Joel pressed, "If he manipulated you into talking about your uncle, your mother, or maybe some detail you remember from back then, it's nothing to be ashamed of. The man's a car salesman. He's *good*. So, damn it, please tell me what you talked about."

As a warning to back off, I replied, "He did mention Audis. How do you like your new A6, Joel?"

Ransler about lost it when I said that. "Why are you so damn defensive?" But then he took a breath and tried to make amends. "You're right, I'm a hypocrite, couldn't say no to this car. I love the way it handles, and he gave me a hell of a deal. But what you don't know is—"

My phone beeped—a call from Birdy Tupplemeyer—so I cut him off, saying, "Hang on a sec." When I answered, the line was dead. An accidental call, probably, but I wasn't going to take that chance. For all I knew, she was parked in that cemetery again and in trouble. So I hit *Redial*, but Birdy's phone went immediately to voice mail.

"I know, I know," Joel said when I came back. "You're supposed to be on Sanibel in fifteen minutes and we can't solve this in a phone call. But did you hear what I said about the appointment Chatham had with Mrs. Helms? One of my guys found it on a slip of paper today—in her handwriting. If that doesn't convince you, nothing will."

The special prosecutor had kept talking, apparently, when I'd switched lines. I asked, "An appointment for when?" but then said, "Let me call you back," because now my cell was vibrating— a text message from Birdy.

"Wait!" Joel said. "The appointment was for last Friday afternoon. Chatham was supposed to be at the Helms place an hour before you were attacked." Then he said, *"Hannah?"* concerned by the silence that was my response.

I felt dazed. "I'm here," I replied. "What are you telling me?"

"The truth," Joel said.

"I . . . I can't believe that Mr. Chatham tried to kill me. Is that what you mean? Today, he was so sweet. No one's that good an actor."

"That's not what I'm saying. It doesn't mean the old man came after you—although he's still pretty spry. Could have been a coincidental robbery like we thought. Or *he* was the axe man's target— Mrs. Helms was already dead by then, remember. What concerns me is, I told him about the attack and he intentionally withheld information. For christ's sake, don't say anything because tomorrow I'm going to question him formally." Joel waited through another silence before asking, "Are you okay?"

No, I wasn't. I felt like a fool. "He should have told me he'd been at the Helms place before I got there! But it's my own fault. I'd never met the man, but I trusted him anyway."

"Hannah, you don't become a millionaire car dealer by sounding insincere. I intended to tell you in person, but, frankly, well . . . you're so damn stubborn sometimes, I got pissed off."

I couldn't think straight. I was due at Dinkin's Bay in ten minutes and also concerned about Birdy. Now this.

In a gentler voice, Joel said, "Give me a call later. Then how about dinner tomorrow night? Your friends at the marina don't have to know."

I wanted to end the conversation and regroup, so told him, "Sure, dinner," and soon hung up, but sat there for several seconds before reading Birdy's text.

Two texts, actually. The first had been sent half an hour earlier, but I'd somehow missed it, which was ironic. The message only added to the chaos in my head:

Spoke with G. R the Lance is poison, stay away.

G was Birdy's friend *Gail*, who had, apparently, finally opened up about Rance the Lance.

Hard to imagine that her second text could be equally as disturbing but it was.

Am here but need help. Can't T watch damn dog?

T for *Tomlinson*. Just as I'd feared, Birdy had returned to Carnicero to look for artifacts and bones. I started to type a reply but then called her instead. It wasn't dark yet, so maybe she was still parked in the cemetery, waiting for the sun to go down.

This time, Birdy answered but wasn't in her car because she spoke in a whisper, saying, "Can't talk! Are you on your way?"

For no reason, I whispered, too, saying, "You promised you wouldn't go there by yourself!"

"No, you *told* me to promise. Smithie, just listen! Today they dug holes and built a wood thingee around the spot. So I think they're pouring cement tomorrow."

"Footers," I said. "Yeah, they'd have to frame it in first. Is that what you mean—a wooden thingee?"

"So you've got to come!" Birdy whispered. "Tonight's our last chance." Then I heard, "Oh shit, someone's coming. I'll text you."

She hung up.

I slapped the steering wheel and started my SUV but was too agitated to drive. I had to do something. Calling 911 was too extreme, so I texted her a warning message: *If I don't hear from you in ten minutes, am calling police.*

Birdy's smartass reply arrived almost immediately: *I am the police. Hurry up!*

No smiley face this time.

I typed a reply—*On my way*—and hit *Send* because I felt sure Tomlinson would approve.

NOW I WAS DRIVING EAST, away from Sanibel Island, and listening to Tomlinson support my decision, saying, "No worries, the

Creature from the Black Lagoon arrived an hour ago. The delivery van guy was in such a rush, I doubt if he stopped to whiz between Macon and Punta Gorda. Said something about the dog chewing through the bulkhead and eating his iPod."

My cell was on *Speaker*, sitting on the dashboard, so I raised my voice a little to reply, "I should have been there but I'm worried about Birdy. Did she tell you what she had planned for tonight?"

"Birdy?" Tomlinson asked. "Oh—*Bertie*." Then I heard yelling in the background, and he laughed, "God, I hope someone's taking video."

"Of *what*?" I asked.

I heard Tomlinson holler, "Anyone have a camera?" before he told me, "The human comedy, Sister Hannah. Nothing can touch it." And hollered again but this time covered the phone, yelling, "He's going to need a bigger boat! Rhonda . . . Hey! I *know* you two have a camera."

"Tomlinson, tell me what's happening!" The temptation was to put the phone to my ear, but I wasn't going to do it in traffic.

Finally, he returned, still laughing. "The dog was swimming out the channel, towing a canoe. You know, with the bowline in his teeth? So Jeth gets in one of the rental kayaks to chase him down. I didn't see how it happened, but now Jeth's in the water, the canoe's swamped, and the dog's got the kayak. You were right, Hannah, the name Largo sucks. We've got to pick out something better that fits."

I asked, "Is Jeth okay?"

"Wait, I'm trying to get a better angle. It'll be dark in twenty minutes, but I can make out the kayak. Yep . . . dog's headed for

Woodring Point, going like a bat out of hell. But like a ghost ship, you know? No one aboard. Hey—what about this? We call him Sinbad."

I had been looking forward to staying in Dinkin's Bay but now genuinely regretted my decision to drive to Carnicero, a place that was frightening, not fun. Hoping Tomlinson would change my mind, I said, "Maybe I should turn around and help find the dog."

"Not if Bertie's in trouble," he said. "Tell me what's going on."

When I'd finished, he asked a few questions, then complimented Birdy, saying, "I love the way that woman's mind works. Most cops are outlaws at heart, but, god, I never thought I'd get naked with one. Yeah . . . you can't leave her hanging out there."

As we talked, I caught a green light at the intersection of Gladiolus and Tamiami Trail, traffic a stream of headlights in the pearly dusk. I planned to take Interstate 75 north across the Caloosahatchee and Peace rivers, then exit near Glades City. Thinking about the route reminded me of Joel's warning to stay out of Sematee County, which I shared with Tomlinson because the coward in me was still looking for an excuse.

"Did they arrest the guy?" he asked, meaning Harris Spooner.

I had to admit I'd forgotten to ask Joel and then added a lie to my cowardice, saying, "I'll call and find out." I wasn't going to do it—and not just because Birdy's friend thought he was poison. Joel had said something that was stuck in my subconscious, a few troubling words or a phrase. The harder I tried to recall what it was, though, the deeper the fragment sank, so I knew it was best to leave it alone until it resurfaced naturally.

Tomlinson asked, "Do you have an address for the shrink's

clinic or the cemetery?" Then jumped ahead, saying, "Screw it—I'll meet you there. The crazy dog doesn't listen to me anyway. The only reason he minds Doc is because they both have tunnel vision. To the dog, everyone else is just frivolous background noise. Uhh . . . speaking of Doc—"

I said, "Wait a second," because I was merging into traffic on I-75 and his sudden change of tone told me I was about to hear something important. It seemed to take forever before I was in a free lane and could put the phone to my ear. "I'm back," I said, and realized the damn thing was still on *Speaker*. So tapped the button and asked, "Is Doc okay?"

"Far as I know," Tomlinson said. "A letter came for you today. Doc's handwriting—block printing, in other words. No return address."

"But he *has* my address," I said. "Why would he send it to Dinkin's Bay?"

Now Tomlinson was uneasy. "Uhh . . . actually, it came in an envelope addressed to me. Your envelope was inside. Mine was typed, so I don't know who sent it, but yours is definitely from Doc. No postmark, of course—but what's new?"

"No *postmark*," I said. "That doesn't make sense."

"Welcome to the wacky world of Dinkin's Bay," Tomlinson replied, then got serious. "I'll be there in an hour, hour and a half, so don't worry about it. I'll bring the letter. We'll talk then."

"Not so fast," I said. "If the letter's not postmarked, it means . . ." *What?* I wasn't sure, so shifted to what was worrying me. "Is something wrong with Doc? I don't mind if you read the letter. In fact, I hope you did."

"I tried," Tomlinson said, dead serious. "Even held it up to a candle—you would've noticed the scorch mark. Thing is, Hannah . . . Well, what you should know about Doc is . . ."

I pictured the man tugging at a strand of hair while he edited his wording. Finally, he got it out. "There isn't a more dependable friend in this world than Marion Ford. But his friends have to get used to dodging the same questions we can't ask him. Understand?"

Of course I didn't understand. The statement was so nonsensical, it seemed to be a plea for patience and understanding—either that or Tomlinson was a lot drunker than he sounded. I replied, "If you've been drinking, I don't want you on the road. So the moment I hear from Birdy, I'll call or text. Sound fair?"

I thought I'd let him off the hook, but he remained serious and no less cryptic when he replied, "I'll give you an hour, then I'm coming. And Hannah? Remember what I told you about the dog—because it's true."

TWENTY-FIVE

When Birdy texted again, I was only a mile from Glades City and the junkyard owned by Harris Spooner, so I was feeling tense and alone on this dark country road, until I read her message:

On way home, no luck. Will call when reception better. Sorry!!! ☺

I felt like saying *Yippee!* a word I've never used, and my spirits, which had been low, rebounded. I checked my mirrors, engaged my flashers, and found a place to pull off the road. First, I texted Tomlinson, telling him there was no need to leave Sanibel. I checked mirrors and door locks again, then tried to call Birdy, but her phone went instantly to voice mail. It was 9:15 p.m., still early enough to rendezvous for a drink. We couldn't be more than a few miles apart if she'd just left the cemetery. So I left a message, then replied to her text: *Am near Glade City exit, how about glass of wine? Where U?*

As I hit *Send*, I noticed car lights behind me and was relieved when I saw that it was an eighteen-wheeler. Even so, I put my SUV in gear and kept my foot ready on the accelerator until the truck went flying past.

When it was safe, I took a deep breath, telling myself, *Relax, you'll be out of Sematee County soon.*

It wasn't just the nearness of the junkyard that caused my nervousness. During the drive, the missing fragment of what Joel Ransler had said resurfaced—but only *after* I'd recalled another troubling remark.

Your friends at the marina don't need to know, he had confided after asking me out to dinner. I'd been so preoccupied at the time, I had not only accepted his invitation, I had been oblivious to Joel's easygoing sneakiness. Worse was his assumption that I was willing to lie to my own friends.

Rance the Lance is poison, Birdy's friend had told her. I had been reluctant to pass judgment based on the opinion of a woman I didn't know. Why would I? Joel had rescued me from a tight spot and he'd been kind to Loretta, had even won her loyalty—something few ever accomplish. He was flirty, true, and charming, but I *liked* the attention. I wasn't going to deceive myself by pretending it wasn't a factor. His attempt to lure me into lying to the man I was dating, though, had tainted my opinion of him. Maybe Joel wasn't poison, but he wasn't someone I would trust—not unless he had misspoken and brought up the subject on his own to explain.

There! I had at last retrieved the item nagging at my subconscious.

Wrong. Believing it freed my mind enough to allow a more sinister fragment to surface. I had been driving north on I-75 at the time and saw a digital sign that flashed *Venice Exit 15–20 Minutes,* a traffic update courtesy of Florida DOT.

Fifteen minutes . . . Fifteen minutes . . .

It was enough to jar the fragment loose. I *remembered*—remembered sitting in the Publix parking lot and defending Mr. Chatham when Joel had said, *We can't solve this on the phone and you have to be on Sanibel in fifteen minutes.*

Joel was right—but how did he know I wasn't on Sanibel? I had told him I wanted to pull over, so he could have assumed I was driving and had yet to reach Dinkin's Bay. I had also told him I was supposed to be there by eight, but how had he *known* I hadn't crossed the bridge onto the island?

Was I being paranoid? I argued it back and forth while still on the interstate. Maybe Joel had used the word *Sanibel* as a synonym for *Dinkin's Bay*. Maybe he had heard the whoosh of fast traffic and knew the speed limit on Sanibel is thirty-five or slower. That was possible, too. But what if Joel Ransler was, in fact, stalking me?

It was a crazy idea that seemed less crazy when I thought it through.

Joel claimed that Loretta had told him Ford was out of town, but I hadn't confirmed that she had. As a special prosecutor, he would also have access to the GPS devices that police use to track suspects. Maybe he had hidden one somewhere on my vehicle. He could have done it at the junkyard or at the funeral.

On the other hand . . . there was someone who'd had an even better opportunity to plant a GPS: Mr. Chatham, or his driver, Reggie, while the limo was parked behind my SUV. Joel could have convinced one of them he wanted to protect me. Or maybe . . . maybe it was Harney Chatham who wanted to follow my every move. Either was possible if my paranoia wasn't paranoia. It depended on which man was telling me the truth.

That was *why* I had been prepared to speed away when I saw truck lights in my mirror.

Now, sitting alone on a dark asphalt road, I contemplated getting out to have a look: use a flashlight to check the undercarriage of my SUV, then pop the hood and search the motor area, too.

No . . . not here, I decided. When I rendezvoused with Deputy Birdy Tupplemeyer, that was the time to look. Pick some nice bright spot, not this lonesome place where my headlights isolated weeds growing in the ditch, the silhouettes of trees miles beyond.

BEEP!

A text from Birdy. She was replying to my invitation to meet for a glass of wine—what a relief to pick up a phone that linked me with a familiar person. *Can't Smithie, almost home. Call U tomorrow.* ☺

As I read, the relief I felt turned to disappointment—then a creeping suspicion. Why the smiley face? It was an affectation she used, but usually when sending a cheery message.

I reread her earlier text:

On way home, no luck. Will call when reception better. Sorry!!! ☺

Same thing—a smiley face that didn't fit. I fanned through a dozen previous texts to confirm the oddity and I was right.

I tried calling Birdy again but got voice mail on the first ring. I became more suspicious. Reception was good in the Fort Myers area. She should have answered if she was nearly home. Unless . . . unless she was still in Sematee County and someone else was using her phone—someone who had read our previous texts and was trying to convince me to turn around.

You're hyperventilating, I realized. *Calm down. No one but Birdy calls you Smithie. It has to be her.*

There was an easy way to confirm that my fears were groundless—a seemingly safe way, too. The cemetery where Birdy would have parked was only three miles down the road.

Keep your doors locked, pull in, take a quick look, then drive home.

I did it. Put my SUV in gear and continued down the road but took the precaution of leaving a long voice mail for Tomlinson.

I wanted someone to know.

TWENTY-SIX

At the caution light, where the Hess station was still a beacon for migrant teenagers, I turned right. No traffic either direction, but, suddenly, car lights appeared behind me. I was doing a comfortable sixty and the lights were gaining on me fast—a car, not a truck. No reason to be alarmed, but I did pay attention. I slowed a bit, expecting the car to pass. Instead, it rocketed to within a few car lengths, blinding me with its high beams, then dropped back to a safer distance.

There was oncoming traffic now: an eighteen-wheeler behind a vehicle with only one headlight—a motorcycle, I thought at first. No . . . it was a commercial van, the kind used to haul migrant workers, with a bad light on the passenger's side. Maybe the driver behind me was fooled, too, because he chose that moment to pass. Bad decision, because the semi and the van were both flying. There was a foghorn blare; the van swerved, but the car was fast enough to make it with fifty yards to spare. I noticed that the van was towing farm machinery but didn't get a good look at the car until it was in front of me, rocketing away. It appeared to be a Mercedes sports model, not an Audi A6, which put me at ease again.

For the next two miles, I had the road to myself, but soon slowed to forty because I didn't want to miss the turn into what had once been a church. In the far, far distance, I could see the illuminated sign of the rehab clinic, so I knew it was close. Even so, I missed the turn. Too much foliage and moss-heavy trees to notice that small opening. Normally, I would have said *Shit* but didn't because the clearing within appeared to be empty. My headlights would have surely sparked off the BMW's red reflectors, so Birdy's car wasn't there.

Good!

To make certain, I pulled to the side of the road and checked my mirrors, ready to turn around. Half a mile down the road, from the direction of the Hess station, the van with the bad headlight was already returning. That puzzled me until it slowed and disappeared north up an unseen lane, so maybe the driver had missed his turn, too—a migrant worker, possibly, towing machinery for a local farmer. There were tomato fields and citrus north of the cypress strand, as I had seen on Google Earth.

Even so, when I swung my SUV around, I kept my eyes on where the van had vanished while also watching for the overgrown entrance to the church. I was going to pull in only long enough to confirm that Birdy's car was gone but didn't want anyone to see what I was doing.

That's not the way things worked out.

I TURNED into the church, my headlights panning along the wooden wreckage . . . illuminating trees and then gravestones that protruded like vertebrae from a tangled hide of vines—all the dark elements I expected to see, plus something unexpected: Birdy Tupplemeyer's car.

The BMW was parked in the same hidden spot, facing the cemetery, the foliage so thick, I hadn't seen its reflectors from the road. The reflectors were glittering now as I tapped at my high beams—which were already on—and pulled closer, seeing the convertible from behind, the car's top up, engine off. I continued to creep closer until I was only a car length away, and that was close enough.

My god, I thought. *What have they done to you?*

I should have called 911 before doing anything else, but I couldn't. It was because Birdy was still in the car. Through the rear window, I could see the silhouette of her head. She appeared to be slumped forward, face against the steering wheel. I knew she wasn't sleeping, but, absurdly, I rapped my horn a couple of times.

When my friend didn't move, I jumped out yelling her name—"Birdy!"—and ran to her, my cell phone in hand . . . didn't stop, in the glare of my SUV's headlights, until I had reached the little car. I yanked at the door handle, expecting it to be locked, but the door flew open, banging hard on its hinges. When it did, I knelt inside and put my hands on her shoulder, saying "Birdy . . . Birdy, are you okay?"

The interior lighting of a BMW is muted, but the overhead console is a triad of bright LEDs. The LEDs flared when I opened the door, but it wasn't until the woman lifted her face and leered that I realized my hands were not comforting my friend Liberty Tupplemeyer.

It was Dr. Alice Candor slumped low behind the wheel.

"I told you I'd have your head one day," she said, a purring reminder that pierced like a blade.

Candor was a big woman, big enough to grab my wrist and stop me momentarily when I tried to jump back. Just long enough for a hypodermic needle to appear in her other hand, the syringe lucent with golden liquid when she jabbed the needle into my neck.

I was in shock but too strong to give Candor time to empty the syringe—at least, I hoped that was true. I wrestled her arm away, which sent my cell phone flying. Then took a few steps backward while my fingers explored the burning sensation near my jugular and I felt blood.

Was this really happening?

Yes. Candor had just stabbed me with a needle . . . *No!*—not just stabbed, she had injected a drug.

I tried to yell *What was in that?* but coughed the words.

Now the woman was out of the car, walking toward me, the hypodermic in her hand and saying, "Calm down, I'm trying to *help* you," her manner blending sarcasm with a lie she had probably spoken a thousand times.

My fingers were assessing my wound while I backed toward the cemetery. The needle had entered closer to my throat than my jugular vein. Blood was trickling down my neck, and I felt as if I couldn't speak without coughing. I did cough while demanding, "Where's Liberty Tupplemeyer? She's a deputy sheriff—you're in a lot of trouble, lady!"

In the lights of my SUV, Candor's face was white as a mushroom, but it wasn't because I had frightened her. She was enjoying herself, holding the syringe like a cigarette as she continued to stalk me. "You're starting to feel dizzy, aren't you, Hannah? Probably a little nauseated, too. But I can make that go away if you'd just let me help."

The doctor was right. I did feel a queasy dizziness. Another effect, though, was a weird blooming sense of invulnerability, and what I saw in the syringe gave me hope. It was still half full of the drug she had tried to inject, the liquid now silver, not gold, in the harsh lighting.

I replied, "Go to hell!" then turned and tried to run, wanted to follow the bright corridor of headlights through the cemetery into the trees. Alice Candor was fit for her age, but it would be easy enough to lose her—I wasn't invulnerable, despite what the drug was telling me, but I was fast. After that, I could double back to the safety of my SUV—use my cell phone, once I'd found it, or flag down a car.

Trouble was, I couldn't run. I took two or three wobbly strides but had to stop.

"Tired already, dear?" Dr. Candor was only a few yards behind, mocking me, her shadow huge on the ground as projected by the headlights of my SUV.

No, I wasn't tired. I felt fearless and euphoric, but my legs had lost contact with my brain. The sensation was like being drunk and trying to escape through a vat of syrup. I tried running again . . . stumbled, then had to grab at something to steady myself—a grave marker, I realized. When I felt the coldness of the stone, the memory of Birdy falling on a grave flickered through my mind. She had said something about not being superstitious, which I had ignored because I was more concerned about the pumpkin-sized mound of sand next to her.

Where was it?

My eyes began to search. There had been several of those mounds in the cemetery, and I didn't want to make the mistake of stepping in one.

Behind me, Candor was experiencing a mood swing. "You're as pathetic as that idiotic police bitch. Any idea how disgusting it was for me . . . *me* . . . to add a goddamn smiley face to a text? Like some airheaded mall twat. I graduated *cum laude* from Johns Hopkins!" The woman laughed, astounded by her own behavior but smart enough to appreciate the irony.

When she said that, I stood and faced her but had to shield my eyes because of the headlights. "Where's Birdy?" I asked.

"Who?"

"The sheriff's deputy," I said. "Did you give her the same thing? What's in that needle?"

Some warmth came into the woman's voice. "You like it, don't you?"

I had to cough to clear my throat. "I've never felt this way before. Where's Birdy?"

"Miss your little friend, huh? I can take you to her. Would you like that? All you have to do is roll up your sleeve."

"Is she hurt?"

"Of course not! She had some . . . *Christ!* . . . some episode about an Indian graveyard—a type of transference hysteria—so I had to sedate her. Perfectly legal, and it was for her own good." The woman came a step closer. "You'll feel much better in a second. I *promise*."

In silhouette, the syringe Candor held stood erect at face level, in contrast to the curvature of her hair, which was pinned back and businesslike, suitable for a physician who was making rounds. I touched a hand to the gravestone to confirm my location, then took two slow steps back while replying, "Those headlights are blinding me. I'll do it, but I want to know what you're giving me first."

Alice Candor followed, my tone triggering another mood swing. "Shut up, goddamn it, or I'll stick you in the throat again!"

Because I had expected to spend the evening at Dinkin's Bay, I was wearing jeans and a favorite blouse—a cross-dyed long-sleeve with Navaho patterns, copper and desert primrose. I braced my thigh against another gravestone and unbuttoned my left cuff. "You'll have to come to me," I said. "I feel like I might pass out."

It wasn't true.

I WAS EVEN MORE unsteady now, but the weird euphoria I'd felt had been transformed—transformed into fear because I knew the doctor was lying and I had to do something. Birdy Tupplemeyer *wasn't* okay. She wouldn't have allowed someone to use her phone to trick me and she certainly wouldn't have given Candor the keys to her new BMW.

Alice Candor, who had graduated *cum laude*, believed me,

however. She waited until my sleeve was rolled high to come a few steps closer, the hypodermic in her right hand while she used her left to reach for my wrist. I remained passive until her fingers made contact, then everything changed. I jumped away from the arc of the hypodermic and, at the same instant, grabbed the doctor by the left arm and pulled her off balance. There was a slingshot effect that allowed me to swing the woman in a circle while my fingers anchored themselves in her wrist. Candor gave a whoop of surprise; she screamed, but I held tight and continued to spin, using my weight as a fulcrum—a children's game of crack the whip. My dizziness wasn't a handicap in such a game and I wasn't playing.

Two full circles was all it took before the woman's legs went out and she was launched face-first toward the ground. As Candor fell, I tried to yank her toward a mound of sand I had seen earlier. It wasn't a direct hit, and maybe not close enough, even though the mound was huge—pumpkin-sized.

Now dizziness *was* a handicap. If I had been able, I would have run to my SUV. I couldn't, but I also couldn't risk the possibility that Candor had held on to the hypodermic. So I dropped my knees onto her back, which knocked the wind out of her—what wind was left anyway. Candor rasped out profanities and battled to get to her feet while I battled to get control of her arms.

Did she still have that damn hypodermic? The woman had landed in shadows behind the gravestone and I couldn't see.

Yes—she had it. But the doctor was shrewd enough to wait until she had wormed to her side before swinging it like a dagger.

The first blow hit me in the abdomen. The sensation of a needle piercing muscle was more frightening than the pain and I knocked her hand away before she had time to press the plunger. She swung again, but I caught her wrist this time and held tight.

I wasn't going to give her another chance. The only weapon I had was a few feet away, so I used my free hand to grab Dr. Alice Candor by the hair and dragged her to the sand mound. Still holding her wrist, I forced the woman's face deep into the sand and she instantly dropped the hypodermic. Even so, I wasn't foolish enough to reach for the needle and I held her there for only a few seconds . . . then I crawled away in a rush.

A fire ant nest was not a place to linger.

I was staggering toward the lights of my SUV when the screaming started. I glanced over my shoulder and didn't want to look again. As I had told Birdy Tupplemeyer, fire ants attack in mass, their bites like burning coals. Dr. Candor was covered with them, her face a crawling mask of black. She was running in crazy circles while she clawed at her eyes and shrieked for help.

The woman tried to abduct you, even kill you, I reminded myself. *Maybe she killed Birdy.*

I couldn't convince myself to leave her, though. It wasn't in me. I couldn't abandon a person who was terrified and in pain—even someone like Alice Candor. People died from fire ant bites.

When I felt a series of stings on my left ankle, it was a reminder. I slapped the ants off my shoe, then went staggering toward the doctor, calling, "I'll help—stop running!" But I was thinking, *You're a fool, Hannah Smith . . . a fool.*

No doubt about it, because, moments later, a van roared into the clearing—a commercial van with only one headlight and pulling machinery.

The driver was Harris Spooner, his ZZ Top beard angelic silver when he leered at me through an open window. Walkin' Levi Thurloe was beside him, riding shotgun while staring straight ahead.

The machinery they were towing was the tire shredder.

TWENTY-SEVEN

Harris Spooner was in a rage but speaking to someone in authority so tried to sound respectful as he said into a phone, "I know . . . I know, but shit happens. If she hadn't swung at me, she'd still be alive. And now Dr. Candor is having a reaction 'cause of them damn ant bites. Eyes all swollen—gezzus, a mess. So it's not like she can give the woman a shot and bring her back to life."

When he said that, I knew the body I had been placed next to was Birdy Tupplemeyer. Until then, I had only feared the possibility because she had been wrapped in plastic and covered by bags of trash, all thrown there in one heap by Spooner or Walkin' Levi.

Either man was strong enough to do it, as I'd found out. When I tried to fight my way to my SUV, Spooner had grabbed me by the shoulders, lifted me off the ground, and shook me like a rag doll while screaming, "Cops searched my trailer 'cause of you! Now you've pissed off the doctor, so it's not like I don't have a *reason*."

I stopped fighting then. It was smarter to pretend I was woozy, almost unconscious, from the drug Alice Candor had given me. The last time I'd seen the doctor, she was having trouble breathing but still coherent and mad enough to tell the men, "Get rid of

that vicious bitch, too, or no more fentanyl! Either one of them
could've ruined it all."

Meaning, they should kill me, then put my body through the
shredder along with Birdy. When I heard that, I was so shaken it
had taken all my willpower not to struggle while Levi used what
smelled like anchor line to tie me, then duct-taped my mouth. It
was my hope he wouldn't tie my wrists and ankles as tightly if I
was passive.

I was right. Levi did as he was told—tied my hands behind my
back, then lashed my legs—but he'd left the knots so loose I was
now wondering if it was because I had defended him from bullies when we were younger. If that was true, maybe I had an ally.
Levi hadn't said a word to me—or anyone, for that matter—but
had handled me gently while lifting me into the back of the van,
which had no seats, and was empty but for a bunch of tools, and
what might have been garbage sacks piled on the body of my dead
friend.

Another point in my favor, I hoped, was that Harris Spooner
was sporting white earbuds and Levi was still missing his. I had
managed to knock the iPod from Levi's shirt during our struggle, and Spooner had called Levi the foulest of names when Levi
attempted to retrieve his favorite source of music.

But did any of that matter? Alice Candor had a hold on both
men, as I found out when Spooner said into the phone, "I don't
give a shit what you say, *she's* the one who fills our prescriptions.
Levi's jonesing so bad, he's shaking—and I'm *right there*. So I hope
you told the clinic to send something along when they come get
her. No . . . a couple of vials, not just patches!"

There was a long silence. Finally, Spooner said, "Even if you get a judge to sign, she's gonna be a problem," which confused me. There was a third woman somehow involved in tonight's events? It sparked a brief hope in me that it wasn't Birdy they had killed— but that ended when he got back to Dr. Candor, saying, "She's sitting in the goddamn BMW with the air-conditioning, what do you expect? Now I've got to get rid of that, too—as if I don't have enough shit to deal with! Car's gonna have to sit here 'till midnight unless you find Mica and he comes with the wrecker."

When he said that, I wondered: *Why didn't he mention my SUV?* Did the person he was speaking with know I was in the van? Spooner didn't offer any clues when he told the person, "Damn it, at least four vials! After what we're doing for that quack tonight?"

For several minutes, I had been lying in darkness, the van's engine running, while the men waited for someone from the clinic to arrive with transportation and a shot of Benadryl, which Dr. Candor had ordered. Now another drug, fentanyl, had been added to the list.

Fentanyl. Was that what Candor had injected into my neck? It was addictive, obviously, and not long-acting because my sense of euphoria was long gone. No wonder Spooner and Levi were so desperate. No matter how many times I'd stood up to the bullies, I realized, Levi would do as he was told.

But what about the person Harris Spooner was talking to? It was someone Spooner had to at least pretend to respect, so maybe the person would help me. Only two possibilities came into my mind: Joel or Mr. Harney Chatham. Alice Candor had known I ignored the false texts from Birdy's phone—probably last-minute information, so she'd had no choice but to be here waiting for me. I already suspected that Joel or Mr. Chatham had hidden a GPS on my vehicle, so only they could have warned her. But would either man allow me to be murdered, then put into a tire shredder?

No . . . Joel had a temper, but he liked me. Mr. Chatham's tears for my mother had been real. It wasn't *possible*.

I had been working at freeing myself from Levi's knots but now concentrated on the duct tape, using a loose floor rivet as a cutting edge. Scrape the tape from my mouth and I could shout out Joel's name, yell a reminder that Loretta's daughter was about to be killed.

Too late—and pointless, it turned out.

"I'm not doin' shit until you get here," Spooner told Joel or Mr. Chatham. "If I go down for this, you're going down, so get moving." Then he said in a rush, "Guy from the clinic's here," and hung up the phone.

I was lying on my side. Car lights sailed across the roof of the van; a window opened to allow a muffled conversation. A minute later, I heard air bubbles being tapped from syringes, then the *Awwwww* sound of a man who felt relief.

"Let's get 'er done!" Harris Spooner said, sounding optimistic for a change.

Walkin' Levi replied, *"Good."*

JOEL OR MR. CHATHAM *would be there to witness my murder?*

I still couldn't believe it, but that's what was going through my mind as I felt the van jolt onto pavement, turn right, and gain speed. Spooner had given one of them an ultimatum. I had heard him clearly enough. *If I'm going down, you're going down . . .*

It was sickening to know I could have been so easily fooled. *Me*—the fourth Hannah Smith, in five generations of women, to die because of poor judgment when it came to men. I wanted to scream, throw myself against the walls and beg God for another chance. I had told Mr. Chatham the truth about church attendance. I went weekly because I believe in God's mercy and in the power of prayer. After such devotion, why was He allowing this to happen? And why had He destined the women in our family to repeat the same fatal error? It wasn't fair!

Life isn't meant to be fair—so grow up and get on with it.

My Uncle Jake, who was not a churchgoer and who had killed three men in the line of duty, had often said that. Something else he often said was *God helps those who help themselves.* Both embraced a *No excuses, keep fighting* philosophy that had guided his life, so had guided mine, too, especially during my rough stretches. It was something to cling to now and calmed the panic that was overwhelming me.

You're not going to let them do this to you, I decided. *Get to work!*

I did. It was hard enough to breathe after a needle in the throat, so I had finished nicking away at the duct tape. The tape hung from my face but no longer covered my mouth. Now I focused on freeing myself from the rope.

When Levi had tied me, he'd used what I was convinced was an anchor line. Good braided nylon that had the smell of copper bottom paint and saltwater. He hadn't cut it—people who know boats seldom cut good anchor line—so the rope lay scattered beneath me like spaghetti. That made it difficult to judge which sections to deal with. My hands were behind my back so I had to make decisions based on touch. Levi had allowed my wrists enough room to move, but not enough to yank my hands free. He'd used what, so far, were good knots, except for an attempted bowline that had cinched down on itself and might require pliers to untie. Then he'd finished by connecting my hands and ankles with half hitches so I was trussed like a steer at a rodeo.

My fingers, though, had already solved the problem of the half hitches. I loosened a final hitch and kicked my legs free of my hands. My wrists and ankles were still bound, but I has halfway there. Next step was to pull my knees into a fetal position, then maneuver my feet through my hands—sort of like skipping rope. Once my hands were in front of me, I could free my ankles, no problem.

That's what I was doing when I felt the van brake and heard Harris Spooner say, "Shit! I just thought of something. If the cops stop us, we're meat. We've gotta stay closer to home."

Just as suddenly, he yanked the van to the side of the road. Because I was balled up like a contortionist when he did it, I tumbled sideways while tools went clattering across the floor. When we were stopped, I realized I had been spared hitting the wall by a mound of trash and the body of Birdy Tupplemeyer.

Poor dead girl, I thought, pressing my cheek against the plastic. *You're still warm.*

Through the screened bulkhead, I heard Spooner once again say, "Shit!" Then he sought counsel from Levi. "It'll take forever to turn this sonuvabitch around. Think I should use the Hess station again?"

In a flat tone, Levi replied, "Good."

Spooner said, "*Good?* Guess that's what I deserve for asking a damn retard. We got a headlight out, dickweed. You ever hear of something called the po-lice? I'm gonna swing this wagon train around, then tell the man there's a change in plans."

The shredding machine, I realized, made turning difficult. I was also remembering the first time I had seen the van. It had disappeared north onto an unnoticed farm lane that might lead to tomatoes and citrus groves but also had to pass close to the cypress pond. Because of the bad headlight, Spooner was being smart and had chosen an alternative spot to get rid of our bodies.

The pond I'd seen last night, a black mirror of lily pads and glowing red eyes.

Alligators eat them all, I had joked to Birdy after she had asked about snakes on Cushing Key.

I pressed my check to the plastic again and whispered, "I will *try . . .*"

TWENTY-EIGHT

I will try to stop them from shredding your body . . .

That's what I meant, which was the best I could do. A promise to a dead friend is still a promise and I was soon glad I had hedged because the unseen road wasn't a road. It was a fire trail, possibly, rough, with lots of potholes. Spooner drove fast anyway, so I took a beating while I tried to untie myself. I bounced high off the floor several times; could hear the thunk of my friend's head hammer against metal—an indignity worse than a strip mall cemetery.

But I kept at it.

If the pond had been farther from the main road, I might have had time, but the van crunched to a stop after only a couple hundred yards. I had freed my ankles and was using my teeth to loosen knots at my wrists when I heard Spooner tell Levi, "Get your ass out there and stand so I can see you in the mirror."

A door opened and slammed shut. I felt the transmission clunk into reverse. Then the van began backing toward what I knew was the pond because Harris provided a running commentary. "Not there, goddamn it, the driver's side! Find you a patch'a dry ground—yeah!—now closer to the water. Don't let me sink them tires, Levi. Okay . . . okay . . . but, goddamn it, where I can *see*, dickweed! This bitch weighs a ton-plus!"

While the van continued backing, I worked faster, using my teeth to pull a series of half hitches free. The anchor line was short by most standards, used for shallow commercial fishing, I guessed, but maddeningly long for what I had to do. Each knot required that I extract several yards of rope through a loop before I could move on to the next knot, so my head fanned back and forth—bite the rope and pull . . . bite the rope and pull. Two or three more loops and I'd be able to part my hands. Once my hands were separated, and if I didn't run into another bad knot, I would soon be free.

Then what?

I didn't stop what I was doing, but my eyes shifted to the tools that had been sliding around in the back. It was too dark to identify much, but the shape of a spade-headed shovel is distinctive.

There was my answer—use the shovel to brain the first man who opened the sliding door, then run. Spooner was too old and fat to catch me. We weren't far from the cemetery where my SUV was parked. If someone had taken my keys, there was also Birdy's BMW.

Would that work?

No . . . I hadn't thought it through. What if it was Levi I had to outrun? He was twice my size, all muscle, and the legs of a man named Walkin' Levi would be in good shape.

There was something else wrong with the plan. Even if I managed to escape and bring back help, it wouldn't be in time to spare Birdy Tupplemeyer's body the obscenity of being spewed into a

pond where alligators were waiting to feed. The thought was horrifying yet didn't alter a more compelling fact: if I had no choice
but to run, I would run. I wasn't going to die to save a dead friend.
But was there a better option?

Yes . . . a new scenario popped into my mind:

*Hit the first man with the shovel, jump behind the wheel, and
drive off!*

I liked that. Just me and Birdy, towing a one-ton tire shredder
in a vehicle that had a bad headlight so was just begging to be
stopped by police. If a squad car didn't appear, there was always
the Hess station three miles down the road.

The van stopped. Spooner got out but left the engine running—
maybe to supply power to the shredder.

Good. Easier for me to steal the thing!

A second later, though, my confidence was shaken when
Spooner said to Levi, "Put this on—the hood and gloves, too,
dumbass, unless you want blood 'n' shit all over your clothes. You'll
have to use an axe or that auger will jam."

Terrifying words to hear, but then I comforted myself with a
detail that might buy me enough time: Spooner had told Joel, or
Mr. Chatham, *I'm not doing shit until you get here.* Spooner had
changed their meeting place, too, which would mean more delay,
hopefully. Thus far, no headlights had pierced the van's windows.

Don't quit, I told myself. *You're almost there.*

It was true. I had cleared the last half hitch, so could now separate my hands enough to work at the knots on my wrists. After
that, all I had to do was deal with the jumbled bowline loop that
Levi had used as a starter and I would be ready.

It almost happened. I had wormed my left hand almost free and was on my feet when the van's back doors flew open. Instantly, I collapsed into a ball and tried to pretend I was still tied and unconscious. Thank god no dome light, but had Spooner or Levi seen me? I didn't know which man had opened the doors and it didn't matter. I lay there curled next to Birdy's breathless body and tried not to breathe. My ears remained alert, however, and noted the clank of tools being moved as if the man was making a selection—looking for an axe, perhaps. Soon, I hoped, the doors would slam closed.

They didn't. It was Harris Spooner, multitasking, talking on a phone, while he searched for the tool he needed. Attempting deference again, too, so it was Joel, or Mr. Chatham, on the other end who listened to him explain, "Done told you! The woman had enough drugs in her to drop a horse but tried to scratch my eyes out anyway—then kicked me in the nuts!" After a pause, Spooner sounded proud of himself when he added, "My knife, of course. The crazies would'a heard a gun."

In my mind, I scooted closer to Birdy, but, in fact, I lacked the courage to move. What came next, though, was so infuriating, it was hard not to react. Spooner saying, "The doctor says she'll sign a paper to prove the woman was crazy. You get a judge to postdate it, then folks'll believe she run off and left all her shit where she lives."

I had to run, too, I realized, and stop worrying about my friend's body. And I would the first chance I got because Spooner was suddenly giving directions, saying, "Yeah, you're at the right place. That fire grade's rough, but ain't too bad—only couple a hundred yards. You in the truck or your good car?"

Had Joel mentioned owning a truck? That's what I was wondering but didn't much care when Spooner yelled to Levi, "Fire up the shredder, dickweed! I can see his lights!"

Through my eyelids, I saw nothing but darkness. And I remained hidden in that darkness for another full minute before the approaching vehicle illuminated the van and Harris Spooner saw that something wasn't quite right.

I felt his weight sink the floor beneath me as if taking a closer look. He was, and a moment later he hollered, "You messed up again, Levi! Mr. Chatham's gonna have your—"

That's all I heard before the tire shredder woofed, then shrieked into readiness. I was already lunging for the van's side door.

TWENTY-NINE

I jumped from the van expecting starry darkness so was instantly disoriented by all the light—a Coleman lantern hissing near the pond; headlights of a truck that had just arrived, its beams framing a scene from a nightmare: Levi, cloaked in a rain poncho, hood up like the Grim Reaper, but holding an axe, not a scythe. Behind him was the pond, its surface blacker for red eyes floating near the shredder, which was trailer-sized, painted yellow, the machine's feeder box a yard higher than Levi's head.

I froze for an instant, my hands partly tied, stumbled, then put a foot on the rope I was dragging and gave a yank. My left hand pulled free. I was struggling to free my right hand when I heard, "If you run, girl, I'll put you in there alive!"

The tire shredder, Harris Spooner meant, a machine so loud the man had to scream to be heard. He was coming toward me, his arms spread as if to herd me back into the van. He was draped in a poncho, too. Add a sun mask, shark's teeth bared, either he or Levi Thurloe could have been my earlier attacker. Spooner's hood was down, though, so his beard and yeti-sized face blazed in the light of the truck's high beams.

The truck. Only fifteen yards away, the silhouette of a man's head watched us from behind the steering wheel. It was Harney Chatham. Had to be. I had heard Spooner say Mr. Chatham's name—even a monster like Harris Spooner conceding his respect—and I knew the former lieutenant governor was my only hope. I began to slide toward the truck while facing Spooner, then I turned and ran, yelling, "It's me! Loretta's daughter!"

Even blinded by the headlights, I saw the driver stiffen when he recognized me. The reaction gave me hope. No doubt Harney Chatham was a monster, too, but he couldn't deny the bond we shared and at least the few small honesties that linked us to my mother.

Or could he?

I was only a few strides away when the truck started backing up, the man's hands working in a blur at the steering wheel.

I hollered, "At least talk to me!" but Chatham wouldn't do it. He spun the truck around in reverse, then shifted into forward and floored the accelerator. Came so close to clipping me that I finally got a good look inside and was momentarily bewildered—I had been wrong about the person driving. Even so, I ran along for a few steps, banging at the window, and pleading for help while the truck fishtailed away.

I would have kept running, too, but that's when Harris Spooner caught up to the anchor line I was dragging and nearly yanked my arm off. My feet flew out from under me and I landed hard on my side. Spooner didn't give me a chance to get up. Instead, he turned and looped the rope around his waist like a plow horse and began towing me toward the pond while he screamed at Levi, "You ain't just an idiot, boy. You're *retarded*."

The sound of the fleeing truck had already been consumed by the whine of the tire shredder. I had no hope the truck would return. The driver had been Mr. Chatham, true, but it was *Delmont* Chatham, drug addict and collector of antique fishing gear, not the former lieutenant governor.

I was on my own and I knew it.

The rope was now knotted so tightly around my wrist, I feared my wrist would break if I didn't pull myself along as Spooner dragged me Clydesdale-style. So that's what I was doing, scrambling along on my knees, using my one free hand like a crutch, to actually help a man who intended to kill me. The pain was bad enough, but the humiliation was worse.

God helps those who help themselves.

The actual phrase didn't come into my mind but the spirit of its meaning did. Crawl to my own execution? No, by god, I would not! I had to do something. Question was *what*?

We were almost to the shredder when Harris provided the answer. He stopped for a moment to touch one ear, then the other—adjusting his earbuds, I realized. The bastard was listening to music! No explaining why I found such cold-blooded behavior intolerable—he had already knifed Birdy Tupplemeyer to death, after all—but it was the spark I needed.

It was also the opportunity because, for just an instant, the rope went slack. When it did, I rolled to my feet and charged the man.

IN HIGH SCHOOL, I'd been a middle-distance swimmer and played the clarinet, not football. Even so, I have tried to ignore enough Super Bowl games to know how small players dealt with bigger men. Plus, I'm a sizable woman and I can *run*.

Because of the tire shredder—or possibly the music he was enjoying—Spooner didn't hear me coming. He sensed a lack of resistance, however, and was turning when I hit him and crashed full speed into the back of his legs. I used my shoulder, tried to stay low so I could roll like a football player when his three hundred pounds of muscle and blubber came crashing down. But, instead of falling, Spooner only staggered to his knees while I ricocheted off like a Ping-Pong ball and landed on my butt.

I felt dazed—a *Now what?* moment that lasted only an instant. Spooner screamed a profanity and lunged for my ankles. When he did, instinct and panic took over. I snaked the rope clear as I got to my feet, then sprinted away. I also resumed chewing at the knot that had become a tourniquet above my right hand.

The knot was beginning to loosen!

It was darker now that Delmont Chatham's truck was gone— just the gas lantern and the van's solitary headlight, but they created a basin of dusky visibility. I had no idea where Levi had gone. He had abandoned his station near the shredder, which offered some hope and caused me to risk angling toward the van. Back to plan A: jump inside, lock the doors, then my dead deputy friend and I would attempt our first carjacking.

But the anchor line seemed determined to have me killed—and so did Harris Spooner. Once again, he snagged the rope's bitter end, which spun me and slammed me onto the ground. For Spooner, it had been a close call, apparently. He thought about it for a moment, then came up with a solution—he looped the rope around his waist again but this time knotted it, which made it impossible for me to run away—not as long as we were tied together.

I had to get my hand free!

Spooner didn't give me the chance to do that either. He kept the rope taut as he walked toward me, coiling the line with each step, taking care not to allow any slack now that he had outsmarted me and I was so near the shredder. Moving slower, too, doing things right, a man who didn't mind letting his confidence show. No—not just confidence. Spooner was letting his mind settle, savoring the moment. It was in his mountainous swagger, his relaxed way of moving now that he had me cornered. Harris was already enjoying what came next.

What came next was him pulling a knife as I struggled to my feet and asking me, "Don't that rope hurt your wrist? Let me cut 'er off for you!"

A joke. He had to holler over the noise, which only added a taunting quality that pleased him. The man's ZZ Top beard parted, a wedge of dark teeth grinned. Knife in hand, he came toward me, adding another loop to the coil even though only a few yards separated us. I maintained that distance by backing away, working furiously the whole time at the knot, which was now loose enough to slide off my hand—*if* the man made the mistake of allowing me a foot of slack. I couldn't count on that, so I was also prepared to run if Spooner charged.

But where?

THIRTY

Behind me, the shredder remained hitched to the van; the van's lone headlight a dusty beacon to the road. To my right, the Coleman lantern showed red eyes waiting in the water, plus something else that was unexpected: Levi Thurloe had reappeared, still hooded like the Grim Reaper and carrying the axe.

I was debating which was a better risk—gators and an axe or a known woman killer?—when Spooner noticed Levi, too. It caused him to pause and yell, "Where the hell you been?"

It was the distraction I'd been waiting for. I dug the fingers of my left hand under the knot and pulled the loop wide . . . only to have the loop instantly reseal when Spooner snapped the rope tight.

The man's eyes had never left me.

"Second thought, think I'll feed her to my dog!" he called to Levi, then surprised me by giving the rope a mighty yank as if hauling in a cast net. No . . . it was a tug-of-war trick because when I planted my feet, he dropped the rope, which sent me backpedaling into the shredder. The noise of the machine was so loud, I felt nothing when I crashed against the metal sheeting and fell.

It didn't matter. A slack rope meant freedom. I pulled another length toward me in reserve, slid the loop off my wrist, then got up—but too late. Nearby, the gas lantern illuminated every detail: Levi and Harris Spooner were converging on me, two huge men in monkish rain ponchos, both carrying cutting tools; to their left, red eyes aglow where steam tangled with shadows above the pond—a vision from hell.

I screamed, "Levi, you've got to help me!"

In reply, Walkin' Levi shouldered the axe and kept coming.

Without looking, I backed myself against the shredder and took a quick look at the thing. I was hoping I could scramble under the machine, which sat on a frame braced with trailer tires. It was possible, but what if I got stuck? There was only a foot of clearance, and even the noise issued a lethal warning: the whine of worn gears, the chatter of cutting teeth fed by a spindle that augered relentlessly, indifferent to what might fall into the hopper.

I didn't have to look to know the hopper was above me: a flanged open rectangle, *Moline Industrial Shredder* stenciled on the side. The memory of the tire Mica had fed into it was too graphic to forget.

Yes . . . crawling under the machine was my only escape. And that's what I was preparing to do when the rope at my feet jogged a fresher memory: *A slack rope means freedom.*

Was that true now?

I had dropped to my knees to crawl under the trailer but risked a glance at Spooner, who smiled his yeti smile, confident he had me cornered. Definitely no need to hurry now that he was only a few steps away. Even if I did dive under the machine, he could wait there with his white-handled fillet knife—a cheap stainless knife he had probably used to stab Birdy Tupplemeyer. Levi, with his axe, could wait on the other side.

Spooner was right. For me, there was no escape. No wonder he was savoring the moment, not bothering to rush. But there was something else the man had not bothered to do, I noticed—the rope was still knotted around his waist.

Crawl under the shredder that would soon consume me? Or fight back by taking a risk?

Spooner made the decision for me when he stood alert for a moment, then hollered, "Levi, you see them blue lights? Cops out there on the highway! Shit! Let's finish up here in case I'm right!"

Police? It was more likely a squad car had stopped some trucker, but I couldn't wait even if help was on the way. I jumped to my feet, rope in hand, and began throwing loops over my arm while I kept my eyes on Spooner. He was close enough to grab me with one step and a lunge if he wanted. But he didn't; just stood there, surprised, while his brain tried to explain my behavior.

Funny. That was the first expression that registered on the man's face. But the smile faded gradually as his eyes moved from me . . . to the words *Moline Industrial Shredder* stenciled above my head . . . then finally, finally to the rope knotted around his waist, and that's when Harris Spooner made the biggest mistake of his life. Instead of cutting the rope, he turned, knife in hand, to look at Walkin' Levi, as if to say, *No problem!*

Levi misunderstood . . . or pretended to. He was standing the length of an axe handle away from Spooner and that's what Walkin' Levi used to break Spooner's arm, an axe handle. He flipped the tool around and swung it like a baseball bat, hit his tormentor so hard that the knife and a tangled white blur of earbuds went spinning into the air.

The ZZ Top giant didn't fall, only gave a woofing scream . . . grabbed his dead arm . . . then staggered a couple of steps while his crazy eyes searched for someone to blame.

Me, that's who his eyes found, and I was ready when he came at me. Holding the rope, I jumped away, then tossed the whole coil high toward the stars. The hopper was the size of a bathtub and impossible to miss.

I didn't miss . . . nor did I stop running even when Spooner screamed, "Somebody help me!" his voice piercing the percussion thump of his own body being tractored over sheet metal, then spun higher by an auger toward the feed chute above him. Alice Condor's pleas for mercy were stuck in my mind, but my real fear was that Levi Thurloe was on my tail. If he caught me, the man I had protected from bullies in childhood might have spared my life a second time, possibly would have even murmured, *You're nice,* but I wasn't taking that chance. I had been lied to enough for one night.

Even minutes later, when I flagged down the sheriff's cruiser bouncing toward me, I wasn't convinced I was safe. My suffocating fear didn't provide a clean breath until I recognized one of the two deputies who jumped out to reassure me. One was a man wearing a uniform, his gun belt shiny as plastic. The other deputy—a person I knew and trusted—was dressed in hospital scrubs and still groggy from drugs.

It was Birdy Tupplemeyer—a sight so shocking but also welcome that it dulled my guilt later when police told me the name of the woman I had left behind, wrapped in plastic.

THIRTY-ONE

From Venezuela, Marion Ford had written, *Sorry, delayed. I miss you. When I get back, interested in buying a place together? We'll need more room.*

Ten days after opening the note, I was aboard my tidy floating home, dressing to see Ford for the first time since his return, when I heard the ting of an incoming text. It was from Joel:

Found the shark mask, I know who it was. NOW will you talk to me?

I had been ignoring the man, true, but I had also spent my nights worrying about the identity of the person who had attacked me at the old Helms place. It wasn't paranoia, or the aftershock of minor needle wounds to my throat and abdomen that caused me to be afraid. My reasons were all based on mistrust, but my mistrust was grounded in fact.

Harris Spooner had survived the shredding machine by the grace of his own body weight and the limits of even good anchor line, so now he was only chained to a hospital bed, which was the fuel of nightmares. Walkin' Levi had also been added to my fears when he was transferred to a psych ward for "observation." Mica

Helms was safely behind bars, but there was a fourth suspect, too, who police had yet to find, let alone arrest: Delmont Chatham, collector of antique fishing gear.

The special prosecutor's text message, however, was a bait too powerful to resist. I called him.

"It wasn't Spooner," I said when Joel answered. "I was right about not killing his own dog, wasn't I?"

He replied, "How are you feeling?" sounding like he cared.

"Busy," I said, "but a little nervous at night. That's why I'd like to skip the small talk. Where'd you find the sun mask?"

"It wasn't Harris," Joel said. "You were right about Levi Thurloe, too. The guy's got the IQ of a butterfly, but his face does brighten a little when your name's mentioned. He says he—"

"Levi *likes* me," I interrupted, "which is flattering, I'm touched. But I'd prefer you answer my question, then explain why you haven't arrested Delmont Chatham. That's who it has to be. A drug addict who collects antiques just doesn't disappear into thin air." I had come close to saying *arrested your Great-uncle Delmont* but monitored my irritation.

Joel didn't like my tone. "It might take a few days, but Delmont will show up. On the other hand, you've got nothing to worry about because the person who attacked you is dead. Her body was right beside you in the van."

I was walking through my little boat's galley but stopped when I heard that. He was referring to Crystal Helms, the childhood friend I had left behind in life and also in death.

I didn't want to believe it. "If that's where you found the sun mask, Mica could have planted it in her apartment—no, wait, you said Crystal lived in a trailer. A woman drug addict, that would make it even easier for someone to—"

"It was Crystal," Joel said. "I know you grew up together, but—well, I'll put it this way: children don't recognize the signs of trauma in other kids. You believe that, don't you?"

"Keep talking," I said.

"Hannah, I'm telling you it was Crystal Helms. I had her medical files subpoenaed. Yesterday, I got a warrant and we searched her trailer. We found the mask, the one made by Patagonia, just like you described it. There were bloodstains. We got the results this morning. Remember when I didn't want to discuss what seemed like an unrelated murder? It was an elderly man named Clayton Edwards. Crystal used a knife, then robbed him. But what ties her to the attack on you are bloodstains from the dog she killed."

I felt a shudder while thinking, *Then put his head in the freezer,* but didn't say it.

There was more to come.

Joel said, "Crystal had issues early on. She despised her mother and idolized her father. When Dwight Helms was murdered, Crystal told more than one prison counselor that she went off the deep end. Which could have been just an excuse—even the dumbest con is a genius at making excuses—but not in Crystal's case. She had a thing for freezers. To her, it was a place homemakers used to preserve trophies. I'm not going to tell you what we found in *her* freezer, aside from one of her mother's wigs. All I say is, thank god she'd been out of prison for only a few weeks."

I asked Joel to repeat some of what he'd told me, then said, "It's hard to grasp the idea of a daughter killing her own mother. Are you absolutely sure?"

The man hesitated for just an instant yet sounded confident when he explained, "No other reason for Crystal to be there wearing a mask. Rosanna had called Harney Chatham and asked him to come to the house but then canceled. The phone records mesh with what the old man told me. It's a guess but, the day you were attacked, I think her brother, or Spooner, knew Crystal was having another spell and went looking for her. Brought the dogs along, too. Fortunately for you, they came by boat."

We talked for a while longer. Joel wanted to use this opening to charm me and he did it by giving me credit for recent positive events and there were several. Courts had frozen all assets of Fisherfolk Inc. A local law firm, Carta, Smith, Taminoshan and Volz, had filed a class action suit seeking redress for commercial fishermen who had been bilked. An unknown party had fronted a multimillion-dollar offer for the twelve cottages of Munchkinville with guarantees to residents that were generous but vague— a car salesman's finesse that Joel, as smart as he was, didn't connect with his biological father. Something else Joel didn't know was that same unknown party had entrusted me with monitoring financial emergencies in our community of aging fisherfolk.

After that, recent positive events became more iffy. Alice Candor *might* soon be indicted, but her team of attorneys had kept her out of jail thus far. The rehab clinics that she and her husband owned were under investigation, but the investigation would take months, even years.

"I wouldn't get my hopes up," Joel said. "The governor's office is getting involved and, well . . . let's just say the governor has a personal interest in who controls state medical contracts. The good news is, like I said, we found the shark mask. Mystery solved. How about we celebrate over dinner?"

I replied, "Even if I felt like celebrating, I don't date clients." After I hung up, I went forward to the master berth, where the note Ford had sent from Venezuela was lying open by the reading lamp. I sat and reread the note for the hundredth time, when, for no reason, an unsettling realization came into my mind—from the start, Joel had *known* my attacker was a woman. Early on, he had pressed me until I had admitted I wasn't sure it was a man. Something else: Joel had no problem accepting the outrageousness of a daughter wanting to kill her own mother with an axe.

I picked up my cell, touched *Redial*, and before Joel could inquire about my health, I said, "You lied to me from day one, didn't you! Why?"

"Christ," he stammered, "I thought you'd changed your mind about dinner. Now what?"

"You suspected it was Crystal all along! That means you still haven't told me everything. Answer my question: *Why?*"

There was a long, long silence that gathered a chilly edge before the special prosecutor replied, "Once you get your teeth in something, you don't quit, do you? Did it ever cross your mind I might be trying to spare your feelings?"

"Spare yourself, more like it," I responded. "Harney Chatham is your father, not mine."

Seldom in my life had I said anything so cruel. Instantly, I regretted my words, but there was no taking them back. When Joel replied, it was in his attorney's courtroom voice. "Let's be perfectly clear, Hannah. This is what *you* want—not me."

"I deserve to know," I said, oblivious to the spider's web that awaited.

"Okay—I warned you." Joel cleared his throat, then made me a part of it all by saying, "The women who murdered Dwight Helms have one powerful protector left. You just mentioned his name. But think about your Uncle Jake. He didn't want the women arrested, Hannah. Why would you?"

ROSANNA HELMS had endured one beating too many and had sent her husband to hell instead of prison . . .

Joel didn't say that, nor had he divulged any names, but what else could explain his dark insinuation that more than one woman had played a role?

I finished dressing, put Ford's note in my purse, then sat outside on a deck chair to think it through. It was early evening, the first week in May. Not dark enough for the automatic dock lights to come on yet late enough that across the street Loretta and her friends had gathered on the porch, awaiting the courtesy van that would take them to Friday-night bingo. The burble of their conversation filtered through the mangroves, interrupted by an occasional caw of laughter and the distant hooting of a great horned owl.

Four old friends—minus one—the women were still pressing ahead, enjoying their lives.

Sweet, perky Mrs. Helms killed her abusive husband with an axe, then one or more of her friends helped cover it up.

I had to repeat it several times in my mind just to establish the possibility. It was a difficult concept to grasp. Mrs. Helms had fussed over her clothing and wigs after surviving cancer; her dresses had shared the perfume of peach snuff when I, as a child, had sat on her lap in church. In the privacy of the mangrove homestead, however, the woman had lived in fear. Dwight Helms was a wife beater. So one long-ago night, young Rosanna Helms, mother of two, had fought back . . . was possibly fighting for her life when it happened and had grabbed the first weapon handy. Or she had been terrorized into insanity and had finally snapped.

In the scenario I was creating, what followed was easy enough to believe. Panicked and in shock, the woman had contacted her best friend, Loretta Smith, who then got Harney Chatham, the future lieutenant governor, involved, as well as my late uncle. For two decades, their secret had guarded the truth.

But wait . . . Joel had said, *The* women *who murdered Dwight Helms.* He hadn't said, *The woman and the friends who covered up for her.* He had been in attorney mode and intentionally vague yet had said that plainly enough.

Loretta helped swing the axe?

I sat back and tried to imagine the scene. Couldn't do it, though. Impossible! Yet . . . it was slightly easier to imagine four tough women, all hardened by island life—Epsey Hendry, Becky Darwin, Jody Summerlin, *and* Loretta—gathering to intervene on behalf of one of their own when something had gone terribly wrong.

Then, and only then, did it seem plausible, even justifiable, when viewed from *an eye for an eye*, Old Testament perspective, and that's the perspective I chose to embrace—until I was shaken by a horrifying possibility: Crystal Helms, not yet school age, had witnessed what her mother and friends had done to the father she had idolized.

No . . . I couldn't allow myself to believe it, despite Joel's earlier warning that children seldom recognize signs of trauma in their playmates. Crystal had been quiet, true, but a shock so terrible would have left her catatonic, not soft-spoken.

Catatonic . . .

My thoughts shifted to Walkin' Levi and the rumors of fever or injury that had traumatized his brain. Had he, too, been a secret witness? Levi had been so terrified that afternoon on Pay Day Road, he had jumped from the truck rather than visit the old Helms place. I thought back to my earliest memories of Levi, trying to make the time line work, but couldn't convince myself of that either.

He was afraid of the pit bulls, I concluded, and couldn't blame him. Nor could I blame Mrs. Helms or my mother, or their friends, for doing whatever was required to survive—not after being assaulted by the likes of Harris Spooner.

Those were different times, Mr. Harney Chatham had told me. *People tended to look the other way. Women tolerated unhappiness for the sake of their children.*

Tragic . . . and also admirable, but the saddest form of admiration because, in fact, it only rationalized looking the other way.

Enough of this! I told myself. *Drop it for now.*

Ford would be arriving soon. I didn't want the upset I was feeling to taint the excitement of our first date since his return from South America. So I got to my feet, locked my boat, and went to tell Loretta good-bye. Before I stepped off the dock, I spent a few seconds staring at the concrete mansion that had displaced a shell pyramid and many tons of Florida history.

Doom with a View, Birdy Tupplemeyer had suggested as a name. "What about the *Bone Throne?*"

This was two nights ago when she and my bodybuilder friend, Nathan Pace, had surprised me with a bottle of champagne and gifts to celebrate the completion of my boat and my first night aboard amid the luxury of my own possessions—including a toilet that worked and a shower that sprayed warm water.

The Bone Box, I had countered rather than risk saying her suggestions were too cute for a building that had already attracted so much misery.

The fact was, neither name fit. Birdy hadn't found a human bone the night she had been detained, then drugged, although she had used that lie as a threat, but her lie had backfired. A sadder fact was, even the conch shell artifact she had found wasn't enough to stop the rehab annex from being built. Alice and Raymond Candor were still rich, still walking free, and still had a powerful ally in the state capitol. The Bone Box, their home, would continue to stand through the years despite the centuries of history its spoor had despoiled.

There was a glimmer of future hope, however. If the Candors got into a financial mess, maybe they would accept the cash offer recently made in my mother's name but backed by Loretta's secret lover and protector.

I want you to help make it happen when the time comes, Harney Chatham had told me.

I was unconvinced The Bone Box was a worthy setting. Alice Condor was a venomous woman, and Mr. Chatham himself had said the Devil's seed had been planted inside those concrete walls. If Rosanna Helms had avoided the mistake of returning to a tainted place, perhaps she would now be sitting atop the mound with Loretta and her other co-conspirators.

A gust of tinkling laughter escaped the porch and drifted toward the water as if to remind me: *A woman's not dead until her last friend is buried.*

That's what I was thinking when I heard the sound of a fast boat approaching and turned to see a twenty-six-foot Zodiac with a T-top crossing the flats, a stealthy-looking vessel, *Sanibel Biological Supply* visible on the side when the boat was close enough for me to wave hello.

It was Marion Ford, looking gaunt but tanned and healthy. He didn't bother to double-check his mooring knots before pulling me into his arms, then saying, "I'd like to say hello to your mother before we take off. Okay?"

No . . . but there was no avoiding the inevitable, just as there was no dodging an answer to the note Ford had sent from Venezuela:

Sorry, delayed. I miss you. When I get back, interested in buying a place together? We'll need more room.

I had settled on an answer days ago—a decision based on mistrust and a fear of my own poor judgment. But I wasn't going to force the issue now. Why risk denying myself the pleasure of a night with a man my body was already responding to and for whom I truly cared?

"You can meet Loretta's friends while you're at it," I suggested. "But be careful—you don't want to cross that group of ladies."

DISCLAIMER

Sanibel and Captiva Islands are real places, faithfully described, but used fictitiously in this novel. The same is true of certain businesses, marinas, churches, and other locations mentioned in this book. Hannah and Sarah Smith are icons in Florida's history, and did exist. However, their relationship to characters in this novel are the author's invention, and purely fictional.

In all other respects, however, this novel is a work of fiction. Names (unless used by permission), characters, places, and incidents are either the product of the author's imagination or are used fictitiously. Any resemblance to actual persons, living or dead, or to actual events or locales is unintentional and coincidental.

Contact Mr. White at WWW.DOCFORD.COM

AUTHOR'S NOTE

Special thanks goes to: Ivan Held and Neil Nyren for entrusting Hannah Smith into my care; Wendy Webb, my magic companion, adviser, and friend; Mrs. Iris Tanner, a guardian angel, and to whom this book is dedicated. Also supportive were my partners and pals, Mark Marinello, Marty and Brenda Harrity, and my teammates, Stu Johnson, Bill Lee, Gary Terwilliger, Don Carman, Judd Park Miller, and Victor Candelaria. Once again, thanks to Dr. Marybeth B. Saunders, Dr. Peggy C. Kalkounos, and Dr. Brian Hummel for providing expert medical advice, and also thanks in advance to young Colgan and Levi Dudley for their contributions to Florida. Special thanks go to writer/historian Jeff Carter.

Much of this novel was written at corner tables before and after hours at Doc Ford's Rum Bar and Grille on Sanibel Island and San Carlos Island, where staff were tolerant beyond the call of duty. Thanks go to Raynauld Bentley, Amanda Gardana, Amanda Rodrigues, Ashley Rodehaffer, Amazing Cindy Porter,

AUTHOR'S NOTE

Desiree Olson, Aaron Geis, Fernando Garrido, Joey Wilson, Khusan (Sam) Ismatullaev, Kory Delannoy, Mary McBeath, Michelle Madonna Boninsegna, Magic Milita Kennedy, Olga Jerrard, Rachel Songalewski, Tall Sean Lamont, High Shawn Scott, T. J. Grace, Yakh'yo Yakubov, Capt. Brian Cunningham, Mojito Greg Barker, Jim Rainville, Nathaniel Buffman, Crystal Burns, Donna Butz, Gabrielle Moschitta, Maria Jimenez, and Sarah Carnithan.

At the Rum Bar on San Carlos Island, Fort Myers Beach, thanks go to Dan Howes, Andrea Aguayo, Corey Allen, Nora Billeimer, Tiffany Forehand, Jessica Foster, Amanda Ganong, Nicole Hinchcliffe, Mathew Johnson, Janell Jambon, C. J. Lawerence, Josie Lombardo, Meredith Martin, Sue Mora, Kerra Pike, Michael Scopel, Heidi Stacy, Danielle Straub, Latoya Trotta, Lee Washington, Katlin Whitaker, Kevin Boyce, Keil Fuller, Ali Pereira, Kevin Tully, Molly Brewer, Jessica Wozniak, Emily Heath, Nicole English, Ryan Cook, Drew Fensake, Ramon Reyes, Justin Voskuhl, Anthony Howes, Louis Pignatello, John Goetz, and Clark and Kristen Hill.

Finally, I would like to thank my two sons, Rogan and Lee White, for helping me finish, yet again, another book.

—Randy Wayne White
Sanibel Island, Florida

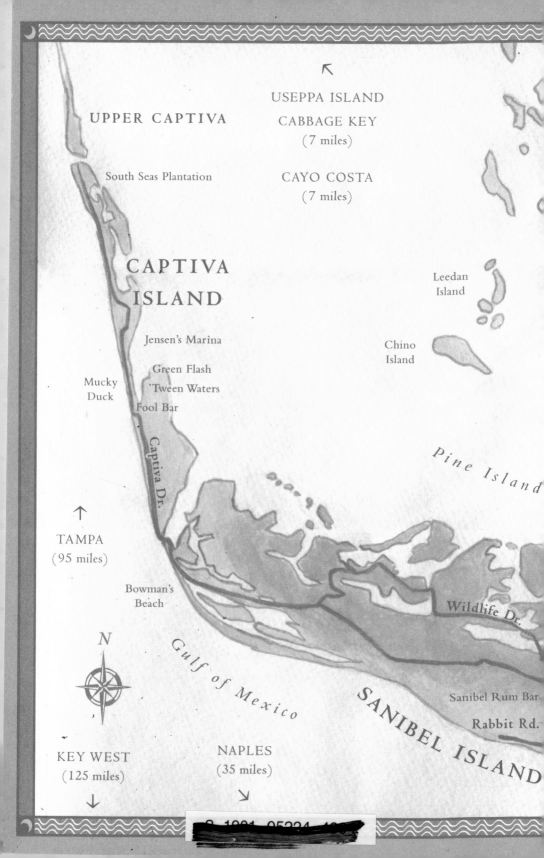